Silhouette®

1241
$4.25 U.S.
$4.75 CAN.

SPECIAL

D0031943

ALLISON LEIGH

A WEDDING FOR MAGGIE

MEN OF THE
DOUBLE ·C·
RANCH

Silhouette®

ISBN 0-373-24241-7

9 780373 242412

50425

"Are you running, Maggie Mae?" Daniel asked, blocking her.

"Don't, Daniel."

"Don't what?" His big hand cupped the back of her neck. Strong and so incredibly warm. Alive. "You remember the first time I called you that?" he murmured.

"Daniel. Please."

She knew what was coming.

"Stop," she whispered.

He paused, his jaw tight. "Really?"

Maggie knew he would. That it would only take one word. Daniel Clay was an honorable man. If he weren't, he would never have stopped at one kiss three years ago. He would have taken what she'd been so close to giving him. But he hadn't.

He'd lcft his home and family instead.

An explosion of heat engulfed her. It had been so long, so very, very long since Maggie had felt a strong male body pressed against hers. "What are we doing?"

His hands pulled her up hard and tight against him. "Finishing what we couldn't before," he finally gritted.

Dear Reader,

Special Edition is pleased to bring you six exciting love stories to help you celebrate spring...and blossoming love.

To start off the month, don't miss *A Father for Her Baby* by Celeste Hamilton—a THAT'S MY BABY! title that features a pregnant amnesiac who is reunited with her long-ago fiancé. Now she must uncover the past in order to have a future with this irresistible hero and her new baby.

April offers Western romances aplenty! In the third installment of her action-packed HEARTS OF WYOMING series, Myrna Temte delivers *Wrangler*. A reticent lady wrangler has a mighty big secret, but sparks fly between her and the sexy lawman she's been trying very hard to avoid; the fourth book in the series will be available in July. Next, Pamela Toth brings us another heartwarming story in her popular BUCKLES & BRONCOS miniseries. In *Buchanan's Pride*, a feisty cowgirl rescues a stranded stranger—only to discover he's the last man on earth she should let into her heart!

There's more love on the range coming your way. *Finally His Bride* by Christine Flynn—part of THE WHITAKER BRIDES series—is an emotional reunion romance between two former sweethearts. Also the MEN OF THE DOUBLE-C RANCH series continues when a brooding Clay brother claims the woman he's never stopped wanting in *A Wedding For Maggie* by Allison Leigh. Finally, debut author Carol Finch shares an engaging story about a fun-loving rodeo cowboy who woos a romance-resistant single mom in *Not Just Another Cowboy*.

I hope you enjoy these stirring tales of passion, and each and every romance to come!

Sincerely,

Karen Taylor Richman
Senior Editor

Please address questions and book requests to:
Silhouette Reader Service
U.S.: 3010 Walden Ave., P.O. Box 1325, Buffalo, NY 14269
Canadian: P.O. Box 609, Fort Erie, Ont. L2A 5X3

ALLISON LEIGH

A WEDDING FOR MAGGIE

Silhouette®

SPECIAL EDITION®

Published by Silhouette Books

America's Publisher of Contemporary Romance

For Amanda and Anna Claire.
I love you.

 SILHOUETTE BOOKS

ISBN 0-373-24241-7

A WEDDING FOR MAGGIE

Copyright © 1999 by Allison Lee Kinnaird

Printed in U.S.A.

Books by Allison Leigh

Silhouette Special Edition

Stay... #1170
The Rancher and the Redhead #1212
A Wedding for Maggie #1241

* Men of the Double-C Ranch

ALLISON LEIGH

cannot remember a time when she was not reading something, whether cereal boxes or Hardy Boys mysteries. It seemed a natural progression that she put her own pencil to paper, and she started early by writing a Halloween play that her grade-school class performed for her school. Since then, though her tastes have changed, her love for reading has not. And her writing appetite simply grows more voracious by the day.

Born in Southern California, she has lived in eight different cities in four different states. She has been, at one time or another, a cosmetologist, a computer programmer and an administrative assistant.

Allison and her husband currently make their home in Arizona, where their time is thoroughly filled with two very active daughters, full-time jobs, pets, church, family and friends. In order to give herself the precious writing time she craves, she burns a lot of midnight oil.

A great believer in the power of love—her parents still hold hands—she cannot imagine anything more exciting to write about than the miracle of two hearts coming together.

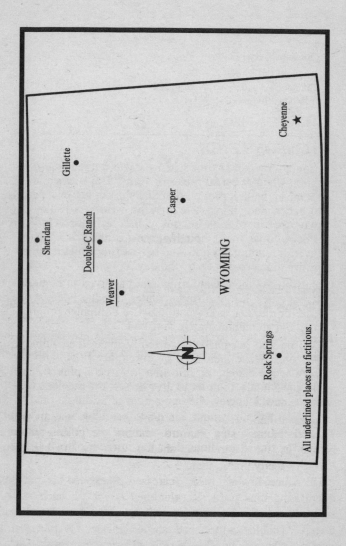

WYOMING

Sheridan
Gillette
Double-C Ranch
Casper
Weaver
Cheyenne
Rock Springs

All underlined places are fictitious.

Prologue

It wasn't easy for him to leave his home.

The only way Daniel managed it was to throw the essentials into a duffel, announce that he was going and walk out the door. No warning. No preparing anyone. He just did it. Given a chance, they'd try to talk him out of going. So he left the only way he knew.

He'd hitched up the horse trailer and was loading Diablo when he saw Maggie.

The setting sun behind her made her look like an angel. Then she took a step forward, leaving the golden-red aura behind as she entered the shadow cast by the big barn. "You're really going, then."

Her voice, low and husky, caressed. Beckoned his thoughts down dangerous paths. He slammed down the latch on the trailer as surely as he slammed down a wall on impossible dreams. Diablo snorted and shifted inside. "I told you I would." She was hugging herself, her slender palms smoothing over the arms of her ivory sweater. His eyes followed the movement.

"You shouldn't—"

"I have to." He reached for his duffel and yanked open the pickup door, shoving the bag across the bench seat.

"It's your home," she protested, following him to stand on the other side of the opened door. "I'll—"

They'd already had this argument. The facts hadn't changed. He cut her off. "You need it more than I do. You. The new baby—" His throat closed.

Maggie made a soft, distressed sound. "Where will you go?"

Daniel shrugged. It wouldn't matter how far he went. The pain would just go with him. But as long as he knew there was an end in sight, he could survive.

Her lashes swept down, hiding her glistening blue-green eyes. "Will you come back?"

The question seemed to hang suspended for a long moment before echoing into the twilight.

He could have told her he'd be back in a heartbeat if she gave the signal. He could have told her he would give them six months. Half a year. But to say the words would put pressure on a situation that wouldn't tolerate any more. He couldn't do that to her. Wouldn't do that to her.

So he climbed into his truck, and she pushed the door until it latched with a quiet click. They stared at each other through the closed window, words wanting to be spoken, yet remaining unsaid.

She brushed a hand across her cheek and looked away. A reddish ray of sunset glinted on the narrow gold band on her finger.

Knowing he shouldn't, he rolled down the window, anyway, and hooked his palm gently behind her neck. Her hair felt like satin against his callused skin. She stepped closer to the truck, moistening her lips. "I wish...oh, Daniel. You shouldn't—"

"Don't." He shook his head slightly. He knew all about *shouldn't*s. Talking about them wouldn't change them. He brushed his thumb over her lips, not sure if he was silencing more words from her or not.

Maybe he just couldn't help himself from touching her lips.

The truth was he *couldn't* help himself. So he had to go. Pure and simple.

Maggie caught his wrist between her hands, her thumb rubbing over his knuckles. Once again he dragged his attention from the glint of gold surrounding her ring finger, only to get snagged in the wet depths of her turquoise eyes. Six months, he reminded himself, grimly hanging on to the thought. Six months ought to be long enough. To accept what was and what wasn't. To adjust.

Six months. Then he'd come back and stake his claim. No matter what.

Her eyes widened as if she'd caught a glimpse of his thoughts. She moistened her lips, averting her gaze. Then drove a knife into his gut when she pressed an unexpected kiss to his knuckles before stepping away from the truck. "Take care of yourself."

All he could do was nod. She was stronger than he was, because words for him wouldn't come anymore. Daniel was leaving her with everything that mattered to him. His family. His ranch. Though he was determined to do it because it was the only thing he could do, he'd wanted to hear her ask him to stay. Not because this was his home. His family. But because *she* wanted him to.

He'd wanted to hear her tell him he was wrong and that she didn't need space. Time. But she didn't.

He started the truck, thinking stupidly that the sound of the wheels crunching over the gravel was about the most damned depressing thing he'd ever heard.

He watched her in the rearview mirror as he drove away.

No. It wasn't easy leaving his home.

But leaving *her* just might kill him.

Chapter One

Three years later

"Mama, is we gonna see Unca Matt?"

For what seemed the tenth time, Maggie Greene nodded at her daughter's question. She turned from the airplane window where she'd been studying the rugged landscape so far below, trying to ignore the tightening knots in her stomach. She looked at the small photo album that J.D. held on her lap. It held a dozen photos, and the pages were worn at the corners from J.D.'s constant handling.

Maggie tapped her finger on the photo of her brother-in-law, big and brawny and blond next to his slender, auburn-haired wife. "You remember Uncle Matthew. He and Auntie Jaimie and Sarah visited us earlier this year."

J.D. nodded, her shoulder-length blond curls bouncing. She flipped another page, skipping right over the photo of her father, who was nothing *but* a photo to her despite Maggie's careful explanation that very morning. She stopped on the picture of Matthew—Unca Matt—and another man, each holding their young daughters on their shoulders.

"Whozzat?" J.D. pointed at the second man, who was more leanly built than Matthew, but no less an imposing figure with his carved features and his thick long hair pulled back in a low ponytail. The family resemblance between the two men was striking.

Though Maggie had explained before, J.D. was just now beginning to recognize the differences between the Clay brothers portrayed in these photos that Maggie's sister-in-law, Jaimie, had sent to J.D. a few months ago. "That's Uncle Matthew's brother Jefferson. He is Leandra's daddy. Remember?"

"I'm bigger than 'Andra. And Sarah."

"Yes," Maggie agreed absently, her eyes straying out the window again. She lifted her plastic cup and sucked the last few kernels of ice into her mouth, chewing furiously. She wasn't used to flying. At all. But she knew by her plain wristwatch and by the change in pitch of the engines that they were nearing their destination.

"And that's Twistin and that's...I forgot, Mama."

"Tristan," she corrected. She looked again at the photo that she knew to be well over three years old. Because it was the last time all five of the Clay brothers had been at the family's Wyoming cattle ranch, the Double-C, at the same time. She touched the photo, indicating the man J.D. couldn't identify. "Sawyer, remember?"

"Is he bigger than Unca Matt?"

"Older, yes. But Sawyer won't be at the ranch, munchkin. He lives somewhere else. And Tristan is the youngest." She tapped her finger over the tallest man in the group, who looked head-on into the camera with a wicked grin.

"And that's Dannl." J.D. rubbed her little thumb over the face of the man in the center of the photo.

Maggie's fingers tightened around her empty cup. "Mmm-hmm."

"Why he don't gots light hair like Unca Matt and Jefferman?"

"Jefferson. Daniel's hair is more like his father's used to be," Maggie murmured. She turned her eyes out the window again, blind to the soaring view. "Darker blond." Liquid butterscotch. Shot through with lighter strands of gold whenever he spent time in the sun. And his eyes had been silvery gray, while his four brothers had eyes of varying shades of blue.

She looked down in surprise when the plastic cup she held cracked under her too-tight grip. Sighing, she set it on the tray table in front of her.

"Why I don't gots a picher of Unca Matt's mommy?"

Maggie's eyes returned to the photo, lingering on the spot where her daughter's thumb had been. "She died when they were very young," she murmured.

"Like Monica's turtle died?"

"Something like that."

"That's sad."

"Yes. It is." She blinked and managed to smile down at J.D., kissing her nose. Wondering how old J.D. would be before she understood that one of her *own* parents had died while she was very young. She'd tried to explain it that morning, while she'd been rushing around the apartment, tossing clothes into suitcases and hiring a cab she could ill afford, to get them to the airport in time for the flight. Smart as J.D. was, she was still only three. There were some things too complicated for comprehension.

Maggie was thirty-one. She hardly understood it herself. But the news she'd received only yesterday had been undeniable. "I bet we'll be landing soon," she said to J.D., as much to distract her daughter as to distract herself.

It almost worked. Maggie started gathering J.D.'s scattered crayons and coloring books and discarded blanket, just as the flight attendant began speaking over the speakers and the No Smoking and Seat Belt lights began flashing.

Maggie's stomach churned and her hands trembled as she stuffed her daughter's belongings into the voluminous purse

she'd carried. The task awaiting her at the end of this spon-
taneous journey weighed heavily. Almost, but not quite, out-
weighing her nervousness over being thousands of feet above
ground, with nothing but a wing and a prayer holding them
there.

The flight attendants efficiently moved along the aisle of the
plane, collecting trash. J.D. took great delight in dropping their
cups into the bags, then sat back in her seat, hugging her
stuffed horse, Duchess, to her little body.

Her daughter had been fascinated with every aspect of the
flight, while Maggie had been wishing she'd been able to just
rent a car and drive to Wyoming. But time was of the essence.
So she'd charged their tickets to her seldom-used credit card
and here they were.

Finally, after a landing that thoroughly unnerved her, they
were on the ground. Maggie sucked in one relieved breath
after another, unclenching her hands from the arms of her seat.
She supposed the powers-that-be instructed the armrests to be
made out of that rigid black plastic stuff to prevent finger dents
from being left by nervous passengers.

But while the relief of being safely on the ground coursed
through her, another set of nerves jangled into life. Nerves
because she still didn't know how she was going to deliver
the news that had prompted this hurried trip to the Double-C
Ranch in Wyoming.

Nerves, because within an hour or so, she'd set foot on
Double-C land again for the first time in years. Nerves, because despite the passage of those years, she wasn't sure she
was ready to confront the memories the ranch held for her.
This was the place where her husband, Joe, had left her. Where
Daniel had later left, because of her. Because he'd thought she
needed the ranch more than he did.

J.D. was tugging at her hand, and Maggie realized that the
plane had nearly emptied while she'd dithered and worried.
She swallowed and pulled her big purse over her shoulder,
heading up the narrow aisle with J.D. forging surely ahead.

She'd arranged for the rental car that awaited her, before

they'd left Chicago. Dumping their hastily packed luggage into the trunk of the economy model, she strapped in J.D. and herself, then had to sit behind the wheel for a few minutes. It had been months and months since she'd driven a car.

She lived in the city now. She walked to work. Walked to the bank. When she couldn't walk, there was public transportation. Taking a deep breath, she started the car and drove cautiously out of the lot. She didn't do too badly. The car was less than half the size of the big pickup trucks she'd driven around the ranch when she and her husband had lived there.

But this little tan model did the job. And all too soon, Maggie was turning into the main gate of the Double-C Ranch. Her stomach was tightening into one huge knot that made her wonder if she would even make it to the main house without first having to pull over to the side of the gravel road.

J.D. bounced excitedly, pointing to the horses who lazily lifted graceful heads on the other side of the fencing that separated rolling fields from the dusty, gravel road. "Horses," she squealed.

Maggie couldn't help but smile. J.D. loved horses. In books. On television. In the stuffed version.

Then the gravel road curved into the circular drive that fronted the meandering ranch house. The "big house" as it was generally referred. Maggie couldn't drag her hungry eyes from the stone-and-wood two-story home.

Oh, so long. So very, very long.

The porch that ran the entire width of the front of the big house was just the same as always, with geraniums blooming from the window boxes. Lilac bushes still clustered along one side of the house. The grass, recently mowed, cast its sharp sweet fragrance into the hot afternoon air.

She stopped the car and breathed in that summer scent.

"Are we there?"

Taking a quick breath, Maggie nodded. "Sure are." She reached over to unlatch J.D.'s seat belt.

"Is Sarah here? And Auntie Jaimie and Unca Matt?"

Maggie opened her car door. "I expect so." She certainly

hoped so. Now that she'd arrived, she realized she could have made one colossal mistake. What if Jaimie and Matt *were* gone?

She should have called ahead.

But then, what would she have said? *I want to tell you in person what I learned yesterday. That your brother—my estranged husband—died two months ago?*

Even now, after a solid day to absorb the fact, she felt a sharp burst of shock when she thought of it. Joe Greene was dead. And he'd left as big a mess in his death as he had in his life.

She felt callous thinking it. But couldn't pretend it wasn't true.

She shook back her hair and brushed down the legs of her well-worn blue jeans before rounding the car to open J.D.'s door. She'd have time to adjust to the news, Maggie reminded herself…later. For now, she had to break it to her best friend that her only brother was dead. And had been for over two months.

Blissfully unaware of her mother's tension, J.D. bounced out of the car, immediately scampering toward the wide steps leading to the front door. "J.D., munchkin, wait—"

But it was too late. J.D. had already pounded her small fist on the heavy door, and stood on her tiptoes to press her finger against the buzzer. So Maggie slowly joined her daughter on the front step.

Three years ago, she'd been the housekeeper here. She'd always used the back door. The one with the wooden screen that had had the same squeak since probably forever that opened into a well-used mudroom, and through there to the kitchen where she'd cooked meals for this family of men. She'd used that back door, the same as everyone else had, because she'd been a part of the Double-C.

But that part of her life was over and done.

There wasn't time to worry over yet another detail, for the door opened with a heavy creak, and Jaimie stood there, astonishment filling her emerald eyes. Her mouth parted, but no words came.

Maggie couldn't blame her. In the three years she'd been gone, Maggie had never once visited the Double-C, though Jaimie and Matthew had come to Chicago several times.

Thank heaven for little girls. J.D. launched herself at her favored aunt, latching her arms around Jaimie's legs and hugging tightly. "Auntie Jaimie, we comes to visit you!"

Maggie smiled faintly and nudged her sunglasses to the top of her head. "Hope it's not a bad time."

Jaimie hugged her niece, then reached out and hugged Maggie. "I cannot believe this," she cried. "Why didn't you call? Did you drive? Fly? Oh my stars. Wait'll the others see you."

She straightened, looking down at Maggie from the advantage of several more inches of height. Her auburn hair flowed riotously over her slender shoulders. She was just the same.

Maggie finally felt tears burn behind her eyes. The first since she'd gotten the news about Joe. Then Jaimie hugged her again before dragging Maggie and J.D. into the house.

"The guys are out," she said. "But they'll be in for supper. Holy smokes, will they be surprised! Are you on vacation? Squire is down visiting Gloria," Jamie said, referring to her father-in-law and his lady friend. "You've got to stay until he gets back. Or, better yet, tell me that you've quit that job at the interior decorating place and have moved back home where you belong!"

"I took some leave," Maggie said. Her stomach tightened. Emergency leave. Bereavement leave. She felt guilty at that, because she knew in her heart she was anything but bereaved. She was upset for Jaimie and for what J.D. did not yet understand. But upset for herself?

She realized Jaimie was heading deeper into the house, J.D.'s hand tucked in hers, and she hastily followed. Through the dining room with the still-familiar gleaming table and china hutch, to the kitchen. "Well, one of these days you'll come to your senses," Jaimie was saying cheerfully. "I haven't lost hope. Sit down. J.D., sweetie, I just made some peanut butter cookies. Want one? Then I'll go up and see if Sarah's awake from her nap.''

J.D.'s eyes lit up. She struggled with a chair, inching it out from the oblong table that took center stage in the spacious kitchen, before climbing up. ''Wif milk?''

''No better way to eat peanut butter cookies,'' Jaimie assured. A whirlwind in motion, she set a plastic tumbler of milk and a napkin with a few cookies on it in front of J.D. ''How about you, Mags? Iced tea or something?''

Maggie agreed to the iced tea. When Jaimie sat at the table with her own glass also in place, she knew the time had come.

She circled the icy glass with one hand, running her finger over the slick surface. ''I have some news,'' she began.

''So do I,'' Jaimie grinned. ''And you're going to love it. But you first.''

Maggie drew in a fortifying breath. Only it didn't fortify her. ''I, um, hired an investigator a while back,'' she said, not sure she could explain the impulse that had been growing steadily over the last several months. She'd waited to hire someone only long enough to save the money for his fee.

Jaimie's eyes sobered. She didn't need Maggie to explain why. ''Joe.''

Maggie nodded. ''He, uh—''

''My daddy's wif the angels,'' J.D. announced matter-of-factly. ''Can I have anover cookie?''

Maggie's shoulders slumped. She met Jaimie's shocked eyes. What else could she say? ''I'm sorry,'' she whispered.

Jaimie moistened her lips and rose, automatically providing J.D. with the asked-for cookie, before sitting down again. ''Joe is…dead.'' She frowned, her expression strained. ''When? How?''

So Maggie explained about the report she'd received the day before from the investigator she'd recently hired. About the car accident, two months past. About the memorial service that had already been held. The rest of the details she left out. She was still grappling with them herself. She wasn't sure she'd ever tell Jaimie the entire truth. For to do so would tarnish even more whatever good memories Jaimie had of her brother.

What good would it do to tell Jaimie that Joe had been a bigamist on top of everything else? That he'd married another woman without attending to the tiny detail of divorcing his *first* wife? Of divorcing Maggie. Or that she and Jaimie would have never known of Joe's death if Maggie hadn't hired the investigator. Joe had so carefully covered his tracks, erasing his past as if it didn't exist. As if Maggie and J.D. and Jaimie didn't exist. Maggie had given birth to J.D. and within days he'd abandoned them. She'd had to learn from Matthew—who was in love with Jaimie—that Joe had been embezzling funds from the ranch.

She knew Jaimie was struggling with her tears. And there was nothing that Maggie could do to ease it for her friend.

"Why didn't we hear something sooner? I mean…two months? He died two months ago?"

Maggie moistened her lips, grateful that J.D. was occupied blowing bubbles in her milk. "Joe severed his ties with the Double-C," she said carefully. "I imagine he worked hard at not being found, otherwise I would have caught up to him in the first place. I wouldn't have lost track of him after Chicago. I mean, after what he did…" There was no point in rehashing how Joe had run off with a good portion of Double-C money in his pocket, abandoning his younger sister just as much as he'd abandoned his infant daughter and his wife. "Are you going to be okay?"

Jaimie brushed the tears from her cheeks. "I won't pretend that it doesn't hurt. Despite…everything," she said huskily. "But I think I should be asking if *you* are okay." She leaned across the table, folding her hands over Maggie's. "Thank you for coming here to tell me. I know it's hard for you to come back. This place must be filled with memories of Joe."

There were lots of memories that haunted Maggie, not all of which concerned Joe. But she couldn't very well tell Jaimie that. So she changed the subject. "Why don't you tell me what your news is?"

Jaimie's eyes softened, and she seemed equally relieved that they weren't going to dwell on Joe. Maybe later. Maybe a long while later. "Well," she said, clearing her throat. "There's two things actually. The first is that I'm pregnant. A few months along."

Maggie's eyebrows shot up, and true delight gave a hard shove against graver thoughts. "You're kidding! Oh, this is wonderful. I'm so happy for you. Matthew must be thrilled."

Jaimie smiled even while her eyes still glistened. "He already pampers me unmercifully, and we only found out a few days ago. For certain. And the other good news is—"

Maggie automatically glanced over her shoulder when she heard that achingly familiar squeak and slap of the wooden screen door from the mudroom behind her. Her smile froze in place, however, when it wasn't Jaimie's husband, Matthew, who stepped inside.

It was the one person she'd felt certain *wouldn't* be at the Double-C. The one person she wasn't prepared to see.

"Well, you can see for yourself," Jaimie continued. "Daniel is here. As of yesterday in fact."

Maggie barely heard her. She was too shocked.

The man removed his dusty black cowboy hat and tossed it unerringly over one of the pegs that hung on the wall inside the kitchen. His quicksilver eyes settled on her, as unreadable as a foggy morning. "Hullo, Maggie Mae."

She trembled. Ordered her vocal cords to function. Time seemed to stand still, even though she distinctly heard the soft tick of the wall clock. "How are you?" she managed. *What are you doing here? Have you finally come home?*

His lips quirked, but the quick smile didn't reach his eyes. Not like it once had. Three years before. "Fine."

"J.D.," Jaimie said. "Let's go get Sarah, shall we? She's going to be so surprised to see you."

Maggie threw a look Jaimie's way, but her friend was already heading out of the kitchen, J.D.'s hand tucked in hers.

He hadn't moved. He still stood there, so quiet and so...male. With the dust of a day's work clinging to his boots and the legs of his blue jeans and his wide chest draped with a clinging T-shirt streaked with dirt and sweat. Her breath eked out. "So." Her cheeks heated at the inane comment.

"So."

Feeling at a distinct disadvantage, she rose from the table. But that wasn't any better, because it just reminded her how big he was. Towering over her average five foot six. Never threateningly, though. Never that. She ran her fingers over the edge of the table. "Jaimie told me her news. Being pregnant I mean. It's wonderful."

There was a time when Daniel's mobile lips would have twitched into a grin at her babbling. But now he didn't so much as blink to indicate what he thought. "Why are you here, Maggie Mae?"

At the name—twice now—she swallowed. "I came to tell Jaimie that—"

His eyebrow peaked when she faltered.

"That Joe died," she finished baldly.

His silvery gaze didn't waver. "What a shame."

Maggie twisted her hands together. "I doubt you mean that."

"You're right," he admitted after a moment. "I don't. Not for me, anyway. Jaimie's probably upset. And you, of course."

"Of course," Maggie murmured. He stepped forward, and she nearly jumped out of her skin. He had to have noticed that, but he made no comment. Then Jaimie returned, Sarah and J.D. in tow, and Maggie realized that he once more was all the way across the kitchen from her.

Had he always moved so quietly? So quickly?

"So," Jaimie said. "We're all home where we belong now. Isn't it wonderful?"

"Yes," Maggie managed faintly, dragging her eyes from Daniel's cool expression. "Wonderful."

So wonderful, apparently, that Daniel's homecoming was the main topic of conversation for the rest of the afternoon, through supper and little girls' bedtimes, until Maggie finally pleaded weariness herself, and took herself upstairs to the room that had once been hers for the very brief few weeks. When she'd moved from the foreman's brick cottage that she'd shared with her husband. Because she couldn't bear remaining in the cozy cottage after he'd run off.

She closed her eyes, shutting off the bitter memories.

She knew she should be grateful that the main topic that afternoon and evening *hadn't* been her news about Joe. Yet discussing Daniel's homecoming wasn't any more comfortable. Particularly with the man himself sitting right across from her.

Sighing, Maggie stared at the bedroom around her. Before those weeks when she'd used it as hers, she had cleaned this room and all the others in the big house, because it had been her job.

Now, she was a guest.

The thick quilt on the wide bed was a different one than used to be there, but it smelled familiar and fresh as a spring day. The faded woven rag rugs on either side of the bed covered a wood floor that gleamed soft and smooth from years of bare and booted feet crossing its wide planks.

She wished, for a moment, that J.D. was sharing this room with her. But J.D. was sound asleep, blissfully happy to be sharing a room with little Sarah. She would have been brokenhearted if Maggie had insisted otherwise.

Now that she was in the privacy of her bedroom, however, Maggie's tiredness seemed to be a thing of the past, and she prowled around the room. She unpacked her suitcase, taking as long as she could while she was about it. She turned down the quilt. Plumped the pillows. Nibbled at her lip and tried not to remember that Daniel's room was right next to this one.

She nearly jumped out of her skin when there was a soft tap on her door. Thrusting her hair away from her forehead, she yanked open the door, not sure what she was prepared for.

It was Jaimie, holding out a stack of fluffy, white towels. "I forgot to tell you that the plumbing in the bathroom that's attached to your room is out of commission. Terrible timing, I know, but we didn't fix it since we're planning to remodel up here. You'll have to share the bathroom in the hall with Daniel. Hope you don't mind.''

Maggie took the towels, burying her fingers in them. ''Of course not.'' It was just a bathroom, after all. She and J.D. were just visiting. Here for a few days to deliver the news. Then home again to the life they'd made for themselves.

She could handle sharing a bathroom with someone.

Not someone. *Daniel.*

Daniel of the quicksilver eyes and heart-stopping grin. Daniel who unwittingly had made her want more out of life than she'd had in the past—a failing marriage and a philandering husband.

Aware that Jaimie's green eyes were more than a little perceptive, she set the towels on the gleaming wood dresser next to the door. ''I didn't get a chance earlier to ask you how you're feeling. You know, with the pregnancy and all.''

Jaimie touched her still-flat abdomen. ''Aside from the news about Joe?'' Her smile was strained around the edges, but Maggie knew that strain didn't stem from her pregnancy. Or her marriage. ''Terrific, actually,'' Jaimie said. ''Like I said before. Matthew pampers me unmercifully. I'm going to be totally spoiled by the time the baby arrives.''

The scrape of a boot alerted them to Matthew's sudden, silent presence. ''All settled in?''

Maggie smiled faintly at the possessive arm that he wrapped around his wife's waist. ''Yes.''

He nodded, satisfied, then looked at his wife. ''Thought you were going to bed.''

''I am.''

A slow smile curled his lips. ''You need your sleep.''

Jaimie's eyes caught Maggie's with a *See?* expression. She gave Maggie a quick hug, then turned with Matthew and headed toward the suite at the far end of the hall. Maggie leaned her shoulder against the door frame, watching them even after the door had closed on the couple.

When Maggie had finally become pregnant with J.D., Joe had lost all interest in whether or not she got enough sleep. She sighed faintly and straightened, absently looking toward the stairs. The sight of Daniel standing there made her go still.

She fought the impulse to step hastily into the bedroom and shut the door. Not only would it appear unbearably rude, but something in his expression nagged at her. As if he expected her to do just that.

Her chin tilted and she wished for some witty or pithy comment. But she'd never been particularly witty. Pithy was out of the question. And all that came out again was that embarrassingly awkward, "So."

He slowly climbed the last stair, his hand resting on the wide newel post. "So."

Maggie drew in a steadying breath, letting her eyes study him as they'd been aching to do during supper.

The thick, wavy hair that J.D. had commented on, looking at his photo, was streaked with golden light. Testament to hours spent in the sun, as was the deep bronze cast of tan he sported. His hair was also shorter than it used to be, cut above his collar now when before it had brushed his shoulders.

But his face hadn't changed. It was still as uncompromisingly masculine as it always had been, though perhaps the creases beside his distinctive gray eyes were a little more apparent. A little deeper.

"You're looking good," he said after a moment.

Maggie flushed, certain he was being sarcastic, since she was the one staring at him like he was ice cream on a hot summer day. Besides, she knew she looked a fright with her hair twizzled up in an untidy ponytail from J.D.'s bath time, the yellow cotton vest and matching skirt she'd changed into before supper equally rumpled. While he stood there looking like God's gift to women in his blue jeans and plain white shirt with the sleeves rolled up his sinewy forearms. She crossed her arms about herself. "You, too."

His lips quirked, but his eyes remained cool. And still he made no move to walk past her to his old bedroom. He stood there and watched her without expression while she looked at him. And wondered.

His older brother Matthew was known to be the calm one in the family. Jefferson, also older, was supposed to be the quiet one. She didn't quite know what to make of this Daniel. The Daniel she'd known had been wickedly sexy. Full of the devil. Teasing her over the least little thing. Making her laugh.

But this man was still. Watchful.

She wondered how else he'd changed in three years. If women still threw themselves at him. If he'd ever caught one of them.

She rubbed at the hard, tight little ache forming between her eyebrows. It was none of her business what Daniel did. It never had been.

She'd been married. To Joe Greene. A man who had, in the end, acted criminally against the Clay family.

"Jaimie tells me you're still living in Chicago."

Maggie nodded. Small talk. That was good. She could handle small talk. "I'm a secretary with an interior design firm. And I also manage the apartment building where J.D. and I live."

His smoky eyes drifted over her. "Quite the city girl."

She stiffened, taking exception to some indefinable note in his tone. "It's a decent job, Daniel."

"So you *do* remember my name."

She flushed. He'd always been able to make her feel awkward. It wasn't anything he necessarily did. Except, perhaps, breathing. Simply existing. It wasn't as if he'd ever gone out of his way to make her feel edgy and unsettled whenever he was near.

She moistened her lips, dredging for normalcy. "Your family is happy you've returned."

His eyes didn't flicker. "No more than Jaimie is happy to have you back."

"That's different. I only came to…to tell…ah, visit." Her cheeks burned anew.

"How did you find out about Joe?"

It was the very last thing she'd expected him to ask. She clasped her arms around her waist and moistened her lips. "I hired an investigator."

"That desperate to find him?"

She lifted her chin. She didn't like the word *desperate*. Didn't like what it implied. "Determined. What about you?"

His lips twisted. "Oh, Maggie Mae, I wasn't desperate *or* determined to find our dear Joe. He was our foreman, after all. And when his embezzling came to light, he cut and ran."

As if she needed any reminders. "I meant what brings you back to the Double-C?"

"It's my home."

That hadn't kept him from leaving it three years earlier. *Nothing* had kept him from leaving. "But what did you do?"

"I turned my truck north and drove."

"While you were *gone*."

His eyes went flat. "This and that. Nothing that would interest you."

She stood there blinking when he abruptly said "Goodnight" and strode into his room. Closing the door with a quiet, solid, snick.

Maggie's breath rushed out. She fumbled for her own door. Closed it. Leaned back against it.

Had she changed as much as Daniel? Three years ago, when he'd left the ranch, his home, he'd not been this silent, watchful man with anger bubbling beneath his words. Had he?

Despite the warm night air drifting into the room through the opened windows, she shivered.

Daniel had been…Daniel. He'd been her boss's brother. It wasn't as if they'd had any real type of friendship. He'd been nice to her, like he was to most people. That was all. That was it. Only she'd repaid it by somehow making him leave his home and everything he cared about. It didn't matter how she'd argued with him, insisting it wasn't necessary. That if anyone didn't belong there, it was Maggie.

"*Oh, come on, Maggie,*" she whispered aloud. What was this somehow stuff? She knew why. Exactly why.

They'd shared one kiss.

One time.

Bare days later, he'd packed up his belongings and moved away.

She dragged her thoughts from the memory that was painfully, dangerously vivid, despite the intervening years.

She'd come to the Double-C to tell Jaimie about Joe. She would be here for one week. When the week was up, she'd go back to Chicago, to the life she'd built for herself and her daughter. Whatever had or had not been between Daniel and Maggie was in the past. Where it belonged.

She changed into her pajamas, and climbed into bed, pulling the quilt up around her ears.

Where it belonged.

Chapter Two

Daniel couldn't sleep. He sat in the wide leather chair in the corner of the bedroom he'd had while growing up, and stared at the wall between his room and the one beside his. The one where Maggie slept. No doubt dreaming and grieving, now that her precious husband was dead.

Joe. The name spat through his mind. Dead. Good riddance.

Then, because he was the man he was, he retracted the thought. Hell, he didn't wish anyone dead. Not even a man he'd hated. A man who'd had everything that Daniel had ever thought he'd wanted, and who had tossed it away. Callously. Carelessly. Deliberately.

Elbows propped on the arms of his chair, he restlessly turned a smoothly carved wooden paperweight over and over in his hands as he stared at the wall. As if he could see through it to the woman on the other side.

He didn't know why he was so surprised to find her here. She was family now, her and J.D. J.D.'s "Auntie Jaimie" was married to Daniel's own brother. Just because Maggie hadn't wanted what Daniel had tried to give her didn't mean that she hadn't kept in touch with Jaimie over the years.

He wasn't even particularly surprised that she'd come in person to deliver the news of Joe to Jaimie. It was just like Maggie. So responsible. So conscientious.

His hand tightened over the paperweight.

Thank God the woman was going home in a few days. She'd take her kid and the dull gold wedding ring she still wore on her finger, and go back to her life in the big city.

It was too bad that Daniel hadn't bothered to pick up a phone to tell Matthew that he was coming back. He might have put off his arrival for a week or two. But then, who could have predicted any of this? And even if he could have, what would he have asked his brother?

Oh, by the way, Matt, heard from Maggie lately? Maggie visited lately? Maggie still in love with her husband lately?

He swore under his breath and shoved out of his chair with a squeak of leather and old wood. He plunked the paperweight on the nightstand.

He didn't expect anything of Maggie. He'd tried to help once, tried to make Joe see sense, and it had blown up in his face.

He'd tried to help again, giving her some time to get over Joe. Giving her space. Doing the honorable thing.

He snorted softly. Honorable. There was a good one.

Maggie had walked away from all that he'd offered her—his home and family—in favor of going in search of the husband who'd left her and her infant daughter flat one cool spring morning. She hadn't moved on. Hadn't healed after a failed marriage. Hadn't removed that gold band.

He had figured he was being noble, doing what his heart told him to do. Even now the notion made him grimace. What he'd been was a fool.

Daniel hadn't come back to the Double-C. He hadn't wanted to come back to this place and see the empty brick cottage where she'd lived. Or see someone else cooking meals for the hands in the bunkhouse. So he'd hooked up with some old contacts of his brother and gotten involved in a life that didn't allow time for memories—tender, painful or otherwise.

The irony was that by avoiding memories of Maggie, he'd ended up making more memories that he couldn't face. He might have tried to do the right thing those years before. But what had he done since then that could even remotely be termed honorable?

Not one damned thing.

His brother Jefferson had warned him. But Daniel hadn't listened, even though he'd known Jefferson was right. Daniel had wanted no time to think. No time to feel.

Well, he'd gotten what he'd wanted. In spades.

And now, he was back. He'd driven through the main gate of the Double-C, home again because he had nowhere else to go, and his head had known it was a good choice.

Only who does he find arriving practically on his heels?

Maggie and her little daughter.

Well, this time Daniel wasn't panting after a crumb of Maggie's affections anymore. That was all water under a very old bridge. He didn't look at her daughter and wish for things that could never be changed. For events that could never be undone.

He just wished he could look at Maggie's blue-green eyes without feeling his gut tighten. Without wondering if her pale corn-silk blond hair still smelled of wildflowers. Without wondering if her lips were still as soft as—

"Hell." He yanked open the door and strode down the darkened staircase, instinct with him as he skirted furniture, rounded the table in the pitch-dark kitchen and burst through the mudroom to the warm kiss of midnight air.

He crossed the gravel road separating the house from the corrals. Walked in the still silence toward that neat brick cottage where Curly, the cook, now lived. The garden that Maggie had once nurtured and enjoyed was long grown over with mown grass. No more flowers. No more carrots and cucumbers and whatever else she'd grown in that little plot of garden.

He found himself staring at the spot where the clothesline

used to stand. The line that he'd put up for her simply because he'd heard her mention once that she liked the way her sheets smelled when they dried in the sun.

He closed his eyes, swallowing an oath as he tried to cut the memory off at the pass. But it was too late and it swelled in his mind, until he was standing in just this spot. Only it wasn't the dog days of summer. It was the fresh dawn of spring. And the sight of Maggie stretching on her toes to pin a sheet in place made him forget about the chores awaiting him.

The brisk breeze tugged at his cowboy hat, and he resettled it and slowly crossed the gravel road to the hard, bare ground where the odd patch of snow still lay. The breeze played with the long sheets that Maggie was trying to hang, and his step quickened as one end blew from her grasp, barely held in place by the one corner already pinned to the line. He caught the snapping corner and held it to the line. "Having a little trouble?"

Maggie's eyes sparkled with humor, and she quickly went onto her tiptoes as she reached up to slip several clothespins over the sheet he held securely anchored. "Nothing a few extra hands won't cure."

He couldn't help smiling back at her. "Think these'll do for now?" He held out his hands, palms up.

Her eyebrows rose a fraction. But she didn't hesitate for long, as she bent down and retrieved the next wet sheet from the basket by her feet. She handed him one end and pointed to the line behind them that ran parallel to the one already filled with wet linens. Her movements were practiced and quick.

Reach. Smooth. Pin.

Each time she reached, her soft blue sweater rose an inch at her waist, revealing the narrow leather belt threaded through the loops of her soft blue jeans. Each time she reached, her arms stretching above her head, that soft blue knit tightened against the full thrust of her breasts. By the third sheet, he had to do something. So he grabbed a bunch of clothespins and jammed them in place, himself. "I hung this line too high for you," he said.

She propped her hands on her hips, her head tilting to one side as she turned amused eyes his way. "And just what good would this line do me if it were any lower? The only thing I'd be able to hang on it without them dragging on the ground would be pillowcases."

She shook her head, chuckling, and turned back to her task.

"A step stool, or something, then."

She laughed outright. "Oh, Daniel, don't be silly. I'm not going to drag a step along with me." She nipped up on her toes, slipping a pin over the center edge of the latest sheet. "All this stretching and stooping gets me back in shape after having J.D." She fastened the corner and reached for the last wet sheet in her basket.

"You're in fine shape."

She rolled her eyes and pushed one end of the sheet into his hands. "Easy for a man to say," she replied easily. "You'll never have to learn what a lot of work it is to get back to your prepregnancy size."

"And I say you look fine to me."

She just smiled, but he could see a touch of shyness in her eyes. Better than wariness, he figured. God knew Maggie had reason to be wary, considering her husband had recently abandoned her and their baby girl.

It just wasn't in Daniel to be sorry that Joe had cut out on his family. Maggie was better off without the lying thief. And—

A gust of wind whipped through the sheets and Daniel caught the sheet before it could blow from Maggie's hands. Her fingers felt cold beneath his and before he knew what he was doing, he'd wrapped her fingers in his, warming them against his palm.

And it was as if the ranch disappeared and it was just the two of them. Standing there between the snapping, fresh linens. Was it the same for her?

The edge of the sheet dragged to the ground, but he barely

noticed. And Maggie didn't reach for it, either. He saw her gaze flicker over their hands, then skip up to his face and away.

She moistened her lips and swallowed. But she didn't pull her fingers from his hold.

A lock of hair drifted across her face, and she lifted her free hand to brush it away, but he beat her to it. The glistening strands of blond felt like silk against his rough fingertips as he smoothed it behind her ear. Her lips parted soundlessly.

And though he knew it was too soon, too early for her, he knew he was going to kiss her. And she knew it, too. He could see it in her beautiful blue-green eyes. "Ah, Maggie Mae," he murmured. "I've waited so long."

Ever mindful of moving too fast, even if his heart was pounding like a runaway train, he ran his knuckles along her satin-smooth jaw. Her chin tilted upward and her soft lashes drifted down.

Daniel settled his lips over hers, reining in the overwhelming urge to pull her against him. To twine his hands in her silky hair and never let her go.

Instead he kissed her lightly, gently. She swayed, murmuring his name against his mouth, and he tasted the soft inner curve of her lips. And it was so sweet and so welcoming and her tongue flirted with his and—

She gasped and yanked out of his arms so fast she nearly tripped over the laundry basket behind her. Her cheeks were flushed as she smoothed her hair behind her ears, looking everywhere but at him. "I…you…we—"

She looked at him and he felt sorrow down to his toes at the panic in her gaze. "It's okay, Maggie Mae—"

Daniel dragged his thoughts to the present, but her name echoed inside his head. *His* Maggie. Only, she wasn't.

She was not his. She never had been.

She'd flushed and stammered and stuttered that afternoon. But the gist had been there. And the gist had been a crumb of a husband named Joe, who—despite his recent abandonment of Maggie and his daughter—she wouldn't betray.

Even three long years later, even beyond death, Maggie was still holding to him.

Daniel raked his hands through his hair, shoving away the thought. He leaned his bare back against the wooden rail fence and tucked his thumbs in his belt loops. What the hell was he doing, staring at the cottage like he could move time backward? Hadn't he learned that wishing and wanting were useless notions?

He threw back his head with a long breath and stared up at the velvety sky that soared over the earth. Over the Double-C.

His heritage.

His home.

He was through trying to find something that he'd only ever known here at the Double-C. It had only led to tragedy, anyway.

He was home to stay. As soon as he'd walked in the door of the big house after his absence, Matthew had bluntly announced his plans for expanding again. Daniel hadn't yet agreed, but he would.

He would agree to take on his fair share. It would be a decision made strictly with the head.

The only kind of decision Daniel would ever make again.

So it was a good thing that Maggie and her kid were here only for a few days. A damned good thing.

Some things came back easily, Maggie realized the next morning when she awakened before dawn. She lay in bed for a moment, her attention lingering on the darkened window. It had been several years since she'd needed to rise at such an ungodly hour. But back just one day—less than twenty-four hours—at the Double-C, and she was easily falling into the early-to-rise routine.

More likely it was the knowledge that Daniel slept on the other side of the wall that had nudged her to wakening.

She huffed impatiently and shoved back the covers, slipping out of the bed.

She was awake. She might as well put the time to good use. She tugged on her aging chenille robe and peeked outside her door. Daniel's bedroom door was still closed. But Maggie's nose picked up the faint scent of coffee wafting from downstairs, and she hurried into the bathroom for what was surely the fastest shower on record. Then back to her room—Daniel's door thankfully still closed—where she hurriedly dressed and tidied up the bedroom.

She was just giving the quilt-top a final smoothing hand when she heard a footfall on the other side of the wall.

He was awake.

She closed her eyes. Then she heard the faint creak of a bedroom door, and she froze. But no footsteps passed by on the way to the staircase. No soft knock sounded on her door.

"Get a grip," she said under her breath. She straightened and tucked her damp hair behind her ears. Smoothed her palms down the sides of her khaki walking shorts. Told herself that her hands were trembling only because she needed her morning coffee.

So why, then, did she dash down the stairs like the devil was at her heels when she looked cautiously out into the hallway to find the door to Daniel's room open and the door to the bathroom shut?

Matthew looked over his shoulder when she fairly skidded into the kitchen. He smiled at her as if it was an everyday occurrence and held up the full coffeepot. "Sleep okay?"

Maggie nodded, relaxing. Matthew's presence was as calming and welcoming as Daniel's was unsettling. She removed a sturdy white mug from the mug tree on the counter, and he filled it before sliding the pot back into the coffeemaker.

She leaned against the counter and cradled the mug, inhaling the wonderfully strong aroma. No hazelnut coffee here. No cappuccino or double lattes. Just good old coffee, strong enough to eat the metal off a spoon. She sipped. And hot enough to singe her throat all the way down.

Matthew, his own mug in hand, sat at the table. "What got you up so early?"

Maggie smiled faintly. "Old habits returning, I guess."

He nodded easily. "Jaimie's been sleeping later these days. Takes a nap in the middle of the afternoon sometimes, too."

"Pregnancy will do that to you." Maggie set down her mug. She felt strange just standing there, sharing coffee. She simply wasn't used to being a guest in this household. "Why don't I fix you some breakfast."

"You don't have—"

"Please. Makes me feel useful."

He shrugged, smiling wryly. "I'm not about to turn down your cooking, Maggie."

Pleased, she pulled open the refrigerator door and started assembling breakfast. After a few minutes Matthew took his coffee with him, and Maggie knew he was going back into his office beyond the stairs to work. It didn't bother her. In fact, working alone in the spacious kitchen felt...nice.

She'd just pulled a batch of blueberry muffins from the oven when she heard footfalls behind her. She quickly slid the muffin pan onto a trivet, not needing to look behind her to know who stood in the doorway between the kitchen and the dining room. Only one man had ever made the skin between her shoulder blades tighten.

Without looking at Daniel, she poured a mug of coffee and set it on the table in front of the chair he'd occupied before. Before he'd left his home.

He moved behind her, but instead of sliding out his chair, he continued to the pegs on the wall where his black hat hung. Maggie's fingers tightened around the dishcloth she held. "Don't you want to eat something?"

His eyes were remote as he pushed his hat onto his head. "Tell Matt I went over to Jefferson's."

Then he was gone.

She blinked against the stupid burning behind her eyes. "I guess that's a no."

Later that morning Maggie threw herself into Jaimie's plans. They left Sarah and J.D. playing under the watchful eye of

Leandra's mother, Emily, at the neighboring horse ranch owned by Emily and Jefferson Clay. Squire Clay had brought young Emily home to live with them after her parents were killed in an accident. She'd been seven and had really been more ''one of the boys'' than anything else during the time she lived with them before Squire sent her off to boarding school. Of course, she'd grown up, and Jefferson had learned just how very female Emily was.

Maggie had been torn between relief and disappointment when they didn't come across Daniel when she and Jaimie dropped off the children.

But Jaimie's enthusiasm for an afternoon shopping in Casper was too hard to ignore, and Maggie found herself enjoying the afternoon as they shopped and had lunch in a small, pretty restaurant.

They talked about everything under the sun, from pregnancy to calving season, to the rocky relationship Squire Clay had with Gloria Day. Eventually they even talked about Joe. About better times. And Maggie knew that Jaimie would be all right. That the happiness she'd found with Matthew Clay would help her grieve for the brother who, in the end, she'd hardly known.

That evening after supper, Daniel stayed out in the barn until he figured Maggie and her daughter would be long asleep.

And finally, when his back was stiff and his knees ached from sitting so long in one position, he silently went inside.

A light had been left burning over the stove. Jaimie's doing, he figured, and poured the last measure of coffee from the pot into a mug. It was barely warm, but he didn't care.

He wandered through the dining room, through the little-used living room. He was glad Squire wasn't back yet from visiting Gloria. It would be all too easy to end up on the receiving end of the old man's sharp eyes, and Daniel just wasn't in the mood for it.

Dan figured it was better if his father never knew what he'd been doing the past few years. It would probably bring on another heart attack. He damn sure didn't need to live with that on his conscience, too.

He headed upstairs only to have his eyes snared by the narrow sliver of light beneath the door of the bedroom that Maggie used. He was all set to walk right on by, but her door suddenly opened and she stood there with the golden light shining from behind her.

Her eyes widened and color flitted over her high cheekbones. She was barefoot. Wearing nothing but a pale yellow sleeveless vest and matching pajama pants that revealed her red-painted toenails.

She looked so warm and soft, so...*female* that it bit into his gut like a hot poker.

He could see her throat work as she swallowed. Could see the way her pulse beat visibly in her neck. He deliberately let his gaze glide along her bare, too-thin arms, to her fingers, delicate, long and tipped in sexy red. He looked until he found what his eyes sought. The dull glint of a gold wedding band.

He needed to go into his room. Shut the door, with him on the inside and her on the outside. Definitely on the outside. Meeting here twice like this in as many nights was nearly more than he could stand. "Can't sleep without the noises of the city?" His tone was quiet and dry as dust, and judging by her expression, about as friendly.

"I was going to check on J.D."

He looked across the wide hallway to his niece Sarah's bedroom. "Sounds quiet to me."

"Ah, yes. Yes, it does." Her eyes shied away from his. "I guess I'll turn in, then."

He didn't know what devil prompted him to touch her bare shoulder. But he did. And she went still as a church mouse. He fancied he could actually hear her breathing cease.

"Don't."

He paused, his eyes on her shoulder. Despite her plea, he ran his fingers down to her elbow, before severing the contact. "You're too thin."

She smiled, but it looked forced. "You know the saying. You can never be too thin or too rich." The words fell flat.

He lifted her hand, tightening his hold when she would have drawn away. He felt the cold band around her ring finger. "Is this the new city look for you?"

"What if it is?" she demanded faintly.

He let go of her. "You're too thin," he said again.

"So I've lost a few pounds," she murmured, her shoulders hunched defensively. "Your shoulders are wider." Her cheeks pinkened. "So what? Time passes. And why are you angry?"

He lifted his eyebrows. "I'm not angry."

Maggie's lips twisted. She dared a look up into his smoky eyes. "Right."

He smiled suddenly, eyes sharp and a dimple slashing alongside his wolfish smile. "I could pretend to be angry," he said softly. "Then we could kiss and make up."

Maggie's heart tripped. "Very funny."

His smile disappeared as quickly as it had appeared. "Has the city taken away your sense of humor, too?"

"Joe claimed I *had* no sense of humor," Maggie retorted thoughtlessly.

"Ah, the sainted Joe."

Maggie dragged her eyes away from the impossibly wide stretch of his shoulders beneath his usual T-shirt. "Daniel, please."

"You brought him up, Maggie Mae."

Her breath stalled, and she closed her eyes for a moment at the name. "Don't."

"Don't tell you how my heart bleeds that Joe's six feet under?"

She winced. "Don't call me that."

"What?"

"Maggie Mae," she managed huskily.

His eyes were depthless disks of silver in his bronzed face. He seemed to stand even closer, though she was certain he hadn't moved. "Margaret Mary never seemed to fit you," he said.

It was also a name that Maggie had never liked. She'd been named after her mother. And heaven knew that Maggie wanted to be nothing like her mother, not even to carry the same name. But it was Daniel, only Daniel, who had ever attached the "Mae" to the "Maggie" that she preferred.

"Maggie Mae used to suit you," he added. "Maybe Margaret is more suitable now. Is that what they call you at your office? Margaret?"

"No," she said tightly.

His head tilted and he smiled faintly, as if the whispered conversation, if you could call it that, amused him. "Go back to bed, Maggie, and sleep the sleep of the innocent. Little girl Greene is sound asleep."

Maggie felt anything *but* innocent. Not with him standing so close that she could breathe in the warmth of him. "J.D.," she managed. "Her name is J.D."

"You are all hung up on names tonight, aren't you."

She moistened her lips and looked him right in those unreadable silver eyes. "And you're angry, no matter what you say. What is it, Daniel? The money? Joe didn't leave me with any of it. Perhaps if you saw my apartment, you'd believe that."

His eyes went glacial, and she found herself backed into her bedroom, the door shutting in them both. Her breath climbed down her throat, nearly choking her.

"Is that what you think? That I want the money back?" His teeth flashed, white and fierce. "Tris and Matt tracked down most of it. Or have you forgotten? We could have prosecuted Joe, and we chose not to."

She inched away until she bumped the dresser. "Because Matthew fell in love with Joe's sister. And I haven't forgotten anything."

"Really."

She closed her hands over the edge of the dresser behind her. "Really."

His brooding eyes rested on her lips, and it took everything she possessed to suppress the urge to moisten them. "Then you remember that afternoon, too."

"Wh-what afternoon?"

He tsked, mocking. "You never could lie worth squat."

"Considering everything, I'll take that as a compliment."

"How long before you go back to Chicago?"

"We leave Sunday," she said stiffly, aware that he considered that day to be none too soon.

"Today is Tuesday." He looked over her shoulder, toward the bed. "Wednesday, actually."

"You don't want me here."

"No, I don't," he said smoothly, and Maggie felt her stomach tighten.

"I didn't know you were back until it was too late." *Or I wouldn't have come.* The rest of her thought remained unsaid. But he knew it as well as she did.

"Oh, Maggie, I am well aware of that." He lifted his hand toward her, his jaw tightening when she flinched. But he continued the motion, drawing a lock of hair away from her cheek. "Well aware," he stressed.

He lowered his hand at last, but he still stood far too close for her peace of mind. If she drew in the deep breath her starving lungs cried for, her breasts, covered only in the thin cotton, would brush against his snug T-shirt. She swallowed, pressing back against the dresser. "I think you should go." Her whisper shook.

He smiled and there was nothing humorous about the expression. He leaned over her, resting his big hands alongside hers on the dresser. "I'm done going. I'll leave that for you." He straightened suddenly. "Do you miss him?"

Confusion swept over her. Then mortification when she realized he was referring to Joe. "Yes."

He nodded, and walked out of the room, opening and closing the door behind him without a sound.

Maggie hugged her arms around herself, shivering. It seemed she could lie convincingly, after all.

She walked toward the bed, her thoughts jumbled. Sitting

on the nightstand beside the bed was her voluminous purse, and before she thought twice, she'd dragged it onto the bed beside her and removed a business-size gray envelope from its depths. She drew out the letter on its matching, conservative gray stationery and reread the contents. She knew the words nearly by heart, even though she hadn't been in possession of the letter for a full week yet.

Some things didn't need much time to sink in. Apparently this report from the investigator she'd hired was one of them. After all, it wasn't every day that you learned your husband, prior to his death, had become a bigamist.

Maggie closed her eyes, trying to summon a picture of Joe in her mind. But the image was fuzzy. The most clear thing was his eyes. The same deeply green eyes that he'd passed on to their daughter.

She sank back against the soft pillows. J.D. She would concentrate on J.D. Her precious daughter was the one good thing to come out of her marriage. It was Joe's loss that he'd never realized that.

She drew in a slow breath and carefully folded the letter, replacing it in the envelope. She *didn't* miss Joe. She hadn't for a very long time. Maybe her pride kept her from admitting it to others, Daniel included, but she admitted it to herself at least.

She pushed the envelope back inside her purse and set it aside once more on the nightstand. The light caught on her narrow wedding band and she paused, staring at it as if she hadn't seen it in ages. Perhaps she hadn't.

She'd been wearing the ring since Joe placed it there shortly after her seventeenth birthday. She'd thought when he'd done so she would find the things she'd missed in her life. She'd been wrong. She'd kept the ring on since Joe left her, more for J.D.'s sake than anything. Her daughter, inquisitive and bright, had seemed satisfied when she'd asked Maggie why she didn't have a daddy like some of her friends. Maggie had told J.D. that she did have a daddy. She'd showed J.D. the few pictures she'd kept from her elopement and the wedding band. She certainly hadn't continued wearing it because she'd expected Joe to come back to her. And the ring had discouraged a few male advances that Maggie had been all too happy to avoid.

Yet suddenly it was too much.

She dashed out of her room into the bathroom, barely managing not to slam the door in her haste. She scrabbled with the water and the pretty little floral bottle of liquid soap. Her breath felt harsh in her chest as she squirted the slippery soap around the ring. She twisted it. "Come on. Come on."

It didn't want to budge over her knuckle. She added water and more soap.

The ring fell into the sink with a *ting.*

Going still, she stared at it for a long while. Then she picked it out, slowly rinsed away the suds and dried her hands. She returned to the bedroom and tucked the band into her wallet. She supposed there might come a day when J.D. would want it. Mostly Maggie just wanted it out of sight.

Then, her thumb rubbing over the very bare place where that ring had been for so long, she climbed into bed.

And slept.

Chapter Three

Before Maggie knew it, Saturday morning dawned, bright and clear. She knew it was a perfect day for the weekend picnic that Jaimie had planned. But she could hardly look forward to it. Because, though she and Daniel had managed to avoid each other since that late-night, well, discussion, she knew there would be no way to avoid him at the picnic.

She twisted her damp hair up off her neck and clamped a tortoiseshell claw-type clip on it to hold it in place, then went to make sure J.D. was dressed.

Not only was J.D. dressed, but she was plowing her way through pancakes at the kitchen table with her cousin Sarah on one side of her and Squire Clay on the other. He'd finished his pancakes and was working on the newspaper crossword puzzle.

He glanced up, his craggy, carved face splitting into a smile. "Well now, child, don't you look purty as a picture."

"Thank you." Before she knew what she was doing, she'd

grabbed the coffeepot and refilled his mug. "Where is Jaimie?"

"She started feeling poorly right in the middle of flipping pancakes." Without taking his attention from his puzzle, he poured a measure of coffee from his mug into the delicate china saucer that sat beside it, then drank the piping hot brew from it instead of the mug. "You just gonna hover there, girl, or sit down and eat a pancake or two?" He glanced up. "Might add a little curve back to your arms."

What was this preoccupation with her weight? But she pulled out a chair and sat. Her stomach was too nervous to eat a pancake, though, and she reached for a piece of dry toast instead.

Squire finished off his one saucerful, then poured some more. "We haven't had time to jaw much, you and I, since I got back yesterday. Jaimie's kept you pretty busy."

Maggie tore off a corner of toast and nibbled. "She has a lot of energy."

He grunted in agreement. "Keeps my boy Matt on his toes."

She smiled. "I noticed."

"Guess you probably noticed, too, how Weaver's growing," he said. "You hear about the new doc in town?"

"Jaimie mentioned her."

"Worked real hard to get the doc to come here," he continued. "I'm a mite proud of it." He continued on, his voice deep and graveled and familiar, and gradually, without having to ever say a word, Maggie felt herself begin to relax.

"You're looking a tad peaked, child," he said, his sharp eyes not unkind. "I hope it's not 'cause you're grieving too hard over Joe."

So much for relaxing. A gnawing guilt spread through her because she knew that she wasn't grieving at all. And she should be. Despite everything, he'd been her husband.

"He was heading down a bad road," Squire went on, shaking his head slightly. "No good was gonna come of it."

Maggie stiffened a moment before Daniel spoke behind her. "I think that can wait for another day, Squire," he said.

Squire harrumphed, but the subject was dropped, to Maggie's relief. Her meager interest in the toast disappeared with Daniel's presence, and she rose, clearing the dishes.

Daniel stood in her way, though, when she turned to set everything in the sink. "That's not your job anymore," he said irritably.

"I'm just clearing the dishes," she returned evenly.

"You're a guest."

"And that means I can't wash a few dishes?" She'd cooked breakfast three times, but Daniel had consistently disappeared just like he had that first morning.

"Leave the girl be, Dan," Squire said. "I swear, boy, you got ants crawling over your nerves. What's griping at you?"

Maggie, hands filled with syrup-sticky plates, looked up at Daniel. She knew what was griping him, and *she* was it. His attitude couldn't have been more clear. He didn't want her around whether she was doing her job or being a guest. She slipped around him to the sink, accidentally brushing against his arm. Felt him very carefully move out of touching range.

The plates hit the sink with more clatter than she'd intended. She flipped on the water, drawing in a shaky breath. Unfortunately, relief was not in sight, because Daniel sat down and started forking pancakes onto a clean plate for himself.

For lack of anything better to do, Maggie squirted dish soap into the sink and set to work on the bowl, dried with pancake batter. "Where is Jaimie?"

Matthew strode into the room, heading straight for the coffeepot and draining it of its last drops. "She's not feeling too hot at the moment."

Maggie dried her hands and started a fresh pot of coffee, one look at Matthew's rather pale face telling her that he wasn't feeling too great himself. "Morning sickness?"

He nodded, gulping at the coffee like it was his lifeblood. "She told me to get out before she hit me over the head with her blow-dryer."

Squelching a chuckle, Maggie opened cupboards until she found a box of saltine crackers. She slipped several free and pushed them into Matthew's hand. "Take those to her." He nodded, turning, and she grabbed the coffee mug from him first. "The smell," she explained. "Jaimie told me she's particularly sensitive to strong…aromas in the morning."

"Oh. Right." Crackers in hand, he bolted out of the kitchen, and she heard him thundering up the stairs.

"Mama, can Sarah and I go outside and play wif Sandy?" J.D. asked, looking up from her empty plate.

"Yes, but you have to stay on the grass around the house. Wipe your hands and faces, first."

"You'd think that boy had forgotten what it was like to be around a pregnant wife," Squire muttered. He shook his head. "And I hear that other long-haired son of mine is just as bad."

Maggie couldn't keep back her chuckle this time. And was astounded when Daniel met her gaze, his own amused. Simply amused. No under-the-surface anger. No glint of something she couldn't name. Just…amused.

The very sight of it made her heart lurch.

"How bad were *you* whenever Mom was pregnant?" he asked Squire.

The man grunted. "Not as damn bad as my sons."

"They're just getting started on their families," Maggie said, smiling. "You had more practice." Then she had to hold her breath, realizing belatedly that Squire had lost his wife when she gave birth to his youngest son, Tristan.

But Squire didn't seem to be thinking about that. "What about you, young lady? Seems to me your J.D. could do with a baby brother or sister."

Maggie flushed. "I'd sort of need a husband first, I think," she managed equably. "Besides, you know what kind of difficulty I had with J.D. I think she's all I was meant to have."

Squire snorted. "Time'll tell, won't it." He scooted back his chair and rose, tall and straight. "I'll go keep an eye on the young 'uns." He hooked his gray Stetson off its peg by the door and settled it on his silvered head, then thumped through the mudroom and out the screen door with its familiar squeak.

Maggie turned back to the dishes, her gaze skating over Daniel, who was slowly poking his way through his mountain of pancakes. She felt a sudden sigh, wishing she didn't remember that he preferred waffles. Or that, if he did have pancakes, he liked them smothered in eggs. Over easy. No doubt, if Jaimie had been able to finish what she'd started without being hit with a bout of morning sickness, she'd have prepared just that.

Wiping her hands again, she put the cast-iron skillet on the stove and took the bowl of eggs from the fridge. Within minutes she set three eggs, perfectly done, alongside his plate.

His quicksilver eyes skipped over her and back to the eggs. "Thanks."

It was grudging. But he said it. He hadn't stomped through the kitchen without so much as a sip of coffee like he had those other mornings. "You're welcome."

She turned back to the dishes and was nearly finished when he carried his plate and utensils to the sink and handed them to her. Her relief was short-lived, however, when he leaned his hip against the counter and crossed his arms. "There is a dishwasher, you know."

She didn't bother responding.

"So would you want more kids?"

At that she dropped the dishcloth, splashing suds and lukewarm water over her arms. "Excuse me?"

His jaw tightened. "You heard me."

She fished around for the cloth and set to scrubbing the last coffee mug, as if she was trying to remove the glaze. "It's not something I've thought about."

"Liar." He took the mug from her soapy hands and rinsed it, then set it in the dish drainer.

With no more dishes to focus on, Maggie loosened the drain and started wiping down the counters. "Why do you care?"

He shrugged. "I'm only making conversation, Maggie."

Her lips firmed. "Now that we're finally leaving tomorrow, you're making an attempt at civility?"

His eyes glinted. "Well, well. The angel has grown claws."

And right now they were curled around the wet dishcloth, just dying to heave it in his mocking face. "Who would have thought?"

"So?"

"So...*what?*"

"Do you want more kids?"

Maggie swallowed. "I always wanted a large family," she finally said evenly. Truthfully. She wanted for J.D. what she herself hadn't had as a child. Brothers and sisters. Two parents who loved each other. Who cared for their children and were *there* for them. But J.D. had only Maggie. It wasn't the way she'd planned, but then little in her life was. And J.D. didn't seem to be suffering too much. Because Maggie would do anything for her daughter. Anything. She never wanted J.D. to grow up wondering what it was about her that made her unlovable.

"Even after being so sick with J.D.?"

She stopped wiping. "It doesn't really matter now, does it," she said bluntly. "My husband is dead." Then, because she didn't want to think about that anymore, she flicked a glance his way. "You're more likely to have children than I," she pointed out. And because it was a thought that plagued her, "Maybe you already do," she added. "You've been gone three years, after all."

His expression tightened and something hard and painful flitted through his eyes. "Do you see me with a kid hanging on my leg?"

Maggie shrugged. "It's easy enough to be a father without having the child around to raise." Wasn't J.D. proof of that? Joe had contributed his genes to their bright, beautiful daughter. But he'd certainly never contributed his time.

Daniel suddenly loomed over her, his expression thunderous. "I can assure you, Maggie Mae, that if I did have a child—which I don't—that child and the mother would be with me. I don't desert what's mine,'' he said, so softly and fiercely that Maggie felt her knees wobble. And she wondered what was wrong with her, that she could feel her stomach tighten with...anticipation?

She cleared her throat. ''Well, bully for—''

''Morning, guys.'' Jaimie sailed into the kitchen, her morning sickness apparently a thing of the past. ''Oh, Mags, you cleaned up the kitchen. Bless your ever-loving heart.'' Her bright green eyes darted from Maggie to Daniel and back again. ''Uh, everything okay here?''

Daniel snagged his black hat in a motion nearly identical to Squire's earlier, thumped it on his head and strode outside, slamming through the screen door.

Later that afternoon Maggie didn't know if the success of the picnic owed more to Jaimie's preparedness or the enthusiasm of the Clay family. Probably a good measure of both.

The children were having a blast, splashing and whooping it up in the swimming hole with Nikki Day, one of Gloria's daughters. Nikki and her twin, Belle, had driven up with Gloria for one last summer fling before they started their final year of college. Both young women were every bit as friendly as their mother. But Maggie found herself watching the way Belle and Daniel whiled away the afternoon, talking in their own corner of the tree-shaded retreat.

When the barbecue had been doused and the food had been eaten—except for a few remaining cupcakes and cookies that still sat on the wide table that Jaimie had enlisted her husband to cart out to the swimming hole in his pickup truck—and the adults were sprawled about on blankets and chairs complaining about the heat and having scarfed too much food, talk grew more hilarious. Stories became more outrageous of the stunts the brothers had pulled while growing up.

Jefferson yanked open the cooler that was in the back of his truck and passed out frosty long-neck beers to his brothers, then dropped onto the checkered blanket next to his wife. ''I think the worst thing was when Dan bought his first bike. He was only thirteen. Remember that, Matt?''

Daniel rolled his eyes, leisurely twisting open his bottle.

Matthew chuckled. ''I don't know how he convinced someone to sell him that old motorcycle. But damned if he didn't get it and ride it home.''

''Oh, I remember that,'' Emily put in, propping her elbow on Jefferson's middle, grinning slyly when he grunted. ''That was after I came to live at the Double-C. Didn't you take a spill, Daniel?''

''The first of many,'' Jefferson drawled.

Maggie folded her legs underneath her and tried not to watch Daniel too closely. Nevertheless, she caught the way he returned Jefferson's brotherly taunt. ''I remember the first time you smoked a cigar,'' he remembered smoothly, watching Jefferson grimace at the memory.

''How about when you sneaked that girl up to your room.'' Matthew directed that at Daniel.

Squire harrumphed. ''I remember that.''

Gloria chuckled beside him.

Belle looked up at Daniel beside her. ''I think I'd like to hear more about this one.''

Daniel shook his head, his lips twitching. ''No. You really don't.''

Jaimie sat forward, her legs crossed. She dropped the daisy chain she'd been making. ''Oh, Daniel. Such a history you have.'' She glanced back at her husband. ''Details. Give me details.''

''Before the girls get out of the swimming hole and we can't talk about these things,'' Emily added, laughter in her voice.

But before Matthew could launch into the story, Daniel set aside his beer bottle and stood. ''Think it's time to swim,'' he announced and ripped off his T-shirt.

Everyone laughed. Everyone but Maggie, who was simply struck dumb when Daniel stepped past her, shucking his jeans to reveal plain black boxers beneath. He knifed into the swimming hole with a flash of bronzed muscles and hair-dusted legs.

Jaimie giggled and leaned back against Matthew. "I think you embarrassed him."

Matthew snorted. "Daniel? Are you kidding? He has no shame. Trust me. I know my brother. He's the guy who once had three dates in one night. All different women. Pulled it off, too."

"Until I found out about it and grounded him for a month," Squire reminded. "Not that it did any good considerin' the way he would climb outta his bedroom window and sneak off to town. Your brother always had one of two things in his hand. A girl or a pool cue. Sometimes both."

J.D. clambered out of the water and scampered over to Maggie, water flying everywhere. "Mama, come swimming. *Please.*"

Suddenly, Jaimie stood up and tugged off her loose T-shirt to reveal a skimpy purple bikini top. "Sounds good to me," she said and ran into the water wearing her denim shorts and the bikini top. "Come on in, Mags," she called.

Emily stood up and unbuttoned her denim dress, dropping it on the grass. Her pregnancy was only slightly more obvious in the brilliant red one-piece she wore, and she joined the crew in the water. From somewhere, a bright blue beach ball appeared, and it bounced around from swimmer to swimmer, with even the little girls joining.

Maggie watched, smiling faintly, as J.D. flopped her arms toward Daniel, and ended up on his shoulders. If his strained grin was any indication, J.D.'s little starfish fingers were clinging a little too hard to his chestnut-wet waves. It wasn't long before Belle, Gloria, Jefferson and Matthew joined in.

"Better git in there, girl, before they splash out all the water."

Maggie looked over at Squire where he lazed in a lawn chair. His only concession to the heat was unbuttoning his chambray shirt two buttons, instead of one, and drinking iced tea instead of coffee. "What about you?"

He raised his eyebrows. "Child, I fenced off this swimming hole for my wife and boys. Not 'cause I like to dip in it. Git to it now. Go on."

Feeling more self-conscious out of the water now than in, she pulled off her dress and kicked off her sandals. She walked over to the flattish boulder that projected over the water on one side and sat down on the end of it. Stuck her toes in the water. Maggie knew it was springfed, but still the chill startled her, and she yanked her foot right back out.

"Chicken?"

She looked down to see Daniel's head beside one side of the boulder. "Maybe." She turned her eyes away from the gray glide of his eyes, even more silvery now that his hair was water-dark wet and slicked back from his chiseled features. J.D. had moved on and was propped on her "Unca" Matt's left shoulder, while Sarah perched on the right. Leandra clung to her daddy's shoulders. All three were shrieking at the tops of their lungs.

Daniel drew her attention when he flicked water over her foot, hovering over the surface of the water. "You won't drown," he said. His eyes met hers, and the laughter and chatter and childish squeals seemed to fade into nothing.

"How do you know?" Water lapped at his broad, muscular shoulders.

His jaw cocked slightly to one side. A shadow flitted through his steady gaze. "I won't let you."

Leaving Maggie wondering what, exactly, they were talking about. And then it didn't matter, because she scooted forward and slipped into the water, catching her breath at the cold. She paddled, keeping her head above water.

Daniel's hand met hers beneath the cold, silky surface, making her breath falter. His fingers slid between hers, and he tugged her toward the center of the swimming hole, out of the shade and into the narrow wedge of sunlight that was all that remained of the hot afternoon sun. J.D. spotted her and flopped from Matthew's shoulder, dog-paddling her way across the distance. "Mama!"

Maggie went under the surface when J.D. launched herself into her arms, and she came up blinking and sputtering. J.D. grinned at her, all smiles and wriggling little girl, and feeling lighter than she had in a long while, Maggie gently flicked water into J.D.'s face. And splashed a little harder into Daniel's.

His eyes gleamed, and suddenly a massive water fight ensued, everyone splashing everyone, until laughing and sputtering and exhausted, bodies climbed out of the water. Falling onto towels and blankets. Bundling into clothes because now that the sun was below the horizon, it was too cool to sit around wet.

Maggie lingered near the water's edge, listening to the vehicles head out. J.D. and Sarah were spending the night with Leandra. When all was quiet again, when all Maggie could hear was the lap of water against fragrant earth and leaves sighing in the trees, she gathered her long skirt around her legs and sat down on the boulder that still retained the warmth from the day's sun.

She leaned forward, drawing her finger along the surface of the water, creating ripples in the glassy surface.

Daniel saw her just before he started walking home. Looking like an angel in a drift of pale green, she was drawing her name upon the water. The sight hit him hard and low and hot. Pure want drove through him and he let it.

Let it because it beat back the guilt and the darkness inside him.

He was glad he'd ditched his wet trunks before pulling on his jeans. But then again, perhaps cold, clammy swim trunks were what he needed against the throb in his gut.

Who was he fooling? He wasn't *letting* the want do anything. It was ruling him. There wasn't any place he could banish himself to. There was only Maggie. And him.

Alone.

Her head suddenly lifted, a wild thing scenting danger. Her finger drew back from the water. ''I thought you'd gone with

Nikki and Belle.'' The area seemed utterly silent in contrast to the enthusiastic noisiness earlier. Her voice sounded intimate in that silence.

''They're driving straight on back to school. Squire'll take Gloria home. Why?''

She lifted her hand, touching her throat with her red-tipped fingers. ''No reason. You and Belle just looked...cozy.'' She dropped her hand to her lap, folding it into her other. ''Everybody has already gone back.''

''I noticed.''

''Oh, right. Of course.''

''You're nervous.''

''Don't be ridiculous.'' She sighed and unfolded her legs. ''I should get back.''

''J.D.?''

''Hmm? Oh, she's thrilled to be spending the night with Leandra. She and Sarah.''

''Quiet night under Jefferson's roof tonight.''

Maggie smiled faintly at that. ''Actually, I think those three will fall asleep as soon as their heads hit the pillows. The swimming, you know. It takes the starch out of them.''

He watched as she slipped her narrow feet into her strappy little flat sandals. ''How about you?''

''I didn't swim so much as get splashed to kingdom come,'' she murmured. She flicked her hands down her dress and started to walk across the lush clover. ''J.D. had fun today.''

For such a large man, he moved very silently. One minute he was three feet away, the next, he stood right next to her. Invading her space. Making her throat knot. ''Did you?'' he asked.

''Yes.'' She sidestepped.

He followed. Blocked.

''Are you running, Maggie Mae?''

''Don't, Daniel,'' she whispered.

''Don't what?'' His low voice was intense. She couldn't bring herself to look at him.

His big hand cupped the back of her neck. Strong and so incredibly warm. Alive. "What?" he asked again.

She swallowed the gargantuan knot in her throat, unable to answer, and tried not to tremble. Then his hand moved, slipping along her jaw, stealing her breath and her sensibilities in one smooth glide. His eyes, shadowy in the deepening dusk, focused on her lips. "You remember the first time I called you that," he murmured. "When you were hanging out those sheets after J.D. was born."

"Daniel. Please."

She knew what was coming. God help her, she wanted what was coming. Just as she'd wanted it *then*. His thumb brushed over her lips and her breath stalled, then returned, choppy and uneven.

"Stop," she whispered.

He paused, his jaw tight. "Really?"

She knew he would. That it would only take one word. A nod. And he'd abide by what she'd said. Despite Daniel Clay's hell-raising reputation, he'd been an honorable man. If he'd truly been the wild Clay boy they'd talked about in Weaver— the one who was never without a woman, a pool cue or a whisky—he would never have stopped at one kiss three years ago. He would have taken what she'd been so close to giving to him. But he hadn't.

He'd left his home and his family instead.

"No," she breathed on a half sob, half sigh. She was weak. What else could explain the insanity that made her go on her sandaled toes and press her lips to his?

An explosion of heat engulfed her. His arm went from her neck to her waist as he turned the tables, his lips covering hers. He tasted of springfed water and male and dark, hot want.

And it had been so long, so very, very long since Maggie had felt a strong male body pressed against hers. And never, not even that never-forgotten afternoon while wet sheets blew and snapped around them, had she felt *this* male body pressed so intimately against hers.

Her eyes burned behind her tightly closed lids, and she slipped so easily, so thoroughly into the hot web he spun of her senses.

"Say my name," he murmured against her lips. His hands slid wickedly along her back. Skimmed her hips. Dragged up great handfuls of gauzy, misty green fabric.

She wanted to weep for the sensations buffeting her. "Dan…iel. Oh, what are we doing?"

His hands closed over the backs of her thighs, pulling her up hard and tight against him. His lips engulfed hers. "Finishing what we couldn't before," he finally gritted, when he lifted his head, allowing her to haul in a shaky breath.

"No, I can't…can't—"

He tossed aside the clip from her hair and whisked her dress over her head, silencing her with another mind-melting kiss. His tongue licked flames of wickedness along her earlobe. Trailed over her shoulder and drifted along the damp fabric of her strapless swimsuit. "Tell me to stop, then," he murmured as he rolled the clinging fabric down. Down, down, until the evening dusk breathed upon her bare breasts. "Tell me you're not trembling for me. Aching for me. I've been thinking about this every night, sleeping on the other side of that wall from you. And you have, too."

Her knees went to water, but it didn't matter, for his arms lifted her right off the ground, his hot lips finding with unerring accuracy one turgid nipple, then the other. She cried out, her dismay disappearing in a puff. She wound her arms around his shoulders, marveling indistinctly over the incredible strength of them. Of the supple, satiny feel of skin stretched taut over rock-hard muscle. Her blood sang in her veins.

"Tell me I'm wrong. Tell me to stop," he repeated, and her skin shivered beneath his gruff, gritty demand.

She bent her head over his, holding him to her breast. "I can't," she cried softly. Her eyes burned. "Oh, Daniel. I can't."

His breath hissed audibly, and she felt herself being lowered to the ground. But his hands didn't let her loose. His hands slid to hers, where she knew he noticed the absence of her wedding band as his touched paused. Lingered over her bare finger. "Here, then. Now. One time. We'll finish it. Then we'll put this behind us. Once and for all."

She trembled wildly, feeling vulnerable and exposed with her bathing suit baring her flesh to his eyes. Never—not before, during or after thirteen years of marriage—had a man looked at her with such thorough determination. Such naked want.

Maybe he was right. Once and they could move on. Maggie back to her life in Chicago. Daniel to…whatever it was that met his needs.

Unable to get a word out of her tight throat, she managed a nod and laid her palm against his chest, so defined in the plain white T-shirt. He felt so warm that his heat leaped through the cotton knit, igniting her palm and working right up her shoulder. To her heart.

She didn't know what to expect then. She reached for her swimming suit, but his hands stopped her and drew her palms back to him, pushing them under the hem of his T-shirt, flattening them against his ridged abdomen.

Maggie choked back a gasp, her fingers greedily pressing against the rock-hard muscles. Feeling them leap beneath her touch. Madness careening through her blood, she yanked his T-shirt upward, struggling to get it over his shoulders. Off his head. Throwing it thoughtlessly, carelessly to the ground when she succeeded, and crying out when he yanked her against him, pressing her bare breasts to his bare chest.

An oath whispered through his clenched teeth, his hands cradling her hips, moving her against him. Then her swimsuit was gone. Somewhere on the ground alongside his shirt and the jeans he shrugged out of and the scuffed athletic shoes he kicked off.

He moved into the water, pulling her with him. His lips closed over her nipples as they beaded, near to pain in the water that, somehow, strangely, didn't seem as cold as it had earlier. His limbs tangled silkily with hers, his hands guiding her legs around his hips, cradling her against him, driving her mad as she felt his heat, his strength brushing so intimately against her.

His lips burned over her temples. Her jaw. Her mouth. "I can't wait," he growled.

"Don't." He went absolutely, painfully still, and she writhed against him, needing him when he denied her the ultimate satisfaction. "Don't wait," she gasped, her mouth open against his shoulder.

He exhaled roughly and sank into her with a low, feral sound.

She arched back, a soft cry on her lips, and shuddered, her body straining against his. Reaching. Reaching.

He was tall enough to stand on the bottom of the swimming hole, and she realized with some remote portion of her mind that he walked right out of the water, laying her back against the clover-soft ground, his hard, hot body keeping the night air at bay. She sank her teeth into her balled up fist, holding back a whimper as he thrust into her.

He lifted her hand and tugged it away from her mouth, catching it, and the other, above her head. "Say my name," he said again.

Mindless. She was simply mindless. "Daniel," she gasped, biting back a low moan.

"No," he said tautly. "Don't you hold back on me, Maggie Mae."

She didn't think it possible, but surely she felt him clear to her heart and beyond. Her heart raced and her breathing stalled.

"Let it out," he breathed against her breast. "I want to hear you."

She couldn't hold it in. The moan started low and soft. And when he turned, pulling her atop him and anchored her hips with his strong, guiding hands, it grew in her throat, until it was a desperate, keening cry. He was no more quiet than she, she realized dimly. And somehow, the fact that she could make this big, strong, somehow angry man, groan with pleasure, undid her. She rocked wildly against him, instinctively seeking that which she'd never experienced. Not in her entire life.

And when the pleasure came upon her, twisting her, flinging her into the wind, it was Daniel's arms that kept her safe. Daniel's heat that anchored.

Daniel's flesh that pulsed deep inside her, filling her.

Making her whole.

"Okay, you've got everything?"

Maggie nodded, her fingers crumpling their airline tickets in her tight grasp. She blinked and told herself she wasn't going to cry. But Jaimie was wiping her own eyes, and it was so very hard to blink back the hot, burning tears. Despite the fact that Maggie had rented the car when she and J.D. had arrived, Jaimie and Matthew had insisted on accompanying her to the airport. Matthew had sent the rental car back, instead, with one of the hands.

"I'm so glad you came here," Jaimie said. "Even if it was because of…well, you know." She hugged Maggie tightly. "We'll always visit you in Chicago. But please don't wait so long again to come back here. I wish you'd just come back to stay. Then we wouldn't ever have to do this. This was your home once, Maggie. Couldn't it be again? No, don't answer. I know you felt you had to go and make your own way after Joe left." She pulled back, dashing her fingers over her cheeks. "I'm just rambling. Don't mind me."

Maggie wiped her own cheeks. She knew that she could never return to the Double-C. Not after what she'd done with Daniel under the stars. Not after he'd walked her back to the big house last night and left her standing alone in the doorway to her bedroom, her lips tingling from the light kiss he'd dropped on them before he went into his own room.

Leaving her. Alone.

Matthew slipped his long arm around his wife and lifted his chin toward the gate where the flight attendant was waiting. "You're the last ones," he said.

Maggie swallowed and nodded. She held out her hand for J.D.'s and took a step toward the plane that would take them back to Chicago. Though she'd told herself not to, she couldn't help one last sweeping glance. But Daniel was nowhere in sight.

Obviously he'd decided they'd closed the book the night before. There was no point in lingering over any of the chapters. Put behind them, once and for all, just as he'd said. Finished.

Finished so finally that he hadn't been in the house this morning. Hadn't been on the ranch even.

He'd left. With no explanation. No note. Nothing.

Joe had done the same thing three years earlier. Yet this time it seemed so much worse. Joe's behavior wasn't unexpected.

Yet Daniel's departure hit her blindside.

It hurt. It hurt so badly Maggie wasn't sure she could stand it. But she'd have to. She had a daughter who was watching her with a puzzled, increasingly upset expression. The flight attendant was glancing with no amount of subtlety at her watch.

So Maggie smiled shakily at Jaimie and Matthew and, with J.D. by the hand, stepped through the gate, handing over their crumpled, wrinkled tickets. They boarded the plane that would take them back to their tidy, small apartment in the middle of the building in the middle of a block in the middle of a big, bustling, busy city. A city where she'd never be able to look up into a velvety black sky and wonder at how far the stars could possibly be when it seemed as if she could just reach up and brush them with her fingertips.

A city where she'd have to let her bruised heart toughen up all over again.

Thankfully, J.D. fell asleep partway through the flight.

Maggie turned her face toward the window and let the tears come.

Finished. Just like he'd said.

Chapter Four

*P*regnant.

The word rolled around inside her head, setting off explosions of panic and disbelief and fear. Maggie still couldn't believe what Dr. Rodriguez had told her.

Pregnant.

Maggie knew she'd have to tell Daniel. But she put off notifying him for one night. Then two, as she tried to figure out what words to use.

It wasn't as if Daniel cared for her. If he had, he wouldn't have walked away from her in August without a word of explanation. He wouldn't have returned to the ranch without a word of explanation. He wouldn't have let all the weeks since pass without contacting her.

The third night passed. And the fourth. And finally, a full week after she'd received the news, after J.D. was finally asleep, Maggie picked up the phone and dialed.

Jaimie answered. Delighted to visit. But no, Daniel wasn't around. He was in town. And what was up?

As much as Maggie loved Jaimie, she couldn't bring herself to say the words. She'd tell Daniel first. And then...well, then, they'd see.

So Maggie rambled about J.D. About her job and about the order she'd gotten to provide samples of her handmade wooden Christmas ornaments to a mail-order company. About Gertrude Nielsen, the cantankerous tenant in Maggie's building who made it her life's goal to complain about one thing or another at least once a day to Maggie.

Never knowing that on the other end of the line, sitting on a long couch in the basement with her feet being rubbed by her husband, Jaimie and Matthew eyed each other, wondering what Maggie *wasn't* saying. And how Daniel could be involved. Daniel, who hadn't cracked but two smiles since August.

It was late when Daniel let himself into the kitchen. Everyone had gone to bed hours ago. Tossing his hat on its peg, he quietly went downstairs to the new guest suite he'd finished building a few weeks ago in one end of what had previously been the overly huge recreation room. He left his keys on the breakfast counter of the small kitchen and shrugged out of his shirt, tossing it carelessly aside, then picked up the notepad he'd left there earlier, along with a narrow, rolled tube of architectural drawings. Snapping on the light near his chair, he sat down, running his eyes over the notes that had nothing to do with the blueprints. As he stared at them, trying to see something, anything, he might have missed, he absently picked up the heavy wooden paperweight to run his thumb over its satiny surface.

Coleman Black, his onetime boss, figured Daniel's concentration on building the house was a good thing. That it would be therapeutic.

If it was so therapeutic, then why was he still staring at his scratchings on the notepad? Why wasn't he accepting the truth that pretty much everyone else seemed to have accepted?

Therapeutic. What a joke.

Although Daniel no longer compared every nail he pounded in this house with the poor conditions of that other home he'd shared for a short time, he still couldn't banish the destruction he'd been unable to prevent from his dreams at night.

If he wasn't dreaming about *that,* he was dreaming about Maggie.

His hand tightened around the paperweight. Sleepless nights were pretty much what he deserved, he figured grimly.

As well as Daniel got along with his family, he needed a place of his own. Away from their concerned eyes and the questions they had—so far—been too polite or wary to ask.

His jaw cocked, and he deliberately loosened his fist from the paperweight. At least Jefferson was keeping his mouth shut. Dan figured it was only because Jefferson himself had more than his own share of secrets.

Well, Daniel had gotten over the reasons he'd left the Double-C in the first place. Damn fool emotions had ruled him back then. Look where it had gotten him. Where it had gotten them all.

Too bad he hadn't learned his lesson then. If he had, he wouldn't be needing activities that were *therapeutic* now. He wouldn't be making pointless phone calls and dozens of inquiries—all which led exactly nowhere.

He tossed aside the paperweight and the notepad.

His head was ruling his actions now, he reminded himself. He was back at the Double-C. He was home. To run his land. To finish building his own house. A house to live in. To grow old in. Maybe to even find peace in.

His eyes strayed to the paperweight which Jaimie had casually informed him Maggie had made. Realizing it, he swallowed an oath. That night at the swimming hole had been insanity. Another episode of letting things other than his brain rule his actions. Getting away the next morning was the best thing he could have done. There'd been no awkward morning-afters. No tearful farewells.

They'd finished what they'd needed to finish that night by the swimming hole.

He yanked off his boots before going into the bathroom where he stepped under the stinging, cold shower spray, and tried, as he did every night, to forget the night he'd spent with her under the stars.

After, he hitched the towel around his hips and, with his jeans in a ball under his arm, he headed toward his room. Matthew was coming down the stairs just outside the open door of the guest suite and Daniel stopped short. He'd been certain everyone was long asleep. "What's wrong?"

"Nothing." Matthew held up the bowl of green mint ice cream he carried. "Except middle-of-the-night cravings. Jaimie talked to Maggie tonight," he said. "She asked about you."

He slicked back his dripping hair. "Why?"

Matt shrugged and started back up the stairs toward the kitchen. "Didn't say. I thought you'd want to know." He lifted the bowl, grinning. "Duty calls."

Daniel dumped his jeans in the hamper in his room after his brother had gone. Maggie asked about him. So what? She called and talked to Jaimie faithfully every week.

He dropped his towel and tossed back the quilt and sheets on his bed, throwing himself down. He folded his arms behind his head and stared into the dark room. The problem was, she'd never asked after him. At least, that was his impression whenever Jaimie shared the "Chicago News" over the supper table.

He closed his eyes. But the tick of the clock on his bedside table sounded too loud. He rolled over and thumped his pillows. But he couldn't get comfortable.

"Oh, for Chrissakes." He finally got out of bed, hitching a clean pair of jeans up over his hips. Barefoot, he went upstairs and silently closed himself in Matthew's office. Then, calling himself the fool of all fools, he flipped through Matthew's Rolodex, and dialed.

Her voice, when she answered, was filled with sleep. Had him picturing her, pale blond hair rumpled and eyes soft as the sea. "It's Dan. What'd you want?"

He heard her indrawn breath. Imagined her sitting up, drawing her knees close and cradling the phone with her shoulder.

"I didn't expect…um…how, uh, how are you?"

He leaned back against the desk, crossing his bare feet. "It's the middle of the night, Maggie. What's wrong?"

"What makes you think something's wrong?"

"Why else would you call?" Dead silence weighted down the phone line.

"Actually *you're* the one calling me in the middle of the night," she returned unevenly. Then he heard her soft sigh. "I don't know why you're so angry, Daniel. I didn't know why when I was there in August. I still don't. I don't know why you were gone that next morning. Or why I haven't heard one word from you since."

"I don't like competing with a dead man." The words dropped baldly from his lips. One thing about late-night phone calls. A person said all sorts of things he shouldn't.

"God…it…Daniel, I was *married*. What did you want from me?"

I wanted you to take what I could offer you. To break free of a marriage that was killing you. But they weren't talking about three years ago. They were talking about nine weeks ago. And he needed to be ruling with his head, not his heart.

"I got what I wanted the night of the picnic," he said evenly. "You agreed. We would finish it. We're two adults. Free to do whatever the hell we wanted to do. And we did it. So put your conscience in a box for once, and forget about it."

"I can't."

"Why? Because you weren't faithful to your dear Joe's memory?"

"No." Her voice shook and he had to strain to hear her. "Because I became pregnant that night. I was foolish enough to think you'd want to know." The slam of the phone crashed in his ear.

He stared stupidly at the receiver clenched in his fist. Then he swore and redialed. Again and again. But all he got was a busy signal.

Maggie shoved the phone receiver in the kitchen drawer and stumbled back to her sofa bed. She huddled in one corner of it, burying her face in a pillow.

She would have cried if she could have. But she was numb. Numb.

So if she was so numb, why did her chest ache like it had been cracked in two?

Chilled to the bone, she wrapped herself in her blanket and rocked back and forth, her eyes painfully dry. She sat there, the rest of the night. Until the pearly light of dawn filled her apartment.

She shut off her alarm before it had a chance to sound and went into the bathroom to take her shower. Pregnant or not, J.D. needed to be awakened. She'd need breakfast. Maggie had a job to get to.

She had a life that she'd formed for herself. It had kept her going since Joe's desertion. It would keep her going still.

It took more makeup than usual to hide the dark circles under her eyes. Even her shoulder-length hair wouldn't co-operate, so she finally yanked it back into a tight bun at her nape. Her working wardrobe, though adequate, was far from expansive, and she pulled the bright red coat-dress off the hanger with a sense of bleak irony. She'd forgotten to pick up her dry cleaning this week.

Perhaps it was a sign. She was her mother's daughter, after all. Might as well dress in scarlet.

Working on autopilot, she dressed and fed J.D., gathered up her daughter's stuffed horse and favorite blanket, then dropped her off two floors down with the young mother, who provided child care for several of the children in the building. Monica Miniver would also take J.D. and her own two children to preschool, pick them up five hours later and keep J.D. until Maggie returned from work.

She stepped off the elevator in her building's lobby and

looked out at the wet morning. Well, wasn't that just perfect, too?

Fortunately she lived close enough to Ryker Interiors to walk to work. But she'd left her umbrella upstairs. She went back up to her apartment to get it.

Now she'd be late.

Late.

She felt a wave of hysteria rush over her. Being late for work was the least of her worries.

In the lobby again, she stepped outside, tightening the belt of her raincoat and shoving open the umbrella.

She didn't get two steps before she stopped short. Stared in disbelief at the man climbing out of the taxicab parked crookedly near the curb. He settled his cowboy hat, seemingly oblivious in his faded blue jeans and white button-down shirt to the steady fall of rain. His long legs brought him across the sidewalk to her, and she watched the rain wet the shoulders of his shirt. "What are you doing here?"

Daniel's shadowed jaw tightened. "Do you really want to discuss it here on the sidewalk?"

She didn't want him in her apartment. It was the one place where memories of him didn't assault her at every turn. "I don't think there is much to discuss."

He shook his head, his eyes molten silver. "I disagree."

Maggie stepped aside as a trio of people scurried along, their umbrellas bobbing. Her hands tightened around the handle of her own umbrella, and she shivered with a cold that had nothing to do with the rainy October morning. "You got what you wanted, Daniel. You said so yourself."

"No."

She shivered again. "I have to go to work. It's too bad you've wasted a trip here."

"Call them and tell them you won't be there."

"No."

"Were you always this stubborn?"

She huffed. Scooted again out of the way of more pedestrians. Saw that his shoulders were soaking, the fabric of his shirt heavy with rain. He had to be freezing. "Fine." She wheeled around, collapsing her umbrella as she shouldered her way inside again.

She knew it would be futile trying to conduct their *discussion* in the small lobby. Trembling inside, she led the way to the ancient, groaning elevator. Seemingly unperturbed by the thick silence in the elevator car, he drew off his hat, slicking water from it, then looked up at the floor number display, his big, knuckles-scraped hand idly tapping the hat against his thigh.

She fiddled with her umbrella and mentally urged the elevator to move faster.

Finally it creaked to a stop and she walked down the hall to her apartment. Her fingers shook, and she barely managed to insert the key in the triple set of locks. The door swung open with a squeak, displaying her minuscule home. At least she'd picked up J.D.'s toys.

Sliding a look his way from beneath her lashes, she went inside and dumped her purse and folded umbrella on the round Formica-topped table that sat in the tiny dining alcove. Shoved her raincoat down her arms and left it lying over the back of one of the chrome-and-vinyl chairs where water dripped heedlessly onto the floor.

She knew that his gray gaze was studying her home—finding it wanting, no doubt—and went into the narrow galley-style kitchen where she quickly called her office.

"Okay." She turned to face him after she'd hung up the phone, fixing her gaze somewhere around his left ear. "You satisfied? You've now messed up my day. So discuss away."

"Messed up your—" He bit off the words and placed his hat on the table with inordinate care. "Where is J.D.?"

"With her child care provider." Thank goodness. It had taken J.D. days and days to stop chattering about "Dannl" when they'd returned from Wyoming. Maggie didn't think she could stand more of the same just now.

When his eyes, those smoky eyes, continued studying her with not a word coming from his lips, she turned away, picking up a small block of cedar that she'd forgotten on the kitchen counter. Molding her shaking hands about the silky surface, she moved over to the couch and perched on the arm.

"Why did you leave the Double-C?"

She started. Not sure what she'd expected, but that certainly wasn't it. She looked at the block of wood that she planned to fashion into three Christmas ornaments. A sleigh, an angel and a snowflake, she thought fuzzily.

"Maggie?"

Her shoulders stiffened when he took a single step toward her. "I only had those days of emergency leave," she said evenly. "You know, to tell Jaimie about—"

"I'm talking about three years ago."

Her fingers stilled. "I don't—"

"Didn't you want to stay at the Double-C? You told me once that it was the only place you'd ever felt you belonged."

"That was before Joe—"

"Leave Joe out of this and answer me."

She tossed the block onto the couch, incredulous that he actually thought she'd be able to leave Joe out of anything that had concerned her and the Double-C. "I can't leave him out of this. For pity's sake, Daniel. He *embezzled* money from you and your family. From the Double-C! What was I supposed to do?"

"He did it," Daniel reminded, his voice hard. "Did we ever blame you?"

"No." She swallowed against the growing knot in her throat. "No, of course not." Matthew and Squire had been unfailingly kind. And Daniel—

"So why did you leave?"

She straightened, too agitated to sit...even on the arm of the couch. "Daniel, this is old news. It has nothing—"

His hand closed over her arm, pulling her around to face him once again. "Why?"

Her pulse skittered. "Because I thought if I did, then maybe you'd come back home!" She yanked her arm away. She lifted her chin and smoothed her skirt with damp palms. "Only you didn't," she finished unevenly. "And I needed to find Joe."

"Because you loved him."

Her jaw locked and she looked down at her hands. She really didn't want to discuss Joe. Didn't want to acknowledge the bitterness that swelled within her whenever she thought of what he'd done. "He was my husband."

"He lied and cheated and abandoned you."

She didn't flinch from the facts, even if she did feel the blood drain from her face. "I married him. For better or worse."

Daniel's lips twisted. "More worse than not."

Anger curled through her. "I'd made a commitment. But perhaps you don't know what that really means, anyway!"

His eyes narrowed. "Meaning?"

She crossed her arms, squaring her shoulders. "What have you ever been committed to, Daniel? The ranch? Your family? Maybe you used me as an excuse to leave, but you could have gone back earlier than you did. If you'd wanted to. Why did Matthew hire Joe as a foreman in the first place, when between you and your brother and the regular hands you could have handled the ranch without hiring anyone at all?" She drew in a calming breath but it didn't calm. "Don't you *dare* stand there all high-and-mighty and preach about *commitment* to me. You left your family. The same as Joe left me. End—of—story."

"You'd compare me to that thieving liar." Something came and went in his gray gaze. Something brief. Writhing.

She felt sick. Did she really think Daniel was at all like Joe?

Daniel. Devilish grins and fast motorcycles. Grease on his knuckles from some engine he'd magically coaxed back to life, and rips in his faded blue jeans. Pool games at the bar in town, impromptu bronc busting and buxom women following him around. Daniel, who'd worked hard during the days and played harder during the nights.

And Joe. Charming, quiet, green-eyed Joe. Who had told her nearly every morning of their life together that he loved her. Who had taken lovers. Embezzled money. And still claimed to love her, right up until the day he walked out of her life and proceeded to erase their existence from his life.

Her shoulders sagged. Her eyes burned. "Why were you gone that next morning in August?"

His expression tightened. "It doesn't matter."

She wanted to scream at him that it mattered far too much. But she didn't. She had too much pride to beg for explanations he clearly didn't want to give.

His fingers clawed through his hair, leaving it standing in rumpled butterscotch waves. "For the record, I didn't *abandon* my family. I *left* you on the ranch because I couldn't stick around and not make you mine. Maybe I wasn't the most clean-living guy in the county, but even I drew the line at taking another man's wife."

She flushed at that. "I wouldn't have—"

He raised his eyebrows. "Oh, really?" Then he stepped closer. "Despite that conscience you drag around with you so diligently, we'd have done just exactly what we did at the swimming hole. It was only a matter of time, Maggie, and you know it."

Maggie shook her head sharply. "No."

He smiled grimly. Thoroughly male. Thoroughly assured. "Lie to me if you want, Maggie. But don't lie to yourself." A muscle ticked in his jaw and he lifted his arm, touching his finger to her chin. "I left the ranch. You left the ranch. We just put off for three years what would've happened if we hadn't."

"Fine, then. Like you said, you got what you wanted." Her breath shuddered in her chest. "It's over and done with."

"Not by half, Maggie. Not by half. You see, I did learn something while I was gone." His lips twisted. His finger, warm and dry, outlined her lips.

Shivers crept along her spine. She lifted her chin, trying to escape that finger. But he caught her chin, holding her still. And her breath jammed in her chest as his eyes locked hers into a silvery gray web.

"I want what's mine," he continued softly.

"I'm not yours," she said, hoarse.

"Ah, but that baby you carry is."

"What are you saying?"

"You will marry me."

Chapter Five

She stared at him like he'd lost his mind.

Perhaps he had. But this woman who'd haunted his dreams for more years than he cared to remember, who'd turned down anything and everything to do with him, who twisted his guts into knots still, carried his child.

His.

He wouldn't ever walk away from what was his. Not again.

"I don't love you," she finally gasped.

He shrugged. "I don't love you, either. But our marriage bed won't be cold."

She scrambled away from him. "You're crazy. I'm not going to marry you. I'm not going to marry anyone!" Her eyes darted to him and away again like droplets of water skittering around in hot grease. "Been there. Done that."

"Don't," he warned, his voice hardening. "Don't ever compare me with him."

She pushed at her hair, unknowingly dislodging the tight knot she'd made of it. "Let's be…sensible. Reasonable. I wouldn't try to keep you from…the baby, Daniel. I told you about it, after all. But marriage is…"

"Nonnegotiable."

"…out of the question. I'm sure if we…"

"Got married."

"…discussed this calmly, we could come to some type of—of arrangement."

"You're not hearing me, Maggie. You're carrying my child. We will be married."

Her finely arched eyebrows drew together. "What if I said it wasn't yours!"

He snorted. "Honey, you are desperate, aren't you."

Her eyes glinted like wet shards of turquoise. "I'm being sensible! You can't force me to marry you."

"No, I can't," he agreed smoothly, his eyes drifting about the small, tidy interior of her apartment. "But I'm sure you'll want to be involved in your child's life."

Her palm pressed against her stomach, her expression turning wary. "What do you mean?"

"My child will be raised on the Double-C, not in some apartment in the middle of a city. You can either be a part of that or not."

She blinked. "Are you threatening me?"

"Not at all." He picked up the block of wood she'd been playing with earlier and studied the fine grain. It reminded him of the paperweight on his nightstand. "You know this child will be better off with two parents. On the Double-C, where she—"

"Or he."

He nodded once. "Or *he* can be part of his or her rightful heritage. Use that practicality you're tossing around. You never wanted a city life. You told me so yourself once." He waved his hand at her. "But look at you. You're working in an office. J.D. is at a sitter. You're pale and too thin, and you're living in an apartment the size of a postage stamp. For God's sake, Maggie Mae, you can't even see the damned sky for all the buildings hemming you in. Is this the way you wanted to raise your kids? Why make things harder than they have to be?''

Despite her conviction that his suggestion…*demand* wasn't the answer, she felt herself wavering. Lord, it would be so easy. She rubbed the knot in her forehead and stepped into the kitchen. Away from his gaze.

He followed. ''Come home to Wyoming, Maggie. You and J.D. don't belong here.''

And she stiffened all over again. It wasn't the life she'd have chosen if she'd had a choice. But she'd worked hard for what she'd achieved, whether in the city or not. A life for her and J.D. A home. Stability that she'd never had. Not during her childhood and certainly not during her marriage. She made her own way now and that was that.

He'd reached one long arm over her head and had pulled open a white cupboard door. She knew what he'd see. A few dozen cans of soup. Some dried pasta.

Things that, before, she'd always prepared from scratch with her own hands. Things that, now, she didn't have time for.

He shut the cupboard with a snap. ''You're thinner than I've ever seen you. You look like a stiff wind would knock you over, and you've got circles under your eyes the size of dinner plates. This life isn't for you, Maggie. Admit it.''

She knew she looked tough, but having him point it out rubbed wrong. ''You think working on a ranch is any easier? Up before dawn. Feeding twenty hungry men three times a day during the season? Taking care of orphaned calves in my kitchen. Shoveling snow just to get from the house to the barn? You think that's not any more tiring? More wearing on a person?'' Her voice rose because even as she said it all, she knew in her heart that it was *those* things that she excelled at. *Those* things that had soothed something in her soul.

The more agitated she got, the more still he seemed to become. She snatched a clean glass from the dish drainer and filled it with water that she didn't drink. He was just there. Watching her. Always watching. And though there was a time when she'd thought she understood the shadows and light in his curiously silver eyes, she understood nothing about Daniel Clay anymore.

Except that she was pregnant with his child. And he was demanding marriage.

Wasn't the marriage demand supposed to come from the woman? She set the glass in the sink, quelling the panic that seeped around the edges of her sanity. *Think, Maggie. Think.* It was just so hard to do when he stood so close to her that she imagined she could feel the water evaporating from his shirt.

Daniel was acting out of shock. He had to be. After a few weeks he'd calm down. Realize that he was going to unreasonable lengths.

Her child deserved his—or her—rightful place in the Clay family. Maggie knew that. Daniel could have his place in the child's life. It would take a lot of adjusting. But marriage—

It was simply out of the question, that was all. Out of the question.

"I know how you are about keeping your promises," he said, almost as if he could read her thoughts. "I'm not leaving until you promise to be my wife."

It was no declaration of love. Of undying devotion. Not when it was said so matter-of-factly in his husky, low-pitched voice. But she didn't want a man's supposed everlasting love. It was fine for people like Jaimie. Or Emily.

Maggie, however, had no reason to trust those words. Her mother had said "I love you" to every male in the small Wisconsin town where Maggie grew up. She'd said "I love you, Margaret Mary," before she'd walked out, one cold winter morning, on Maggie and her father. Even her father, who kissed her on the forehead with a sincere "I love you, Margaret Mary," had drowned his unhappiness over his wife's abandonment in one too many scotches before attempting to drive home in a winter storm. And Joe…

It was just as well that Daniel didn't claim to love her. But that didn't mean she'd be fool enough to tie herself in the ropes of matrimony. Daniel would chafe at those ropes within weeks. She was sure of it. Look at how rapidly he'd escaped after their one night of loving.

She started when his long arm reached out. "Who are you calling?"

He continued lifting the telephone, and started punching numbers. "Matt. Tell him that I'm going to be staying here for a while."

She pressed her finger against the disconnect button so fast, so hard, that her fingernail chipped. "No."

"Then give me your promise."

"I don't think I like you anymore."

His lips twisted, his eyes so grim she wanted to cry. "You don't have to like me. You've only got to stand in front of a judge and say 'I do.'"

"But we'd be—"

Again he seemed to read her thoughts. "Living as husband and wife. I've been called a fool a time or two, Maggie. But I'm no idiot. We will be married. With all that that implies." His eyes, so startling with those lush dark lashes surrounding the gleam of silver, focused on her mouth. She cursed the fact that he made her breath quicken. So easily. "You don't have to like me to be satisfied in my bed, either. We've already proven that."

Mortification swept through her like wildfire because she knew it was true. She'd found more satisfaction with Daniel during those hours alongside the swimming hole than she had in a decade of marriage.

"We both want what will be best for this baby. Think about how hard you had it with J.D."

"Exactly." She latched on to that. "Daniel, I'm only…well not very far along, obviously. What if—" the painful possibility plagued her as it had since the moment the doctor had told her she was pregnant "—I did miscar—"

"You won't. You miscarried before you had J.D., I know. But this time you won't."

Her head dropped back and she closed her eyes, praying for…she didn't know what. "You don't know that."

"You've been to the doctor?"

"Yes."

"Who knows your history?"

She swallowed. Nodded. She'd called the doctor the day after he'd told her she was pregnant.

"And?"

"And who knows? This pregnancy could be completely different." She folded her arms around her waist. "Or it could be worse. The first trimester is the most…iffy." It wasn't the greatest explanation, but he got the gist.

"And you're nine weeks along."

She wasn't sure why it hit her so hard. The fact that he knew exactly—without having to think one moment about it—how far along she was. Joe had never…

Oh, God. She was comparing them.

Daniel took up far more than his fair share of the narrow kitchen. She slipped past him, sinking into a chair at the table because her knees were getting shaky. "I'll give you an answer when I'm four months along." He'd have time to realize he was not thinking clearly. They'd come to some other arrangement.

He shook his head. "You'll give me an answer now. I want you at the Double-C as soon as possible. You won't even have to go to Gillette for a doc. You can go to Rebecca Morehouse in Weaver."

Maggie realized she was seriously considering Daniel's outrageous demand. She propped her elbows on the table and lowered her forehead to her palms. Her mind whirled. "What would we tell everyone?"

"Something wrong with the truth?"

She moved her shoulders impatiently. "Like mother, like daughter," she murmured to herself.

"What?"

"Nothing." She sighed and lifted her head. "What about J.D.?"

He finally turned his searing gaze away. "What about her? She'll thrive on the ranch. She already thinks horses were invented just for her."

"If I agree—"

"You will."

"Then I have some conditions of my own."

"You'll be under my roof, Maggie. In my bed. Nonnegotiable."

"Yes, you've made that abundantly clear." And her face felt hot because she simply wasn't used to a man being so…blunt about it. "I'll agree to marry you, if we can wait until I'm in my second trimester. No one but you and I need to know until then."

"I'll ask again. Why hide it?"

"Because too many people will be hurt when—" His eyes met hers and she couldn't finish the statement. *When you change your mind.* "I'd rather we keep it to ourselves for now, that's all."

"You'll come to Wyoming now."

She held her breath, telling herself she wasn't going to agree to this insanity. She wasn't. She really, really wasn't. "Yes." She exhaled the word, feeling dizzy.

"I'm building my own house," he said. "It'll be ready to move into soon."

"Oh." Her teeth nibbled at her lip. She had to clear her throat. "Where?"

"Not far from the big house. I bought out Donna Blanchard's place. Razed the old house and started fresh. Combined the land with the Double-C."

She remembered the spread. Donna Blanchard had been the woman who owned a small piece of land bordering the Double-C. A few years older than Daniel, she'd been divorced and had been hanging on to the land by her fingernails. She'd wanted to move to the city three years ago. It was nice that she'd finally gotten her wish. "We, um, don't say anything about our plans though, until December."

He shook his head. "Third week of November."

"Last week."

"Thanksgiving. Your other conditions?"

She swallowed. "Just one." She looked down at her hands. "That you never leave again without saying goodbye." She looked up in time to see his jaw tighten at the pointed remark.

"Agreed," he said with finality. "We'll be married right after Thanksgiving."

"Agreed," she parroted. Then blinked. Realizing she'd just bargained herself into an agreement of marriage with Daniel Jordan Clay.

But a lot could happen in a month.

A month during which Daniel would surely come to his senses.

He scooped up his hat and jammed it on his head. "I'll make the arrangements."

Flagrant panic exploded in her chest. "Arrangements?"

"You'll want to move your stuff, won't you?"

"Oh…right. Um," she looked blindly at her small apartment. "This is a furnished apartment. We just have our clothes and…personal things. Toys. My saws."

His eyebrows rose. "Saws?"

She brushed at her drooping hair, finally tugging the hairpins free. "I know they're old, but—"

"Maggie, what are you talking about?"

She nudged the block of cedar that he'd set on the table. "My saws. For my wood art. Did you think I just chipped away at it with my teeth?"

She pointed at the wall behind him and he turned, apparently noticing for the first time the narrow hanging. The dark wood had been cut away until all that remained were delicate strands of wood depicting a rearing horse. "You made that?"

"Yes." She also wished that she didn't wait, vaguely anxious, for his opinion.

He lifted his hand, running his finger along the detailed mane. "Reminds me of Diablo."

Maggie looked away, afraid he'd see the confirmation in her eyes. "My father taught me woodworking when I was in school," she said. When her father had been sober, that is. "I took it up again when we settled here in Chicago. I found some equipment at an estate sale, and it reminded me of—" She broke off. It had reminded her of the pride in her father's eyes when she'd so easily taken to a hobby that he, himself, had enjoyed. "I thought I could earn some extra money doing models for Ryker Interiors," she finished.

"I didn't realize you worked with wood so extensively. Apparently there are a few things we don't know about each other, after all."

She didn't doubt that for a moment. She wasn't certain there was a single thing she knew about Daniel for sure. Other than that his touch drove her to madness. And now they were paying the price for it.

He stopped in front of her. "Don't look so dejected, Maggie. You're going back to the Double-C. That, at least, should be something you can be happy about." She thought for a moment that he'd lower his head and kiss her. But he didn't. All he said was, "I'll be in touch," before he walked out the door.

Then she sat there, alone.

Her eyes burned suddenly, and she smoothed her palm over her abdomen. If she really were alone, she wouldn't have just promised to marry Daniel.

A man she had no intention of loving. Because as soon as she did, he'd leave her, too.

Everyone did.

Despite Daniel's confidence that Maggie and J.D. would be ready to travel with him back to Wyoming, they didn't quite manage it, and Maggie and J.D. ended up flying several days after he'd left. There had just been too many details to tie up at the apartment.

Though Maggie suspected she was making a monumental mistake, everything else went smoothly with the move. How could it not?

Daniel hadn't told her who would be meeting them at the

airport. Maggie assumed he'd send one of the hands. She knew he'd probably spared time he couldn't really spare when he'd been in Chicago. That he was working flat-out on the house, determined to beat the coming winter.

She certainly hadn't expected to see Daniel himself waiting at the gate when they walked off the plane.

Her feet dragged to a halt at the sight of him, and all her misgivings and doubts about what she was doing there came surging to the surface. J.D. had no qualms, however. She spotted Daniel immediately and tugged her hand from Maggie's, darting across the exiting stream of people with a delighted squeal. "Dannl," she cried.

Maggie's breath caught as Daniel seemed to hesitate before pulling her up into his arms. After a moment he grinned back at J.D., but to Maggie it looked strained.

What had she done?

After what seemed a decade, they turned in the main entrance of the Double-C. The tires hadn't even stopped crunching over the gravel drive when the wide front door flew open and Jaimie came trotting out, her long hair bouncing around her shoulders. She dashed over to the truck and yanked open the door.

Suddenly the two women were laughing and crying and hugging. Daniel just sat there, watching.

At least he'd gotten this part right.

Matthew joined the women, hugging Maggie. J.D. protested from the back seat, and Daniel turned to help her out.

"Oh, my stars," Jaimie cried when he rounded the truck with J.D. "We just saw you, and I swear she's grown."

"And look at you! You're showing," Maggie countered, laughing.

Daniel couldn't tear his eyes from the sparkle in her blue-green eyes.

Jaimie had crouched down next to her niece, and he turned to see Matthew watching him, a knowing expression in his older brother's ice-blue eyes. "Why don't we take this in-

side,'' Daniel suggested, ignoring his brother for the moment.
''Where it's warmer.''

Chattering away madly, the women headed toward the big
house. J.D. hung back, her green eyes focused on the corral
some distance beyond the house. Her little body fairly shook
with excitement.

''Horses,'' she breathed, as if she'd never seen them before.
Her little sneakers headed in that direction.

Daniel stifled a sigh and followed, not terribly surprised
when his brother did, too.

''Their flight go okay?''

''Yeah.''

''You okay?''

''Why wouldn't I be?''

Matthew snorted softly. ''I don't know. 'Cept that you take
off last week like a bat outta hell, and come back announcing
that Maggie's moving back, spouting about apartment buildings going condo and job layoffs.'' He shrugged. ''No reason.''

J.D. reached the wooden fence of the corral, and Daniel
caught her before she could slip between the rails. She strained
against him. ''Dannl, *horses!''*

''I know. But if you go through the fence, you might get
hurt.''

She gave him a disbelieving look. Daniel heard Matthew
squelch a laugh, and he glanced at his brother.

''Jaimie gives me that look now and then,'' Matthew muttered under his breath.

J.D. suddenly relaxed in Daniel's arms, and she smiled her
singularly sweet smile, taking in both men. ''We ride the
horses now?''

Daniel met his brother's eyes over the little girl's head. Matthew rubbed his jaw and shook his head wryly. ''Man, you
are in for trouble,'' he said, and turned his head when his wife
called him from the house that he had a phone call.

Over J.D.'s blond waves, Daniel watched his brother stride
back to the big house and stop long enough to loop a long

arm around Jaimie and drop a lingering kiss on her upturned lips. Then Sarah joined her parents, wrapping her short arms around her daddy's long leg. Without releasing his hold of Jaimie, Matthew swung Sarah up into his other arm, and the trio disappeared inside the rear of the house.

Daniel sighed faintly and looked down at J.D., his arms tightening involuntarily around her petite little body. She looked up at him, her emerald eyes wide and innocent. Then she smiled that smile that was distinctly hers, and Daniel felt a slice of pain knife through him. He managed to smile back, but it was an effort. He didn't want to remember that once, long ago, he'd wished this little imp had been his child. Didn't want to remember that her real father had left her behind rather than stay and right his wrongs.

But then he had to wonder how much better than Joe he was, considering his own involvement in that and how he'd spent his last few years. How he'd failed another innocent child.

Maybe, just maybe, if he did a good enough job now with J.D. his conscience would finally rest. At least on this one score.

No matter how much Daniel had hated Joe, how close he'd come to separating the man limb from limb for cheating on Maggie, he hadn't expected Joe to run off the way he had.

"Dannl, I pet the horses?"

He looked into J.D.'s hopeful face. "Sure," he said gruffly. He turned her around and set her on the top rail of the fence, keeping his arm securely around her squirming body, and whistled sharply. J.D. practically vibrated off the fence rail with excitement when two horses trotted over.

From the wide, uncurtained window in the kitchen of the big house, Maggie watched Daniel and her daughter. Her fingers curled tightly over the edge of the counter.

Jaimie came up beside her and they both watched as Daniel and J.D. petted the patient mare. Even from within the house they could hear J.D.'s excited laughter.

"I'm glad you're back," Jaimie said.

Maggie couldn't tear her eyes from Daniel and J.D. She hurt inside from the sight, but she couldn't stop watching. "Me, too."

"He's very good with the children," Jaimie continued after a moment.

"Hmm?"

"Daniel. The girls adore him."

At that Maggie finally turned and glanced at her sister-in-law. "They always did," Maggie said drily, surprising herself with the unexpected spurt of humor.

Jaimie's smile grew. "Ah, but this time it's the little girls I'm referring to. Not the adult variety. Although, you must admit that the guy is pretty hard to look at. I mean, those silvery-gray eyes and that bod? A woman has to have a lot of intestinal fortitude to be able to stomach watching him for more than a few seconds at a time. Frankly, I don't know how we tolerate it." Suddenly Jaimie threw her arms around her and gave her a heartfelt hug. "I'm *so* glad you're home," she said fiercely.

Maggie's eyes burned, and she returned the hug. Just then it seemed ridiculous that she'd stayed away for so long. That she'd ever gone away in the first place. After all, it hadn't done any good. Daniel still hadn't come home. And Maggie hadn't been able to find Joe to end what should have ended long before. She'd failed everybody.

"Well, now if this ain't a sight for sore eyes." The deep, booming voice brought the women's attention around to the doorway that connected the kitchen to the dining room and the rest of the spacious house beyond.

Maggie brushed her hair behind her ear with a hand that suddenly trembled. "Hello, Squire. It's good to see you." If anyone had something to say about Maggie moving back to the Double-C, it would be him. Subtlety wasn't one of Squire Clay's finer traits.

But his ice-blue eyes, so like those he'd passed on to Matthew, twinkled. "You don't have a hug for an old geezer like me?"

Jaimie snorted and walked around the huge oak table that sat like a queen in the center of the large kitchen and patted Squire's tanned, lean cheek. "Geezer my foot," she said tartly. "We know your secret, Squire. You just like hugging pretty women."

"Watch your tongue, missy," he returned, unperturbed.

"I'd better see what Sarah's up to," Jaimie said. "It's been quiet for two minutes, which usually means disaster looms."

Alone with Squire, Maggie tucked her hair again behind her ear. She moistened her lips.

"Child, you look like someone's planning on feeding you to the lions," he said as he removed the full pot from the coffeemaker and poured a mugful. Maggie automatically handed him a saucer as he sat down. "You just gonna hover there, girl, or sit down and give your feet a rest?"

Maggie pulled out a chair and sat.

"Guess you're waiting for me to make some comment on you moving back." He pinned his gaze on her. "Am I right?"

Maggie swallowed. "Well—"

"It's none of your concern," Daniel said, striding into the kitchen. He locked gazes with his father. "She's family and that's all that matters."

Squire harrumphed. "Never said otherwise, son."

Maggie studied her twisting fingers.

"Yeah, well I recognize the signs. You're gearing up for something, Squire, so put a lid on it."

The older man grunted again. Then he patted Maggie's clenched hands. "Don't mind him. It's good you've finally come home, child. You've been gone too long. My son is right, if he'd ever let an old man get a word in edgewise. You're family, Maggie. You and that young 'un of yours. Don't you go forgetting that again in the future."

Tears burned behind her eyes. She wondered whether he'd think so kindly of her if he knew the way she'd behaved under the night sky with his son. If he knew the real reason she was here. "Thank you, Squire."

"Mama, Dannl let me petted the horses!" J.D. dashed around Daniel's legs and barreled into Maggie, clambering up on her lap.

Squire chuckled. "Little darlin', you'll get to do that a lot now. And don't forget there's also Matthew's dog and D.C., the cat, and a new litter of kittens to boot."

J.D.'s eyes just kept getting wider and wider. She stared at Squire. "Kittens?"

"Yup. Wanna go see?"

Maggie made a surprised noise when J.D. nodded and hopped off her lap, going around to Squire and latching on to his fingers trustingly when he rose from the table. "Let's get Sarah, too," he suggested.

J.D. didn't even look back at Maggie as the two disappeared through the dining room.

"He'll take care of her," Daniel said quietly.

"I know," Maggie answered quickly. "It's just…well, I didn't expect her to adjust so easily."

Daniel's expression turned mocking. "Disappointed?"

She flushed, not at all sure that he wasn't right.

His long fingers closed over the back of her chair, brushing her shoulder. "We all have some adjusting," he murmured. "Some of it'll be easier than others."

There was no mistaking his meaning, and her heart kicked nervously.

"Maggie, you should come see how we're…oh, hi Daniel." Jaimie fairly skidded into the room in her stockinged feet. "Did you bring in Maggie's bags?"

"No. I'll do it now. That way she can get all settled in her new home." He looked down at Maggie, the corner of his lip curling.

If he didn't change his mind, they both knew that the home Maggie would be settling in soon wouldn't be here at the big house at all. It would be under another roof entirely.

The roof of the house that Daniel was building.

Chapter Six

Before supper, Jaimie showed Maggie the progress she and Matthew had made on their remodeling project. "I still can't believe that Matthew took it into his head that we needed to redo the bedrooms and bathrooms. I mean the man hasn't changed one single thing in this house ever. Of course, there's always been plenty of room, but modernizing will be good. Honestly, though, I never expected the mess. Corky has a fit whenever he comes in to clean."

Maggie glanced at the gleaming hutch that held a beautiful display of lovingly cared-for china from Sarah Clay, the wife that Squire lost decades earlier, as they passed through the dining room to the wide staircase. "I thought Corky was the bunkhouse cook." She was certain that the ageless man hadn't been doing the cleaning when she'd visited in August.

Jaimie nodded. "He is. But Matthew doesn't want me lifting stuff and all that anymore. Corky was willing to add more duties, fortunately." Jaimie chattered on as she led the way up the staircase, describing the progress of the remodeling as they went. "Other than deciding it needed to be done, Matthew left the remodeling up to me. The only thing he was determined to have was that." She waved at a big triangular corner bathtub that stood upright against one unfinished wall. Her eyes sparkled. "Big enough for two, you know."

Considering the size of the Clay men—all over six feet—Maggie could well see that Matthew would insist on a roomy bathtub. She didn't think too closely on the notion of sharing one. It was something she'd certainly never done with anyone other than J.D., when she was a baby.

Maggie turned off that thought. Because hard on its heels was wondering if Daniel would figure sharing a tub was part of his marriage demand.

Her sister-in-law had bent over a sizable stack of boxes containing ceramic tiles, then triumphantly held up a beautiful square of creamy tile. "Here it is. This is going on the floor in our bathroom. Nice, huh?" She rooted around a little more, then came up with a second tile in a deep, lustrous blue. "For the border, just like we talked about. I love this blue color. The master bedroom's going to have the same colors. I've ordered new drapes, too, from that catalog you recommended." She looked at her tiles, obviously pleased. "I've been dying to see how Daniel decides to decorate his new house. He told us you'd agreed to help him with it. Honestly, I really can't believe how fast he got it up." Then Jaimie clapped a hand over her mouth, stifling her giggles. "That didn't come out quite right."

Maggie flushed, catching on. "Jaimie, you know, Daniel—"

"I know, I know. He told me all about it."

Maggie's flush died a painful death as she felt the blood rapidly drain from her face. "He…did?"

"Sure. You could have told me about Ryker Interiors laying you off and your apartment building going condo. You're my best friend, silly. It's not your fault all that happened, and there's no reason to be embarrassed. Of course moving back here was the most sensible solution. And I, for one, couldn't be more thrilled that Daniel got you to see reason. I always suspected you had a soft spot for him."

Maggie blinked. Just what kind of web had Daniel spun? She felt terrible. Dishonest. She didn't like keeping the truth from Jaimie. The entire notion had been a mistake. What would it be like a week from now? Two weeks? If only she'd thought this craziness through. If only Daniel hadn't insisted on that foolish promise.

If only she'd thought to ask Daniel exactly what he planned to tell his family. "Jaimie, there's something you should—"

A door slammed and small footsteps pounded, accompanied by a childish wail. Both Jaimie and Maggie started down the stairs. Sarah latched on to her mother, her little face streaked with tears, her words about broken crayons garbled. "I'd better go quiet the troops," Jaimie said.

The truth would have to wait.

Daniel concentrated on carrying his tack into the tack room. He knew Jefferson was leaning against a stall watching. His brother's stance might be relaxed, almost lazy, but Daniel wasn't fooled. Only thing was, he didn't want to talk about whatever it was his big brother had on his mind. He didn't want to talk. He didn't want to think. He damned sure didn't want to feel.

"Got a call today from Coleman."

Daniel stiffened. So much for thinking he could avoid this. He turned and stepped past his brother who partially blocked the doorway of the tack room.

"He says you didn't check in this week."

He consciously relaxed his hands and looked steadily at Jefferson. "Haven't gotten to it yet."

Jefferson's lips twisted. "I'm the last person to advocate toeing the line with Hollins-Winword," he said. "But you can't ignore Coleman Black. When the boss himself starts checking up on you—"

"I'll call. Now drop it," Daniel said grimly, turning away.

"You couldn't have changed things."

Jefferson's voice stopped him when he'd reached the doorway. Daniel looked out across the gravel road, across the grass and the buildings. But he wasn't seeing his home. He was seeing a small village destroyed. The ravages of fire and—

"No matter what you did, Daniel, you couldn't fight Arturo's men."

Daniel thrust away the vision. Thinking about the devastation did no good. It wouldn't help those he'd failed to protect. It wouldn't help the innocent. If he'd only kept his emotions out of things, he wouldn't be standing here battling down memories he refused to face. "Thought you kept your nose outta the agency nowadays. You retired. Remember?"

"Cole called me, Dan. Not the other way around. You made a deal with him when he got you out of Santo Marguerite and away from Arturo's men. You call once a week, check in or he's gonna call you."

"Or you. Nothing like having big brother around to keep tabs," Daniel gritted angrily. He supposed he should be grateful Coleman didn't send someone out to check on him in person. His former boss made no secret that he wanted Daniel to come back to work as soon as he served out his suspension.

Jefferson swore softly. "It's only a few more months, Dan. Then you're free and clear."

Free and clear. Daniel swiveled around and faced his brother once more. "It wouldn't matter if I'm here at the Double-C *free and clear* or still with the agency. Those people…that village—" He couldn't finish. If he started thinking about the people, the families, he'd start thinking about Angeline. He eyed his brother. "You of all people should understand."

Jefferson's lips compressed. "I understand all right. I know firsthand that bottling it all up doesn't get you anywhere."

"All this because I missed a phone call." Daniel forced a careless smile. "Go on home to your wife and rest assured that I'll do my duty at my earliest opportunity." He saw the gears of his brother's mind clicking behind Jefferson's sharp gaze. And wished he'd just kept his mouth shut.

No, he wished he hadn't ridden out to join his brothers as they repaired fence. He hadn't needed to. He'd planned to work on the house that afternoon. But picking up Maggie had left him restless. Too restless to find relief even through hammer and nails.

"Are you gonna tell Maggie? Tell her about Angeline?"

Daniel managed not to wince, but it was an effort. The likelihood that he'd find any positive news about the four-year-old child was nearly nonexistent. He couldn't even let himself begin to hope that she hadn't died with all the rest. Telling Maggie wouldn't help anything. "What for?"

Jefferson grunted softly. "You're not fooling me, Daniel. I know how you feel about Maggie."

Daniel had had enough. "I don't feel anything, Jeff," he said. And turned on his boot heel and strode out of the barn.

In the kitchen Maggie automatically dumped the dregs of the coffeepot and started a fresh pot brewing. The roast that Jaimie had put in the oven earlier was nearly done, so Maggie started snapping the fresh green beans that Jaimie hadn't gotten to yet. She heard the door open again behind her, and stiffened when it was Daniel who stepped up to the sink beside her and flipped on the water, sluicing it over his hands and forearms. She felt his glance, but kept on snapping beans.

He dried himself, then tossed the dishtowel onto the counter, his movements jerky. Maggie reached for the towel and hung it neatly over the oven door handle.

"Ever proper, aren't you, Maggie."

Her busy hands paused over the bowl of beans. "Ryker laying me off? My building going condo?"

He crossed his arms over his wide chest, making her wonder why the shoulder seams of his red-and-gray plaid shirt didn't simply give up under the strain. "Had to give 'em some explanation," he said, "since you're so all-fire determined to keep the truth under wraps and *you* didn't give 'em a reason." Then his head tilted as he studied her, and the grim darkness in his eyes seemed to lighten. "Though, if you ask me, they're gonna know something's cooking just from looking at you."

Maggie's jaw tightened. Her stomach took an all-too-familiar lurch. "What's that supposed to mean?"

"Just that you're looking a tad more…rounded."

"Fat, you mean."

"Honey, you'd have to pack on a helluva lot more to look even remotely plump. I was talking about your, ah—"

She flushed, barely keeping herself from tugging at the top of her denim jumper. "I get the drift," she muttered. With the long-sleeved sweater she wore underneath it, the jumper was almost uncomfortably tight against her breasts. As soon as she'd learned she was pregnant, it seemed as if her modest chest had decided it was time to flourish.

"Not that I'm complaining, mind you," he added smoothly.

Her jaw loosened, and she shot him a look. It was the type of comment the old Daniel might have made.

"But Jaimie's pretty observant, as are the rest of the folks 'round here. Sure you want to wait until Thanksgiving to spill the beans?"

Maggie turned and pushed the full bowl of green beans into his arms. "Only beans being spilled are those, if you don't hold on to the bowl," she said stiffly.

Surprise glinted in his eyes. "What am I supposed to do with these?"

"Rinse 'em," she snapped, and wheeled on her heel out of the kitchen and straight to the bathroom that was beneath the wide staircase. She'd barely shut the door before the nausea overwhelmed her. When it finally passed, she rinsed her mouth, then sank to the floor and leaned her back wearily against the wall behind her.

Weak tears clung to her eyelashes and she wiped them away with a sniffle. Then looked up with a startled squeak when the bathroom door opened and Daniel stood there. She looked away, her jaw tightening. "Don't you *knock?*"

Unfazed, he joined her in the small bathroom and closed the door. He was so large he probably used up all the oxygen, she thought resentfully. He rinsed a soft blue washcloth in cool water and handed it to her. Then lowered the lid on the commode and sat on it, his eyes unreadable. "Does this happen often?"

Maggie pressed the wonderfully cool cloth to her flaming face. "Three or four times a day like clockwork."

"Is that normal?"

She lowered the cloth. "What? Getting leery of this whole deal already?" He just looked at her and she felt small. "As long as I'm able to keep some food down, the doctor said I'd be okay," she said after a moment.

"And are you?"

"What? Keeping food down?" She folded the washcloth in half. Then half again. "Some. I do better in the middle of the day. It's the mornings and the evenings that are the worst."

"Then we'll have to make sure you shovel in the food at noon, won't we."

Despite her misery, Maggie couldn't help the small laugh that escaped. "Now there's a picture," she muttered. "Just roll up a trough for old Maggie to dive into."

His lips didn't smile. But the few lines bracketing his eyes deepened. "A tad drastic," he murmured. "Unless it's chocolate mousse."

He narrowed his eyes a fraction, and Maggie's heart suddenly chugged. An image of Daniel licking chocolate from her fingertips flitted through her mind. What was she thinking? She'd never done anything like that in her life.

His hand lifted, and she froze when he touched the buckle strap of her jumper, right where it lay snugly over the top swell of her breast. "I wonder what's sweeter," he mused gruffly. "The taste of chocolate. Or the taste of you."

"Daniel." Though the finger touching that buckle was perfectly innocent, the knuckles of his other fingers as they grazed her bodice were anything but. She drew in a shaky breath, nearly gasping when his palm went flat against her ultrasensitive flesh.

"You're fuller," he murmured. "Just like I thought."

She knew she should move his hand away. Protest. Something. Then his hand slid beneath her arm, down her waist.

"How long before you start showing?"

Pushing away his hand, she awkwardly rose in the small bathroom, made even smaller by his long legs taking up half the space. She brushed down her skirt. "Weeks yet." She almost wished it would be sooner. As soon as her pregnancy started to show, she felt sure that whatever attraction Daniel felt for her would die, and he'd call off this foolish agreement. The very day that Maggie's waist had begun to thicken with J.D. had been the very day that Joe had once again started looking elsewhere to satisfy his needs. She flipped on the water and rinsed the cloth.

"Too bad."

Maggie's fingers clenched on the soft blue terry cloth. She shut off the water and looked up, catching their reflection in the mirror over the sink. He'd risen also and stood behind her. His hands slipped to her waist and she dropped the cloth, nervously gripping his spread fingers with hers, halting his sure movements. "What are you doing?"

"I want to touch you."

Her eyes widened and in the mirror she saw as well as felt the color rise in her own cheeks. "You, uh, you already did."

"Not enough."

She swallowed. "We're in the bathroom, Daniel."

"I'm not suggesting we make love here, Maggie Mae," he said drily.

Her color brightened even more. "I should say not—"

"Although, with you on the sink here, we could probably—"

"Daniel!"

Daniel smiled faintly, thoroughly enjoying the outraged shock in Maggie's turquoise eyes. "Don't get your knickers in a knot." Despite her frantic grip on his hands, he shaped his palms around her narrow waist. Then slid to her firm abdomen. He forgot all about his brother and about phone calls and bottling things up as a purely male shaft of possessiveness pierced him. His babe nestled within her taut body. He really did think it was a shame that he'd have to wait several more weeks yet before he could see that flat belly swell with his child.

He hadn't planned this situation. Hell, he was thirty-seven years old, well versed in the facts of life, and he should've known they were taking a chance the night of the picnic. But logic had had little to do with what they'd done together that night.

She might cringe and cry over their behavior. That was Maggie. Always so concerned with what was proper and right.

He, on the other hand, didn't give a flip right now about what was proper. Maggie had been a free woman the night they'd slept together. She'd even finally taken off that wedding band.

And if there was a bone-deep satisfaction inside him that it was his child that had caused the new fullness in her beautiful breasts and the faint thickening of her narrow waist, he wasn't about to apologize for it.

Nor was he about to let her shut him out of one minute of this pregnancy. She'd just have to get used—

"Mags?" That was Jaimie's voice. Jaimie knocking on the bathroom door. "Are you all right? You left the water running in the kitchen."

Maggie's rounded gaze met his in the mirror. Her mouth parted soundlessly. Her horror and embarrassment couldn't have been more plain.

His small spurt of good humor withered. He stepped back and opened the door. "She's fine," he said, walking past Jaimie's surprised face.

In the kitchen he yanked open the refrigerator and pulled out a cold beer. His gaze fell on the phone hanging on the wall. Barely pausing, he twisted off the bottle cap, sending it sailing toward the counter and strode right past the phone and the call he knew he should make, through the mudroom and out the back door.

Dusk was falling and it suited his mood just fine. He walked along the gravel road, stopping at the bunkhouse where the men were already jostling for position at the long supper table. Beer bottle dangling between his fingers, he decided to join them. Sitting across the table from Maggie in the big house, knowing she was pregnant with his child and having to lie about it just didn't sit well. Not on top of everything else.

He knew he drew a half dozen curious looks when he joined the crew at that long table in the bunkhouse. But he was long used to making his own way without explanation or excuses. When the big platter of pork chops passed him, he forked two onto his plate and passed it on.

Maggie didn't know why she hadn't figured out what Jaimie and Matthew's remodeling project would mean. After all, she'd seen for herself the walls that had been torn out.

It just hadn't clicked.

Not until she'd joined Jaimie upstairs as they tucked their daughters into bed in Sarah's room.

When the little girls were finally quiet, Maggie joined Jaimie in the wide hallway. And then it hit her. The bedroom she'd used before was no more. It didn't exist. Nor did Daniel's room. It was all one big open area filled with stacks of lumber and pails of paint.

She rubbed the pinpoint of pain in her forehead that had taken residence earlier when it became plain that Daniel didn't intend to join the rest of them for supper and Jaimie had cast more than one speculative glance her way. "It just occurred to me that I might be bunking in one of the barns."

Jaimie tucked her arm through Maggie's as they headed down the stairs. "Oh, you. Of course not. Before we tore everything out up here, we remodeled the basement. Didn't I mention that? I thought I did."

Maggie couldn't be sure. There'd been so much that Jaimie had chattered on about during their weekly calls, but Maggie had been hardly aware of much except getting through each day.

"You know how the basement was just one really huge

recreation room. Far more space than was necessary, actually. We made a guest suite down there. Two rooms and a full bath. Even a small kitchen and a sitting area. The original plan was that Squire would move down there—more peaceful you know, but he changed his mind.'' She shrugged as if there was no explaining Squire sometimes. ''So now we have a guest suite. There's privacy when you want it, but you're just down the stairs from the kitchen when you don't.''

Maggie felt her stomach tighten before Jaimie continued.

''Daniel did all the construction himself. I'm sure he put your suitcases down there already. The only drawback, of course, is that J.D. is upstairs, and you'll be down.''

''J.D. thinks sharing a room with Sarah is the next best thing to heaven or horses,'' Maggie said faintly. Would Daniel also be sleeping down there in that new guest *suite?* She didn't have the nerve to ask. Wasn't sure she wanted to have her suspicions confirmed.

''Once we're finished upstairs, you can move back up again if you want. We tore out three rooms, of course, to make one plus a new nursery. Daniel will be in his house by then, I should think.''

Maggie's stomach tightened. ''He told me he razed the Blanchard place.''

''Matthew was pleased when Daniel announced he was buying the place. Donna Blanchard had been wanting to sell for years. In fact, Matthew was all set to buy her out before, but…'' She trailed off, her eyes darkening. ''Well, fudge.''

''But my husband had embezzled thousands, and the Double-C had to sit back and regroup,'' Maggie finished grimly.

''My brother, too,'' Jaimie reminded softly. ''But, yes. I'm sorry I brought it up.''

Maggie stared blindly at the banister beneath her hand. ''I expect a lot of people will bring it up one way or another eventually. Nothing like a scandal to set the tongues wagging.''

''No,'' Jaimie considered that. ''I heard that when Donna's husband took off with a waitress from Colbys that the whole town of Weaver was buzzing more. Look, Mags. People don't *bug* me about it, and the same blood that ran in Joe's veins runs in mine. Good heavens, Matthew married me despite what Joe did. This family stands together, and you're part of this family.'' She flashed an encouraging smile. ''Besides, most people didn't even *know* about the money. We recovered most of it, and Matthew didn't press charges. So just stop worrying so much over this. Everything will work out. It always does.''

''You always were the optimistic one.''

''And you were the practical one. So be practical about this. People in this area have enough to worry about in their own lives to make a big deal about what our darling Joe did more than three years ago. He was the one who did wrong. You and I can't walk around being ashamed for what he did.''

Maggie almost said, *Easy for you to say,* but didn't. Because she knew that Joe's actions *hadn't* been easy on Jaimie. Just that quickly, tears burned behind Maggie's lids. Her marriage had died long before Joe lost his life. But he'd been Jaimie's brother. ''I'm sorry he's gone,'' she said. Their marriage had been irretrievably broken. But death?

Jaimie bit her lip. She brushed back her luxurious hair, then dusted her palms against her jeans. ''So am I. He'll never know, now, all that he gave up.'' Then she exhaled loudly, her smile rather bittersweet. ''That's the past though, Mags. You're back now where you belong. So let's just focus on that from now on.''

Chapter Seven

The guest suite, as Jaimie termed it, was really a self-contained apartment, in Maggie's opinion. She'd seen enough design plans at Ryker Interiors to know that the space usage was well planned and the decorating, while not lavish or over-done, was beautifully welcoming in its understated elegance.

She knew the Clays were financially well set. But most of the time, she didn't think about it. The Double-C was a working cattle ranch. Weather and market prices were as much a concern for this spread as any other. Even if Matthew, and Squire before him, had made wise investments during the better years that carried them through the leaner ones. They lived relatively modest, normal lives with none of the airs Maggie had encountered so often in the clients at Ryker Interiors.

Only after everyone had turned in for the night and she slowly wandered through the so-called suite did it hit her again. A remodeling project like this, and the one going on upstairs, didn't come cheap. There was probably little that the Clays couldn't afford to do if they so chose. If Daniel decided he wanted their child on the Double-C, he could no doubt achieve it, just as he'd implied less than a week ago in her Chicago apartment.

Wrapping her arms around herself, she went into the spacious bedroom where her suitcases had been deposited, conveniently laid across the foot of the wide bed. Even unfastened and opened, though the contents had been left untouched.

All she'd been thinking, for the past several days, was how quickly Daniel would change his mind about their marriage agreement. Assuming that once he did, he'd be reasonable about coming to some other sort of arrangement. The possibility still hadn't really hit Maggie that Daniel could end up being the primary caretaker of this child.

She was the mother, certainly. But the courts were favoring the rights of fathers more and more. Daniel was more than able to hire whatever type of assistance he might need. While Maggie—

"No," she whispered. "Daniel wouldn't do that." She snatched an armful of clothing from the suitcase and began hanging them in the closet. He wouldn't take her child. He wasn't that kind of man.

Back and forth she went from the suitcases to the closet to the dresser.

Are you so sure you know what kind of man he is?

She flipped one empty suitcase closed. "He wouldn't," she muttered. She didn't believe that his interest in her would last. But that didn't mean that—

Oh, doesn't it?

"No." She closed the other empty cases and stuck them on the shelves in the closet.

So where is he? He certainly isn't here pushing you to make wedding plans.

She didn't know where Daniel was. He'd left, as usual, without one word, and she didn't like the way that fact gnawed at her. Which was probably why she was worrying herself over something that wouldn't happen.

Daniel taking her child from her.

He might have changed. But he hadn't changed that much. She knew it with everything inside her.

She peeled out of the denim jumper, tights and sweater. Sighing with relief, she bundled into her chenille robe and padded barefoot into the sitting area adjacent to the two bedrooms. Entering the spacious bathroom, she took a long shower.

The mirrors were still half-fogged with steam. But she looked at her reflection, anyway. Touched her waist, laid her palm flat on her abdomen.

Where Daniel had laid his hand earlier.

The veneer of calm that she'd so carefully cultivated vanished and she trembled. How many times had she been disappointed, devastated, in the past?

"What's wrong?"

Gasping, her head whipped around, her wet hair flying. She scrabbled with the lapels of her robe, dragging them together, holding the chenille tightly over her racing heart. "Nothing," she said, ire warring with panic. "My agreement to return to the Double-C did not include you invading my privacy." She tied her belt with sharp, jerky movements. "That's twice you've barged in on me."

Daniel stepped in her path when she tried to brush by. "I thought you might be sick again."

"As you can see, I'm not." She damned her wayward hormones. Surely that was the only reason she felt on the edge of tears yet again.

"If you're not sick, then what is it?"

"Nothing."

"Right. That's why you're shaking."

There was no way she could get past him out of the bathroom and to her bedroom. For whatever privacy he allowed her there. She firmed her shoulders. "Stay out of my head, Daniel."

"Trust me, honey. If I could, I would. What's worrying you?"

Her jaw worked. She didn't want him reading her thoughts.

Her emotions. "I've had two miscarriages before. Two, Daniel. And a difficult pregnancy with J.D." Her hands fisted in the long folds of her robe. "Twice I knew there was life inside me and twice I could do nothing to save it."

"Mag—"

Her eyes burned as she shot him a tight look. "Is that good enough reason for me to worry? Are you satisfied now?"

He gave her a look she couldn't interpret. "Ah, Maggie Mae, why didn't—"

"Save your pity, Daniel. I don't want it and I don't need it."

His eyes iced over. "Nobody said squat about pity. Does it occur to you that you might not be the only one concerned about this pregnancy? I might not have known about both your miscarriages, but I sure in hell remember you carrying J.D. I remember the day you started bleeding and we had to drive you into the hospital."

A knot tightened in her chest. She remembered that day, too. Daniel had carried her from the brick cottage to Matt's truck when Jaimie, who'd been filling in for her at the main house, had gone for help. His hand had been bloodied and broken—he'd never explained why—but he'd carried her heavily pregnant body nearly a mile.

Once at the hospital, it had been hours and hours before Joe had eventually shown up. She'd felt a tiny stab of hope when he'd arrived. It had been the first time that he'd seemed genuinely interested in the welfare of their child. But that stab hadn't lasted long. One look into Joe's eyes and she'd known how he'd spent those absent hours. The only thing she hadn't known was the name of the woman it was this time.

"Nothing's gonna happen to this baby," Daniel was saying.

"You just don't get it, do you—" her voice hitched "—sometimes there's no choice. No choice. You can…eat right. And get enough rest. And take your vitamins. And—"

His hands closed over her shoulders. "Stop. You're getting too worked up."

She jerked out of his hold, appallingly aware that she

wanted to just rest her head against his wide chest. She couldn't start depending on Daniel. She had to depend on herself. Only herself.

"Dammit, Maggie Mae—"

"Stop calling me that name!" And then her stomach rebelled. She stumbled to the commode, too weak and sick to stop Daniel from crouching beside her, holding back her hair.

After, she rested her head on her bent knees. The comfort she drew from Daniel's quiet, watchful presence scared her senseless. Because it would hurt so much more when he no longer offered it. "Go away, Daniel." Her words were muffled against her robe. "Please, just leave me alone."

Daniel's fists clenched at his sides as he looked at her hunched, miserable form. "Is your stomach settled now?"

She didn't answer. Just rose and shakily brushed her teeth.

He swallowed an oath and simply picked her up in his arms when she was through. She wriggled and told him acidly to put her down. He did. Once he'd carried her into the bedroom where he'd put her cases earlier, he settled her on the wide mattress.

Her ankle-length robe had separated, giving him a long view of shapely leg. A view that nearly distracted him from his task. He yanked the quilt up and tossed it over her legs. She popped right back up like one of those Weeble toys Sarah liked to play with. The ones that wobbled but never fell down.

She wrapped her robe tightly around her and stepped past him, going to the doorway and pointedly holding on to the knob. As if she couldn't wait to slam it shut as soon as he moved his rear through it. "I could have walked."

"Fine. Tomorrow, you can do all the walking you want to. Right into Rebecca's office. The sooner you start regular medical care, the better you'll feel."

Her turquoise eyes shot him a look that fairly singed. "Is that so."

"Regular prenatal care is important."

"My, my, Daniel. What baby book have you been reading

lately? I prefer to select my own physician, thank you so much.''

''Rebecca is right in Weaver. If you want to do any *selecting,* you're gonna have to go to Gillette.''

''So?''

''So?'' He curled his fist, because she stood there looking at him so prissily that he wanted to muss her up, but good. Right there in the center of the disheveled bed. ''So, the whole point of getting a doc in Weaver was that people wouldn't have to go so far for medical care.'' Why was she being so stubborn? She'd already admitted she was fearful for the baby. Their baby.

''I went to Gillette before,'' she said without pause. ''There is no earthly reason I can't go there again. Dr. Foster—''

''Is too damned far away. Just because Rebecca started up a practice in a podunk town like Weaver doesn't mean she's not qualified. She comes from New—''

''I don't care where she comes from. I'll choose my own doctor. Dr. Foster knows my history.''

He thrust his hands through his hair, keeping his fingers there because if he didn't, he really was going to do something stupid. ''Rebecca could get your files or whatever from him. Does it occur to you that being so bloody far from your doctor might have been part of the problem before?''

''That is ridiculous!''

He was going to do something stupid. He reached out and peeled her fingers from the doorknob, turning her inexorably to face him. ''Is it? Dammit, Maggie Mae, don't be stubborn about this.''

She glared right back at him. ''You're the one throwing orders around. It's *my* pregnancy, and I'll go to the doctor that I choose!'' What would be the point of seeing the doctor in Weaver? When Daniel changed his mind about his marriage demand—and he *would*—she and J.D. would go to Gillette. Where her old doctor practiced.

''It's my baby, too. Your days of making unilateral decisions are over.''

"Unilateral..." Maggie yanked her shoulders away. Disbelief coursed through her. "This is too much," she muttered. "Joe couldn't stand to hear one detail about J.D., and you're busting into bathrooms and telling me which doctor I can see. What's next?" She tossed her head back, raking her damp hair away from her face. "I suppose you'll want to sit in the exam room while I have my checkups? Are you going to make sure I take my daily prenatal vitamins?" She blinked rapidly. "Rub my back when it starts to ache, massage lotion over me so I don't get stretch marks and tie my shoelaces when I'm so big I can't reach my feet?"

Daniel's eyes were flat disks of silver. "Maybe. I warned you, Maggie Mae. Don't compare me with Joe."

"I wasn't—" *Yes, you were.* Tiredness swept through her with a wildfire's speed and deadliness. "That wasn't my intention. I'm just...I—"

"What?"

"I'm used to handling things on my own," she admitted stiffly. Wasn't that the only way to keep her sanity? Stay in control.

"Those days are over. That's my daughter..."

"Or son—"

"...you're carrying. You might have wrangled this stupid month outta me. But you won't shut me out of one minute of this pregnancy, Maggie. So save yourself the trouble, and don't bother trying."

"It wasn't stupid! And I'm not trying to shut you out of anything."

"Aren't you?"

"No!" *Yes. Yes, yes, yes.* She wanted to go back to the safety of Chicago. Where she didn't have to worry about anything beyond spending time with her daughter, collecting her next paycheck and filling that order for handmade Christmas ornaments. Where she didn't have to worry with every breath she drew that she'd lose this baby the way she'd lost the others. Where she didn't have to look at this man...so strong and warm and male.

And want things that would never be.

"Liar," he said softly.

She wanted to deny it. To hotly refute his accusation. But she couldn't. Her shoulders curved inward. She folded her arms around herself. Around the baby who grew within her. Daniel's baby.

Tears burned behind her eyes. "I don't want to fight with you." She swallowed and looked up into his wintry gray eyes. Why on earth had she given her word that she'd marry him? What kind of insanity had preyed upon her that she'd done something so foolish?

"You're giving a good imitation of it."

"I just want to pick my own doctor. Is that so awful?"

His jaw ticked. "Gillette is too far away."

Knowing he could well be right didn't help her jumbled emotions any at all. "This is my pregnancy," she said flatly. "I'll pick my own doctor."

His eyes narrowed, and Maggie drew in a breath, dreadfully aware that she'd crossed some invisible line of his.

His legs moved, and Maggie stood there, snared without the good sense to move away. She jumped when he closed his hand behind her neck, tilting her face inexorably to his. "Understand this, Maggie. This is *our* pregnancy." His gravelly voice dropped with each word, more fierce for its very softness. "You will be my wife. Get used to it."

She trembled. His anger was palpable. Yet she wasn't afraid. Her nerves felt excruciatingly sensitive. Far too aware of the strength in the palm he cupped against her neck, the long fingers warm against her scalp where they threaded through her damp hair.

She felt his gaze on her lips. And found herself moistening them. "But—" His mouth covered hers, blotting out her words. Her thoughts. Her good sense.

His kiss didn't allow for anything but absorbing him. His taste. His heat. She twisted her hands in his shirt, grabbing for purchase when her knees dissolved.

And then it was over. He straightened, leaving her mindless and swaying.

"Don't try pushing me out of one minute of this pregnancy," he said, his tone flat. "You'll regret it if you do."

Maggie stumbled to the bed, sinking onto the corner of it after he walked out of the bedroom. She was a noodle. Overcooked and jiggling. He, on the other hand, had seemed as cool as a cucumber. Walking away as easy as you please.

She sat there, listening to the faint sounds of him moving around out there. Then the soft hiss of the shower.

Making a face, she donned a nightgown and crawled under the covers. She pulled the spare pillow over her head, childishly hoping that he ran out of hot water.

She'd be late for work. If she didn't get up and right now, she'd be late. But she was so warm. So comfortable. For once the springs in her pullout bed weren't poking her in the backside. She buried her nose in the downy pillow under her head and sank more deeply into the tendrils of sleep that clung to her.

Warm. So very warm. She stretched her legs luxuriously.

And sat bolt upright, staring stupidly about her. She rubbed her eyes and blinked as a yawn split her face. Of course she could luxuriously stretch. This bed wasn't her aged pullout sofa in the living room of her small Chicago apartment.

She had no job waiting for her at Ryker Interiors. No rents she had to collect.

She only had a few weeks in which to wait for Daniel to change his mind about marrying her.

She sat up, pressing her forehead to her drawn-up knees for a moment, wishing that it was as simple as that. She nibbled the inside corner of her lip, then thrust back the covers and stood. The abrupt motion made her sway, and she closed her eyes, waiting for the room to stop tilting. When it did, she smoothed her hand over her abdomen. "Stop that," she murmured.

The room stayed reassuringly steady as she dressed in comfortable jeans and a cheery yellow T-shirt, which she had to leave untucked to hide the button she left unfastened at her waist. She strode into the second bedroom where she yanked the tumbled sheets on Daniel's bed straight. Dragged the blanket up off the floor and settled it across the wide mattress, then reached for the tangled quilt.

And stopped cold. She eyed the bed. The covers had been churned up as if a storm had occurred in the bed.

When she'd been housekeeper here, she'd made all the beds. All of them. Including Daniel's. He'd been so neat that the only evidence he'd slept in his bed had been the dent in his goosedown pillow.

She slowly finished making Daniel's bed until it was as perfectly smooth as the one she'd just made in her bedroom. She gathered up the slips of notepapers he'd tossed on the nightstand and set them neatly on the dresser where they'd be less likely to land once again on the floor. There were phone numbers scrawled in Daniel's handwriting across the half dozen slips. One had a name along with several numbers. Angeline.

She dropped a paperweight that she'd given to Jaimie a few years ago onto the slips. Angeline.

Well, Maggie wasn't fool enough to think that Daniel hadn't had women friends. Was she?

Then she didn't have time anymore to wonder about the women in Daniel's life, or why he slept so restlessly now, because her morning sickness had apparently lain waiting long enough.

Maggie finally felt better and went upstairs. She pulled a thick woolen sweater off the pegs by the screen and pushed through the door. The sun was bright and the air brisk with the bite of coming winter. Maggie stood on the back step, pulling the sweater around her shoulders, and let her eyes drift in the direction of the cottage where she and Joe had lived. The foreman's cottage. Before she knew it, her feet were carrying her across the soft grass and along the gravel road that led to the bunkhouse and the cottage.

She finally stopped about a hundred yards from the neat, brick dwelling. The garden that she'd planted when she and Joe first came to the Double-C was grown over with grass as if it had never been.

She drew in a long, deep breath. It felt so odd being back here. But odd or not, as Maggie absorbed the scent of grass and horse and wide-open space, she knew that she'd finally come home to the only place she'd ever really loved.

Turning on her heel, she headed back toward the big house.

She didn't notice the black pickup truck until she'd nearly reached the back porch. When she did, the portion of calm she'd attained promptly vanished. She hovered in the middle of the gravel road feeling idiotic. She needed to get a grip before she had a heart attack or a nervous collapse.

Taking what must have been her fiftieth calming breath already that morning, she continued toward the big house and up the porch steps. But before she could reach out to pull open the screen door, it moved, pushed open from the inside.

She knew who'd be standing there in the mudroom before she saw him.

"I thought you'd gone," she said, thinking not of his nasty comment about wasting the morning, but of the way he'd torn apart his bedding in his sleep. Of a person named Angeline. She shoved the sweater on a hook.

"I came back."

Chapter Eight

"**O**bviously," Maggie said. She stepped past him into the kitchen, then wondered why. There weren't any chores to busy her hands. Then she noticed the half-eaten homemade cinnamon roll in Daniel's hand. "Didn't you eat earlier?"

His lips twisted. "Worried I'm gonna get fat?"

Maggie blinked. "Hardly." The answer came out involuntarily. The way her eyes immediately went to his lean torso was out of her control, too. The plain white T-shirt he wore clung to every line of him from shoulder to leather belt. She remembered, intimately, the powerful build he possessed. "It's none of my business anyway," she added, knowing she sounded prim and uptight but unable to do anything about it.

"On the contrary," he murmured. "Don't you think a wife should be concerned with her husband's health?" He finished off the roll in one bite.

"I'm not your wife," she hissed.

He swallowed. Licked his thumb. "Yet."

She stared stonily at him, wishing for a smart comeback that never came.

"You about ready to go?"

He stood only a few inches away now, and she imagined she could actually feel the heat of his body. "Go?"

"Yeah. Go. As in drive to my place. Our new home," he drew out the words. "I need to pick out exterior paint, and word has it that you're helping me decide on that kind of thing. Unless you're going back on your promise."

"No," she said stiffly.

His eyes drifted over her face. "I didn't think so," he agreed blandly. "I'll be in Matt's office," he said, without looking at her as he walked from the kitchen. "Let me know when you're ready."

Thirty minutes later, she could put off thinking about the house no longer. Sitting beside Daniel in the cab of his truck, she stared out at where the dilapidated, two-story, Blanchard house had once stood. The original house had been completely razed, just as Jaimie had said.

In its place stood a dwelling that took her breath.

Daniel continued driving around to the rear of the house, then stopped the truck, throwing it into park.

She felt his eyes on her, knew he was waiting for some comment. "It's…remarkable."

While the big house was a comfortable, rambling, old stone-and-wood barn of a house, this house was pure grace. She pushed open the truck door and slipped to the ground, wrapping her arms around herself for warmth in the cool air. She should have thought to have brought a sweater. Somehow, with Daniel around, thinking sensibly became a near impossibility.

She stepped around the truck, her head tilting back as she tried to take in all of the house at once.

She knew that, when finished, the clapboard would be misty gray and that the windowpanes would gleam. It was the house of young girls' dreams…elegant and stately. With a wrap-around porch and gabled eaves.

She could just picture it with rose bushes alongside it, heavy with blooms. In winter, with the snow, pristine white as it drifted around the foundation. It was a house that sang longingly for family. For the smell of bread baking in the oven. For the crackle of a fireplace and for the squeals and chatter of children.

It wasn't at all what she would have expected Daniel Clay to build. With his own powerful shoulders and callused hands. And he'd done it in such a short time. "How did you—" she waved her hand, slowly encompassing the graceful house. "You hadn't started it when I was here in August." He'd only just arrived before she did.

He pulled one of two cardboard boxes of catalogs out of the truck and tucked it under his arm. "I had crews come in for some of it," he said shortly. "Go on in."

The reality of what she was doing came crashing down about her shoulders. She reached for the second box, but he stopped her.

"I'll get it."

"But—"

"I said I'll get it. You're not to carry stuff around."

Maggie blinked. "Excuse me? Is taking orders from you part of our agreement?"

He notched his hat back with a thumb. "It is for this. No lifting. Period. You need something lifted, you find me. That includes carrying J.D. around. Because that's my baby you're carrying inside you. Understand?"

She gaped. "That's ridic—" But he'd already turned away, leaving her to follow as he strode toward the house. Maggie huffed, then eyed the second box. It probably weighed all of twenty pounds, she guessed, reaching for it. She actually curled her hands around the cardboard sides. Then paused.

Not because she was afraid of Daniel's order.

But because her common sense knew that he had a point.

She straightened, leaving the box sitting on the seat, and followed Daniel into the house. Like the big house, this one was built with a mudroom at the rear. Through that was the kitchen and she stopped just inside.

There was a portable light fixture fitted with a bare bulb clamped onto the edge of the unfinished counter and she wondered how many times he'd worked past dark. Now, however, sunlight streamed into the spacious kitchen. Highlighting the high ceiling and making the windows glisten.

Unlike the exterior of the house, which only needed a coat of paint and shingles as far as she could tell, the kitchen was woefully unfinished.

And very chilly, she realized, with a shiver.

She left her purse next to his black hat on a bare wood counter that would, presumably, soon be tiled. She crossed the plywood floor following the sounds of his movements. The dining room. A soaring great room. A sweeping staircase that, when finished, would be a visual feast.

Daniel appeared at the top of the stairs. "Up here."

Butterflies the size of elephants crashed around inside her stomach. She slowly started up the steps. She imagined the bedrooms were upstairs. And the bedroom he would expect her to share.

By the time she reached the top, she was shaking.

"Something wrong?"

She folded her hands together. "Of course not." Considering it came out in a near squeak, she wasn't surprised when he snorted, disbelieving. He turned away, striding along the wide hall. "I thought J.D. might like the room on the end here. There's a bay window. If you think she'd like a window seat, I'll add one."

"Oh. How...lovely." Maggie had always wanted a bedroom with a window seat. To sit in and read and dream. But her room in the aging house of their Wisconsin dairy farm had been tucked upstairs with only two tiny dormer windows.

He stepped toward her, and her thoughts scattered. He was so big and so tall, and in the cool, utter silence of the empty house around them, she felt the very heat of him reach out and enfold her.

Her breath stilled. Inexplicable tears burned behind her eyes.

She suddenly wanted him to tell her that everything would be okay.

But she'd stopped depending on other people the day her mother walked out the door when she'd been thirteen.

She wanted him to hold her and make her feel beautiful and wanted.

But the only reason she was here at all was that she carried his child.

She'd gotten "caught," as the fine upstanding ladies of her hometown church, Augusta Baptist, would have said. Caught just like her mama before her.

Still, she wanted Daniel to touch her. To cup his broad, callused hands around her face. And kiss her.

His head lowered toward hers.

"Yo, Dan!"

Maggie jumped. She brushed her hair behind her ear, turning to look down the stairs. A man she'd never seen before stomped into view.

She felt as shaky as a new calf, but Daniel just headed down the stairs, calm as you please. "Shingles in?"

The man nodded, tipping back his hat to reveal a balding head beneath. "Boys 'n' I'll get to it, if you're ready."

"Sooner the better," Daniel said. "Matt says we'll have snow by Halloween. You know his nose for snow."

Maggie watched him disappear with the other man. The coolness of the house nudged chills down her arms and she closed her arms around herself. She went into the bedroom at the end of the hall, and sure enough—there was a beautiful window just made for a little girl's dream spot.

She drew in a steadying breath. J.D. wouldn't be installed in this room, she reminded herself. Daniel would change his mind before Thanksgiving arrived.

She turned from the room and slowly went downstairs. Already she could hear movement from the roof. Then the rhythmic slap of bundles of shingles landing. The heavy thump of footsteps as men walked across the roof over her head. She returned to the kitchen, slowly drawing out some of the catalogs from the box Daniel had left sitting on the floor. The house didn't extend to furniture yet, and she carried several paint brochures back to the staircase and sat on the bottom step.

Slowly she paged through the brochures. Overhead, she heard the thwack of hammers driving nails.

"Find anything you like?"

She started. "*Must* you do that?"

"Do what?"

"Walk around without making a sound." She pushed to her feet and walked past Daniel back through to the kitchen where she dropped all but one of the brochures into the box.

"Sorry," he said. "I'll try to remember to stomp my feet more in the future."

An unwilling smile crept toward her lips. She didn't want him to make her smile. She didn't want to like him. But she'd always liked Daniel. He'd made her edgy, true. But he'd also made her smile.

How many times had he fixed something around the foreman's cottage that had needed fixing? Her washing machine. The oven. Hanging that clothesline. He'd been the one to place the first shovel in the earth when she'd decided to plant a garden.

He'd been the one to make her wish for a marriage that didn't choke the life out of her. And he hadn't had to say a word.

All he'd had to do was exist. To be.

And now, unless he called it off, she had promised to be his wife. To enter into a marriage with him because of the child they'd created together. Not because of love. Not even because of friendship.

But because she was her mother's daughter and had behaved shamelessly under an August moon.

"Maggie?"

She swallowed the knot in her throat and flipped open the

brochure to the square of misty gray paint. "Here," she said, pushing the brochure into his hands. "You said pick a color. That's it." She pushed the brochure into his hands and hurried out of the house. Out into the chilly sunshine, amid the sounds of the roofers.

Where she wouldn't have to admit to anyone but herself that the gray she'd chosen was the exact shade of Daniel's quicksilver eyes.

That night Maggie decided J.D. should sleep in the guest suite with her. Matthew and Jaimie had driven into Gillette for the evening, and Sarah was spending the night with Leandra at Jefferson and Emily's. J.D. had been invited, too, but to Maggie's surprise had said she wanted to stay with her mama.

However, once it was bedtime, J.D. didn't seem terribly inclined to settle in the bed. She toyed with the pillows, arranging and rearranging them to Duchess's liking. "Is we gonna live here now, Mama?"

Busy folding the small load of J.D.'s clothing that she'd washed late that afternoon after she and Daniel had returned, Maggie's teeth sank into her lip. "We are…visiting," she murmured, setting the shirts and jeans into a neat little pile. "It's late, J.D. Get into bed and settle down."

J.D. climbed to the middle of the wide bed, giving an experimental bounce or two while eyeing her mother. Duchess tumbled to the floor.

Maggie picked her up and handed the stuffed horse to J.D., shaking her head at the bouncing. "J.D."

Her daughter set the stuffed horse back on the pillows at the head of the bed. "Why is my daddy wif the angels?"

Startled, Maggie's hands stopped in the act of smoothing down the quilt that J.D. had rumpled. Of all times— "He was in a car accident," she said carefully. "He was badly hurt."

"He had a bad owie."

"Yes."

"They didn't gots any bandedaids?"

J.D.'s curls were whisper soft when Maggie brushed them from her daughter's forehead. "Bandages weren't enough, sweetheart. So the angels took Daddy to heaven where he wouldn't hurt anymore."

"I don't like owies," J.D. said. "Mama, are you gonna go wif the angels, too?"

Her vision blurred and she sat on the bed, pulling J.D. into her lap. "No, J.D., I am not going anywhere. I'm going to stay right here with you."

J.D. wrapped her arms around Maggie's neck and pressed her warm little cheek against Maggie's. "I love you, Mama."

"I love you too, sweetheart." She heard a sound and looked up to see Daniel standing in the doorway. She turned toward J.D., dashing a hand over her cheeks. "Come on, now. Under the covers," she murmured.

J.D. did so, and Maggie kissed her brow, straightening from the bed.

Daniel leaned his shoulder against the doorjamb. "She okay?"

Maggie nodded.

J.D. spotted Daniel and called his name, holding her arms up, demanding a night-night kiss. Even though Maggie saw a muscle tighten in his jaw, his expression was gentle as he complied.

But when he turned again to find Maggie hovering in the doorway, his face settled once again into his usual unreadable mask. "I ordered the paint you picked. You still haven't told me what furniture you want for the bedrooms, though."

She felt the blood drain from her face at the thought of bedroom furnishings. Of beds. Of sharing one with him.

She pulled the door shut and stood in the living area, squelching a nervous jump when Daniel moved past her to sprawl in his leather chair. One toe of his boot tapped a slow rhythm in the air.

He watched her from hooded eyes. "You gonna hover there all night or sit down and relax?"

Relax. There was a good one. But she sat. Then hopped up again at his next question.

"What did you want to talk about this morning?"

She rounded the couch, her fingers pressing into the upholstery. This morning. When she'd seen his eyes go dark and inward. Before she'd seen his beautiful house and wondered with one fanciful part of her mind what it would be like to actually live there. "It was about J.D., actually."

"What about her?"

"Well, you...she is already fond of you," Maggie managed. "If we get mar—"

"*When* we get married—"

Her lips tightened. "I don't want J.D. hurt," she said bluntly.

His boot stilled. "Why would she be?"

Maggie folded her arms and paced between the couch and the television. "Daniel, J.D. has already lost one father."

"She didn't even know him."

She couldn't deny that. "Nevertheless, I don't want her to lose—"

"You're already planning on a divorce, then?"

She pushed back her hair. "No, of course not." She wasn't planning on a *wedding!* "I'm making a mess of this."

"You won't hear me disagreeing there."

Maggie stopped and propped her hands on her hips. "You're not helping matters any."

Daniel leaned back in his chair, his expression calm. "What do you want me to do differently? I've already lied to my family about what you're doing here. All because you insisted on waiting until Thanksgiving to announce our plans. I'm giving you an opportunity to give your input on the house we'll be sharing for the rest of our days. Just what else, exactly, is it I'm supposed to be doing?"

He made it sound so utterly reasonable, that she wanted to throw something at him. "Don't make her love you and then walk away," she gritted.

His jaw cocked. "You're comparing me again," he said softly.

She shook her head. "No, Daniel. I'm talking about *you*. J.D. thinks you hung the moon and she barely knows you. I just…I—" She broke off, frowning at him. "Don't encourage her."

"I see," he said softly. "You want me to ignore her the way Joe did."

That stung. "Of course not."

"You can't have it both ways, Maggie. Actually, you're not gonna have it *any* way. J.D. is part of our little family unit—" he clipped out the word "—as much as we are. As much as the baby. If you don't like it, too bad."

Maggie's voice lowered, and she leaned over the back of the couch toward him. "I saw the way you looked at her this morning. You were miles away. J.D. is an extremely bright child. How long do you think it'll take before she realizes your interest in her is feigned?"

Daniel's eyes frosted. "Feigned."

"You explain it, then. If it wasn't your lack of interest in J.D., then what was it?"

He shoved to his feet, slowly rounding the couch, but she stood her ground. Even when he towered over her and the toes of his boots nudged her sneakers. "Nothing."

She shook back her hair, crossing her arms. "I don't believe you."

His expression suddenly shifted. If she hadn't been watching closely, she wouldn't have even noticed. It was his eyes. One moment as cold as ice chips. The next, gleaming silver. And the nervousness that she didn't feel in the face of his temper burgeoned to life in the face of this latest expression.

When he lifted his hand and oh, so slowly tucked her hair behind her ear, and his fingers lingered there, she couldn't help it. She hastily stepped back, feeling her cheeks fire at the amusement in his eyes. "Don't do that," she ordered. But it lacked teeth considering the way it came out all shaky.

She rounded the couch, putting the big sectional between them once more.

The corner of his molded lips deepened, as if he was hiding a smile. "There's no need to look at me as if I'm the big bad villain planning to have my wicked way with your pristine, virginal self."

"Then stop smiling at me like the wolf before he huffed and puffed."

"Which one would you be? Straw, sticks or bricks?"

She very much feared that if Daniel chose to blow hard on her, she'd crumble just like that fabled straw and twig. "Bricks," she lied.

Daniel considered her, feeling a shaft of admiration for the way she didn't back down even though he could see the way her fingers trembled and twisted together. He'd only wanted to get her to back off the topic of his reaction that morning.

If there was one thing he knew unsettled Maggie, it was the drugging physical connection they felt for each other. Unfortunately he'd underestimated. Because want—hot and urgent—charged through his blood.

Just then he wanted nothing more than to sweep her off her feet and make her his. And since he wasn't entirely sure he could keep from doing just that, he made himself shrug. "I talked with Rebecca Morehouse," he said. "She's expecting your call."

Maggie took the bait quicker than a starving kitten. And he disliked himself even more than usual because of it. "Is that so?" Her voice, for all its smoothness, couldn't hide her ire. "I suppose you told her *why?*"

"No. I'll leave that up to you when I drive you to town."

Her gently rounded jaw tightened, and her eyes glinted more green than blue. And he realized he could only go so far. "I'm going out," he said abruptly, seeing her blink, wind deflating from her annoyed sails.

Feeling lower than a snake's belly, he scooped up his keys and slid his hat onto his head. "I'll be late. If you need anything, call Curly."

By the time words finally formed on Maggie's lips, Daniel had already gone up the steps that led directly outside. She heard the hollow echo of the door and moved to the high windows that were barely above ground level and stood on her toes, trying to peer out. But all she saw was the reflection of the room behind her.

She could hear, however. Could hear the low growl of his truck as he drove away from the big house. She blew out a breath and leaned against his beaten leather chair.

Once again she'd driven him from his home.

It was well after midnight when Daniel finally threw his truck into park, alongside the darkened house. He sat in the cab of his truck, listening to the engine tick as it cooled. He didn't think of anything particular. Not of the call he'd finally made to Coleman Black. Not the latest string of futile inquiries he'd made about Angeline.

Not even of Maggie. Or the fact that he was going to be a father. Or the fact that he'd just spent two hours sitting on a bar stool in Colbys staring into a whisky from which he never drank so much as a sip.

He just sat there in his truck for a long while, listening to nothing.

Finally, his engine terminally silent, the night thick and nipped with autumn chill, he climbed out of the truck and went inside.

He didn't need to turn on a light. He knew the big house as well as he knew the back of his hand. Still, he hesitated midway down the darkened staircase.

A pool of golden light spilled from the small, decorative lamp sitting on a corner table. Not enough light to fully illuminate the room. But certainly enough to make the huddled form in his old chair visible. He finished descending the stairs, then waited. He realized he could hear the soft cadence of her breathing. She was asleep.

He had to wrap his hand hard around the banister for a moment. Maggie was sleeping in his chair.

He'd manipulated her into coming here with his veiled threats about the baby. He'd fully expected to have her in his bed. Counted on it, in fact, because then maybe he'd get a decent night's sleep again.

But the reality of it hit him with the force of a wrecking ball.

Then the small bundle in his chair shifted. The knit afghan she'd pulled over her folded legs slipped to the floor. He imagined that he could smell the wildflower scent of her. He set his hat and keys soundlessly on the counter and walked around to sit on the couch. Calling himself a fool, he settled the afghan across her again, then relaxed into the couch.

And watched her sleep.

Chapter Nine

Daniel knew his time was up when a full week had passed since Maggie and J.D. returned to the Double-C, and J.D. was determined to ride a horse, for real this time.

It was late afternoon and Daniel had come across J.D., playing with her stuffed horse in the bunkhouse while Curly was busy cooking supper for the hands.

He knew he really was a coward when her little face lit up like a Christmas tree and her eyes zeroed in on him with the force of a laser. He wanted to turn tail and run.

"Dannl, I ride a horse today?"

Curly shrugged his wizened shoulders and kept on shucking corn when Daniel looked to the old man for assistance. Daniel thumbed back his hat and looked down at J.D. She was sitting on top of the long picnic-style table. "Where is Sarah?"

J.D. sighed, her shoulders curving downward dramatically. "Seeping."

Considering that Sarah was past diaper age, Daniel figured that was J.D.'s version of sleeping. "Your mom?"

Another huge sigh. "Sawing."

Daniel's lips tightened a little at that. He'd specifically warned Maggie not to work too many hours a day at her wood art projects. As usual, she hadn't listened. He knew for a fact that she'd been at it since earlier that morning. It had been her excuse for not accompanying him to the building site that morning.

"Dannl?"

He focused on J.D.'s face, sincere pleading in those green eyes despite her melodramatic presentation. Ah, hell. He was supposed to be a big, tough man. What harm could a horse ride do?

He managed a grin. "Sure thing, snooks."

Her face broke into a huge smile and Daniel felt the kick right down to his gut at her strong resemblance to her mother. She pushed to her feet, Duchess for once forgotten, as she jumped into Daniel's arms, supremely confident that he'd catch her. "Right now!"

Daniel couldn't help but chuckle at her exuberance. He looked at J.D. and saw only her. Not J.D.'s parents. Not even Angeline.

Only J.D. And she was a charmer. "Right now," he agreed.

Maggie sat back on her chair and arched her back, sliding off her safety glasses and tossing them on her workbench. She'd gotten a great deal accomplished today toward her Christmas orders, and there was a neat stack waiting to be packaged and mailed. Nothing like having more space to spread herself out in. Even sharing space with two tractors, a torn-apart engine and various other pieces of equipment, she had more room than she'd had in her apartment in Chicago.

She picked up the oval welcome sign she was carving and blew gently, scattering the fine sawdust clinging to it. She'd started the hanging before she could talk herself out of it. She'd give it to Daniel for his home. She had yet to finish carving the words "welcome to my home."

He'd been such a bear when he'd cleared this work space

for her and set up her equipment. He'd lectured her for a ridiculously long time about overworking herself, lifting too much and generally overtaxing herself. He'd sounded so much like Squire sometimes did that Maggie had been reluctantly charmed. After all. If he'd been so adamant about her doing too much, he could have refused to set up her equipment in the first place.

Maggie would have pitched a fit, true. She had catalog orders she was committed to filling and one last small model she'd promised to send Ryker Interiors. But Daniel had made the offer of the machine shed.

She slowly ran her fingertips over the hanging, feeling instinctively for flaws, when she heard J.D.'s distinctive squeal.

Maggie rose and went outside. She'd felt a little strange at first, knowing that J.D. was being watched by so many other people while she attended to her wood art. Jaimie. Squire. Even Curly had pitched in.

But that was just the way it was here. She needed to remember that. Everyone watched out for everyone. It was one of the charms of the Double-C.

J.D. squealed again and Maggie followed the sound around the machine shed to one of the smaller corrals behind the horse barn. And her feet rooted in place at what she saw.

Daniel held J.D. securely in front of him as he rode the same horse he'd been riding the day of her arrival—Spike, she'd finally learned—around the ring.

J.D.'s little fingers were clutched in Spike's lustrous mane, her face glowing. It was quite a while before J.D. noticed Maggie watching, and when she did, she waved so enthusiastically that Maggie felt sure her daughter would have tumbled right off the horse if it weren't for Daniel's steady hands around her waist.

Her fingers curled as Spike plodded to a halt on the other side of the rail from Maggie. Daniel looked down at her from beneath the brim of his hat, his expression challenging. As if he expected her to rebuke him for taking J.D. riding.

Only then did Maggie realize that it was only because Daniel held her daughter on the horse with him that she wasn't coming unglued. If it had been anyone but Daniel, she might well have expressed her unhappiness at not being consulted first.

Maggie knew how to ride a horse. She'd grown up with them, after all.

Yet it was Daniel who was treating her precious girl to her first horse ride. "You look like you're having fun," she said, aware of the surprised look Daniel couldn't quite contain.

She supposed she deserved that look, after her words that night about Daniel not getting too close to J.D. But how could she be upset at this?

"We are," Daniel stated, aware that the words were true. J.D.'s childish ecstasy was hard to resist. Even for a man who was determined to remain detached. "But I think we've been at it long enough for one day."

J.D. started to protest, but Daniel stopped it by wrapping her palms around the reins. "Maybe your mama will get the gate for us."

J.D. held the reins as if she was born to them. "Mama, will you get the gate for us?"

Maggie nodded and trotted over to the gate, swinging it wide. They rode through, and Maggie pushed the gate shut, her expression soft. As soft as the hand she laid for a brief moment on his thigh. As soft as the "Thank you" she whispered, before stepping back from Spike.

Daniel tore his attention away from Maggie and softly clicked to Spike. J.D. laughed with delight as they trotted toward the horse barn. She was even more delighted when Maggie followed them into the barn and spent the next ten minutes chattering away to her mother about her first horse ride in between asking Daniel a million questions about everything from why the horse barn smelled that way to why the horse needed a blanket under the saddle. Was it cold?

Daniel was starting to cast desperate looks Maggie's way by the time J.D. was moving on to questions about the horse's anatomy. Maggie hid her amusement at his obvious relief

when Sarah and Squire passed by and J.D. immediately ske-
daddled off with her new buddies.

"Does she ever stop asking questions?"

"Sure. It's called sleeping." She caught a wisp of a grin
on his face when he gave Spike a last pat and stepped out of
the stall. He swept up his saddle as if it weighed nothing and
carried it and the saddle blanket into the tack room. Maggie
climbed off the bale and followed him.

He glanced back at her when she stopped in the doorway.
"You're not gonna ask me why horses have four legs and
people have two and snakes don't have any are you?"

She shook her head. "No." Sawdust clung to the sleeve of
her sweater, and she brushed at it. "I did have a question for
you, though."

"Great," he muttered. He turned to face her, his hands
propped on his lean hips. "Well, lay it on me. I'm tough."

"Real tough," Maggie agreed. "That's why a tiny little
female person puts a glint of panic in tough man's eyes."

Daniel managed not to flinch. Maggie couldn't know how
her dry jab stung.

"Actually, I was just wondering what happened to Diablo."
He relaxed a fraction. "I gave him away."

Her eyes went wide. "But why? You loved that horse."

Daniel's lips twisted. "He was a horse. That's all." Her
expression told him she didn't believe his words for a minute.
Hell. He'd thought J.D.'s questions were torture. But Maggie
just stood there, leaning against the door to freedom, absently
picking pieces of sawdust from her sweater as she studied him
with her perceptive blue-green gaze. "Somebody needed him
more."

Her eyebrows lifted a fraction.

He looked over her head, thinking he should just brush on
past her, whether she was blocking the way or not. But if he
did try to brush past her, and if she didn't move out of the
way, then he *would* brush against her, and…ah, hell. Answering her question seemed easier.

"I was in Minnesota for a, uh, job at a children's hospital."

PLAY "LUCKY 7" AND GET
THREE FREE GIFTS!

HOW TO PLAY:

1. With a coin, carefully scratch off the silver box at the right. Then check the claim chart see what we have for you — **FREE BOOKS** and a gift — **ALL YOURS! ALL FREE!**

2. Send back this card and you'll receive brand-new Silhouette Special Edition® nove These books have a cover price of $4.25 each in the U.S. and $4.75 each in Canada, b they are yours to keep absolutely free.

3. There's no catch. You're un no obligation to buy anything. charge nothing — ZERO — your first shipment. And you dc have to make any minimum numb of purchases — not even one!

4. The fact is thousands of readers enjoy receiving books by mail from the Silhoue Reader Service™ months before they're available in stores. They like the convenience home delivery and they love our discount prices!

5. We hope that after receiving your free books you'll want to remain a subscriber. B the choice is yours — to continue or cancel, any time at all! So why not take us up on c invitation, with no risk of any kind. You'll be glad you did!

YOURS FREE!

PLAY LUCKY 7 FOR THIS EXCITING FREE GIFT!

THIS SURPRISE MYSTERY GIFT COULD BE YOURS FREE WHEN YOU PLAY

LUCKY 7!

PLAY THE

LUCKY 7

SLOT MACHINE GAME!

Just scratch off the silver box with a coin. Then check below to see the gifts you get!

YES!

I have scratched off the silver box. Please send me all the gifts for which I qualify. I understand I am under no obligation to purchase any books, as explained on the back and on the opposite page.

335 SDL CPRP

235 SDL CPRH
(S-SE-04/99)

Name: _____
PLEASE PRINT CLEARLY

Address: _____ Apt.#: _____

City: _____ State/Prov.: _____ Postal Zip/Code: _____

WORTH TWO FREE BOOKS PLUS A BONUS MYSTERY GIFT!

WORTH TWO FREE BOOKS!

WORTH ONE FREE BOOK!

TRY AGAIN!

The Silhouette Reader Service™ — Here's how it works:

Accepting your 2 free books and mystery gift places you under no obligation to buy anything. You may keep the books and gift and return the shipping statement marked "cancel." If you do not cancel, about a month later we'll send you 6 additional novels and bill you just $3.57 each in the U.S., or $3.96 each in Canada, plus 25¢ delivery per book and applicable taxes if any.* That's the complete price and — compared to the cover price of $4.25 in the U.S. and $4.75 in Canada — it's quite a bargain! You may cancel at any time, but if you choose to continue, every month we'll send you 6 more books, which you may either purchase at the discount price or return to us and cancel your subscription.

*Terms and prices subject to change without notice. Sales tax applicable in N.Y. Canadian residents will be charged applicable provincial taxes and GST.

Her eyes contained only curiosity. So he continued. Completely skirting the reason he'd been in Minnesota, namely Coleman Black and Daniel's first gig with Hollins-Winword, and focused instead on the work in which the hospital specialized. Which was dealing with children who'd experienced severe physical or emotional trauma. He sure in hell didn't expect to see the soft glow in Maggie's eyes when he finished.

"So the boy started speaking again when you took Diablo there to show the kids?"

"He started speaking to Diablo," Daniel corrected.

"But the boy spoke. For the first time in several years."

He nodded.

"No wonder you left Diablo there. You're so generous."

No, he wasn't. Maybe he'd been generous back then. When he'd seen a young boy's need. But time and life had a way of sucking that generosity out of a man. Which was just as well. "He was just a horse."

Maggie just smiled gently. "Whatever you say, Daniel."

He shot her a look. But she merely continued smiling that little smile of hers and stepped from the doorway, opening the path to freedom. Which he took with indecent haste.

Despite Maggie's certainty that the days would drag until Daniel relented on their agreement, she was wrong. There were just too many things going on. Maggie woke one morning and realized with a thorough thump of panic that nearly two weeks had passed since she'd first arrived.

J.D. and her never-ending enthusiasm for everything on the ranch that was new and exciting to her. Even digging up worms with Squire for their regular fishing treks.

Jaimie and Matthew's remodeling project.

Daniel's house.

She and Daniel had fallen into a routine of sorts. He was up and gone by the time she rose around seven. He'd return mid-morning and take her, and occasionally J.D. too, over to the house, or into Weaver or even into Gillette to pick up one thing or another. She'd also, against her better judgment, selected a bedroom suite for J.D.'s room in the house. But the pickled oak set had caught her eye and before she'd known it, she'd shown it to Daniel, who hadn't wasted a breath before he'd ordered it.

The luxury of wealth, she'd supposed.

Then later in the afternoon, he would drop her off again at the big house. She knew that he then spent several hours helping Matthew with the hundred and ten chores that never seemed to be quite finished on the busy ranch while she worked on the wood ornaments she'd promised the mail-order company.

Half the time he came in for supper, when he would jump in the shower to wash off the accumulation of sweat and dust before sitting down at the table with the rest of them. The other half of the time he didn't come in at all until much later. So Maggie fell into the habit of wrapping a plate of food for him and leaving it in the refrigerator in "their" kitchen downstairs.

Not once had she awakened again in the middle of the night to find him watching her from the couch while she'd slept in his comfortably worn chair. Nor had she come across him giving a horse ride to J.D. again, though she knew he'd done so several times since that first.

J.D. was sleeping upstairs with Sarah again. Only Maggie and Daniel were in the downstairs suite. If he'd wanted to take steps toward that "real" marriage bed he'd threatened, he was certainly having no difficulty in waiting until their marriage was a reality.

She was relieved. Of course she was.

Still, Daniel hadn't given any indication of changing his mind. And that didn't relieve her. Of course it didn't.

She flopped back on her pillows, thinking that she was, in all probability, going insane. Since when had she ever been so ridiculously indecisive?

She either wanted out of their agreement. Or she didn't.

She either wanted to be with Daniel. In all the ways he'd said.

Or she didn't.

Insane. That was her.

Shaking her head, she got out of bed, making it all the way into the bathroom before her morning sickness struck. But she was falling into the groove of it again. Get up. Get sick. Take a shower and clean up and start the day.

Like falling off a log.

She stared at herself in the mirror. "Maggie Mae," she whispered to herself. "You really need your head examined."

Her reflection didn't disagree. Smiling wryly at her own foolishness, she stepped into the shower.

She and Daniel were driving down to Casper that morning for an estate sale. It had actually been Maggie's suggestion, when Daniel didn't seem able to settle on what kind of furnishings he wanted for his den.

She should have known that he'd turn her suggestion around and expect her to accompany him. He was the only man she'd ever been involved with who seemed to take it for granted that they'd do things *together*.

She turned her head into the steamy water, rinsing away her shampoo.

Involved with. She was *involved* with Daniel. And the knowledge was beginning to become second nature.

It was a frightening realization.

She climbed out of the shower and toweled off, then realized she'd forgotten her robe in the bedroom. She wrapped the huge terry cloth bath sheet around herself, tucking in the ends, and dashed a comb through her hair before heading for the bedroom.

It was getting distinctly colder outside, and her clothing choices were becoming more and more limited. It seemed impossible to her, considering how early it still was, but she could hardly stand to wear her jeans anymore. Her working wardrobe from Chicago—suits and dresses—were of little use these days.

Perhaps her lilac leggings and the matching sweat—

"Oh!" She stopped short at the sight of Daniel crossing the living area.

Her imagination had his eyes lingering just a moment over her damp shoulders. He continued striding toward his bedroom, yanking off his denim shirt and rolling it into a ball. "I'm gonna grab a shower before we go," he said, finally slowing as he passed by her. He plucked the white T-shirt molding his chest. "Get rid of cow stink."

Maggie hid her hands in the folds of the big towel surrounding her, thinking that he smelled just fine to her. Male and appeal— She frowned. "What?"

His lips twitched. "I asked if you left any hot water, or if I'm gonna be stuck with a cold dunking."

She felt heat rise in her cheeks and cursed her fair skin. She probably looked like a ninny, standing there with her hands clamped in her towel, for all the world like a virgin who'd never seen a man in his T-shirt.

Particularly when she'd touched so much more skin than he displayed now on that August night weeks ago.

"I wasn't in there very long," she managed.

He was silent for a moment. "You okay?"

Except her mouth seemed unaccountably dry? "Fine."

"Not sick this morning?"

"Not *that* fine."

She nearly lost her grip on her towel when he lifted his hand and brushed his thumb across her cheek. An incredibly warm, utterly gentle thumb. "You've got circles under your eyes."

She'd thought she'd looked pretty good these days. Despite her morning sickness, her color was better. And she was, well, to use his words, *rounder.* "No makeup yet this morning," she said dismissively.

His thumb glided down her jaw, then away, and she squelched the yearning that he place his palm against her cheek. "You don't need any paint," he murmured. "You never did. Aren't you sleeping well?"

It was too close to the truth. "Aren't you?" She deliberately turned the tables. "You're the one who rips apart his bed night after night."

She decided she imagined his stiffening. Because he only smiled wickedly and ran his thumb over her bare shoulder in a deliberate caress. "Maybe I'm dreaming about having you there with me."

Daniel watched the flush climb into her cheeks. Sure enough, she backed away from him, giving enough space between them that he thought there was some possibility that he'd live to draw another breath. He hadn't thought about the way his bed looked each morning. Or that she'd probably been making it, rather than leaving it for Curly. Stupid of him. He'd have to start making his own bed again.

Each morning, with dawn still hours away, he was all too glad to escape sleep, where his dreams beat at him with unforgiving precision. And too eager to get up to think about what state he'd left his bedding in. "Where is J.D.?"

Now Maggie looked even more wary. "Jaimie's probably already taken her and Sarah over to Emily's. They're finishing their Halloween costumes. We talked about it at supper last night."

"Right. You'd already made J.D.'s costume before you moved home."

"You were listening."

He shrugged. "J.D. is going to be a bumblebee. Sarah wants to be…oh, that Disney character—"

"Jasmine." Her shoulders shifted restlessly and she started for her own room.

He slid his hand around her arm, halting her. "What's wrong?"

She shook her head, not facing him. "I need to get dressed."

Looking at her, knowing she didn't have anything but silky skin under the folds of that big towel, raised the predictable results in him. It would have been smart to let her go on her way and get dressed. But he'd left smart behind the night he'd seen her sitting beside the swimming hole, drawing her name upon the water. He stepped in front of her, planting his hands at his sides, though the effort not to touch her again was nearly more than he could stand. "Maggie?"

He saw her throat work. Watched indecision flit across her lovely face. Her chin, just pointed enough to make the oval face distinctive, wrinkled. Then she looked up at him, her eyes more blue than green. "I was wrong," she said, and her husky voice curled around his nerve endings. "That night I told you to keep your distance from J.D. That I—" she pressed her lips together for a moment "—I didn't want her to get hurt. Joe never—I'm sorry. I know you don't want me to compare you but he...he never would have taken time out of his busy days to give a horse ride to his daughter. He certainly would've never sat at our supper table and listened to two little girls chatter over their Halloween costumes."

"It was just supp—"

"No. It's so much more than that, Daniel. And I—" She broke off, then went onto her toes, brushing her lips quickly and oh, so briefly against his. "Thank you," she whispered, and brushed by him.

He should have let it go at that. Should have. But couldn't. And he looped his arm around her waist, halting her movements. Then she was against him, her arms wrapped around his shoulders, and her mouth was beneath his, her breath cool and minty from her toothpaste. Her skin, oh, sweet heaven, that skin that was like liquid silk flowing over her bones—

He jerked his head up, staring into her face. What the hell was he doing? Not using his brain, that was for damn sure. He'd read that baby book he'd found of Jaimie's. Though it hadn't said sex should be avoided, he'd figured it out for himself. Maggie's history was too shaky. Until they had the go-ahead from a doctor, he couldn't let things get out of hand.

He forced his fingers to retuck the towel he'd been busily untucking. "You'd better get dressed," he said evenly.

The color that had ridden into her cheeks slowly ebbed. She brushed her wet hair back with a hand that wasn't any steadier than the ones he shoved into his pockets. She nodded. "Yes.

Of course." And turned, closing her bedroom door quietly between them.

He let out his breath on a hiss. Then turned for the bathroom. It didn't matter whether she'd used all the hot water. 'Cause what he needed now was only the cold.

"What about that settee?"

Maggie turned from her perusal of an ancient roll-top desk to see the item Daniel was pointing at in the antique shop. They'd already attended the estate sale and were slowly working their way through other shops in Casper. She cocked her head, studying it for a moment. Then she stepped forward and ran her hand over the scrolled arms. "The wood needs refinishing," she said, stating the obvious. "And the upholstery, of course." She stepped back, looking at him. Hoping that her face didn't show the jitters that had been fluttering around in her tummy since that morning. Since he'd held her. Kissed her.

She focused desperately on the settee. "I, um, think it's a tad delicate for your den."

"In the hallway," he said. "Between the dining room and the great room. Along the wall."

She knew exactly where he meant. He was right. The settee would be perfect for the spot. "I thought we were here to look for stuff for your den."

He settled his hat and smiled a little. "Go with the flow, Maggie."

She pushed up the sleeves of her lilac sweater. "Daniel, refinishing that thing alone will take—" She broke off with a huff when he turned and lifted his hand, bringing the proprietor of the antique shop running. Antique? Maybe a tenth of what was in this place was actually antique. The rest was junk, as had been most of the items at the estate sale.

This settee, though, really was charming. She could just see it with its cherry wood refinished and perhaps a nice tapestry on the—

She turned off the thought. Falling into Daniel's plans for

the house was becoming far too easy. She needed to remember that she wanted him to reconsider their agreement.

He had pulled out his old-fashioned money clip and was peeling off bills, easy as you please, and she wandered through the dusty store toward the front where she looked out the glass door to the street outside. The snow that Matthew's famous "nose" had predicted by Halloween had yet to arrive. But then again, there was still another day.

Then it would be November. Even closer to Thanksgiving.

She jumped a little when Daniel appeared behind her, settling his palm at the small of her back.

"Ready?"

She nodded. "What about the settee?"

"We'll swing by and get it on our way back."

They'd driven Daniel's black truck to Casper. There would be plenty of room in the truck bed for the delicately carved settee.

"You ready for lunch?"

Surprisingly, she was. She nodded, and stepped through the door when he held it open for her. Daniel had parked on the street just a few yards away from the shop, and she'd left her coat inside the truck. Yet the cold air barely penetrated her thick sweater, and the arm he dropped easily over her shoulder heated her even more. The flutters in her stomach jittered around even more frantically.

They started across the sidewalk toward the truck.

"Daniel? Is that you?"

They both turned toward the female voice that called to him. And every bit of pleasure that Maggie had begun feeling from their shopping stopped up inside her.

The woman dashed across the sidewalk, clutching her purse to her side. "I thought it was," she smiled. "I'd heard you were back, but—"

Maggie managed not to grimace when the woman's heavily mascaraed eyes widened with recognition.

"Maggie," she said with surprise.

"Hello, Marlene."

The other woman continued staring at Maggie for a moment, and Maggie felt an unexpected spurt of sympathy. What did they have to say to each other, after all? Talking about Joe seemed out of place, even if he had spent time in *both* their beds. She supposed she could have told Marlene that her one-time lover had died. But with Daniel standing beside her, she just couldn't see herself doing it. "How is Jolene?" Maggie finally asked.

Marlene seemed to nod with relief. "Fine. Just fine. She's in high school now, you know. Graduates in two years. She plans to go to college in California." Marlene shook her head. "Her grades are good, though, so maybe she'll get a scholarship."

Maggie murmured something. Then felt Daniel's hand, warm and strong, close around hers.

"Well," Marlene smiled awkwardly, her eyes taking in the two of them standing there so nice and cozy. "It's…nice to see you both," she said politely.

This time Daniel answered. "Thanks. Say hello to Boyd."

Marlene flushed, glancing Maggie's way again. "We're divorced now," she said. "He moved to Rock Springs when Jolene and I left, um, Weaver." Then made a production of looking at her watch. "Oops. I'm late. 'Bye now." She scurried back across the street, her coat flapping around her legs.

Maggie felt Daniel's gaze but didn't return it. She didn't even have to wonder whether the Switts' divorce had had anything to do with Joe. It had been written all over Marlene's face. Encountering one of Joe's women hadn't been something she'd expected. Though when she thought about it, she didn't really know why not. It had been rather naive of her, considering the trail of women through which Joe had cut a wide swath.

Knowing Daniel's feelings about Joe, she half expected him to make some cutting remark. But he didn't. Merely steered them around to the truck, where he waited until she'd climbed safely up onto the seat. "So what kind of meal you want," he asked when he joined her in the cab.

She pulled her coat across her lap. "Aren't you going to say something?"

He shifted toward her in his seat, his sinewy wrist resting over the top of the steering wheel. "Well, to be honest, I'm thinking Hobo Joe's. I can get Double-C steak there and you can order a salad or soup or chocolate cake. Whatever it is your heart desires."

"About Marlene."

He seemed to sigh faintly. "What about her?"

"Joe—" She didn't know what to say.

He tilted his head and she couldn't see his expression beyond the black brim of his hat. "Was a jerk," he finished flatly. "He drank and he had women and he gambled money he couldn't afford to lose, and he tried to make it up by sticking his fingers deeper into Double-C's pockets."

There wasn't a single thing he said that wasn't true. And it was mortifying.

"But what Joe did that was really, really stupid," he lifted his head, until his quicksilver gaze met hers, "was to walk away from you."

Maggie's eyes burned. She felt caught in the steady strength of his gaze. She couldn't have said a word to save her soul.

Then his wide shoulders shifted again, as if restless and the spell was broken. She blinked and looked out the window, aware of him settling his hat and starting up the engine. "Now what do you say," he asked as if the last taut minute had never occurred. "Hobo Joe's?"

Maggie nodded. Hobo Joe's sounded just fine with her.

It was fine. Despite the fact that it was midday, Daniel had the steak he wanted. Maggie's hunger kicked in so voraciously that she not only ate the garden salad and vegetable soup she'd ordered, but half of Daniel's baked potato and a corner of his steak, as well.

Feeling utterly replete, Maggie mentally crossed her fingers that the meal would stay put. Daniel finished his coffee, and aware that the afternoon was getting mighty close to evening, they went out to the truck. She expected that they'd pick up the settee and head home. But Daniel drove into the parking lot of a shopping center first.

Not until he walked them into the department store did she get her first inkling. He caught her hand in his and led her past cosmetic counters, lingerie displays and dressy gowns already out for the coming holidays and came to a stop in front of a salesclerk in the maternity clothes area.

"We're having a baby," he announced, tapping his hat against his leg.

Maggie felt her face fire. They hadn't even told their family, and Daniel was announcing it to strangers. And not the "she's pregnant" that Maggie would have expected. But "we're having a baby."

The salesclerk afforded Daniel a smile, and waved her hand at the display of clothing surrounding her. "I'm sure your wife can find something to her taste," she said. "There's a chair there by the mirrors, if you'd like to sit and wait while she browses."

"I'm not—"

"Thanks," Daniel said, interrupting Maggie's automatic denial of being his wife. He tugged Maggie toward a mannequin, basketball-size tummy bulging out the front of a bright red maternity dress. "That's pretty," he said.

Maggie spared the dress half a glance. "What are you doing?"

"Getting you some gear that doesn't strangle the kid before she's even born." He pulled a hanger off a rack and held up an orange-and-lime striped shirt. "How about this?"

"I'd look like a circus tent." She snatched the plastic hanger from him and shoved it back on the rack. "I can pick out my own clothes."

He raised an eyebrow. "So pick."

Aware of the salesclerk standing just feet away as she arranged a stack of sweaters on a table, Maggie leaned closer to him. "You know very well what I mean. I'm not going to let you buy me a bunch of maternity clothes."

"Why not?"

"It's not right, that's why not!" She cast an exasperated look over her shoulder, half expecting the clerk to be gaping at them. But the woman was still folding.

She didn't realize that the expression in his eyes had been easy and warm until they cooled. And contrarily missed it. But she wasn't going to relent on this issue. She was already living in his family's home. Picking out furniture for a house she had no real expectation of ever living in. For him to pay for her clothing was just too much.

He dropped his hand over her shoulder, drawing her stiff shoulders against him. Then he lifted her chin toward him, for all appearances a husband displaying affection toward his pregnant wife. "Either you pick out some clothes that fit or I will. And I will damn well dress you every morning in 'em if I have to," he murmured for her ears alone.

"I will pick them out and you can go—go wait in the truck or go to the men's department or something. Because there is no way I am going to pick out my *things* with you hovering about," she said with not one tremble in her voice.

If he hadn't wanted her in that moment so bloody fiercely, he would have applauded. There she stood telling him where to get off, and he wanted her more than his next breath.

He drew in a slow breath. He tilted his head. "Why don't I just wait here," he suggested mildly, and bit back another wave of gut singeing lust when she dashed her hair away from her cheek, eyeing him like she'd expected him to put up more of a fight.

She nodded and went into the dressing room.

He leaned his head against the mirrored wall behind him and thumped his head deliberately against the hard surface. Anything to drown out the soft rustle of clothing being removed behind the door not three feet from him.

She came out, dressed once more in her purplish outfit. Seemed ready to say something, but didn't. She took a few steps past him, and he discreetly adjusted the position of his black hat. "Maggie," he called after her softly. "You bring 'em back here."

By her flush, he knew his suspicions were correct, and that she'd planned on paying for whatever she selected herself. "Or I can come with you," he suggested blandly.

"No!" She swallowed. "No. If I find anything, I'll bring it back here."

When she walked out of sight, he blew out a long breath and glanced up to see the saleswoman watching him.

"Your wife is very lovely," she said. "Your baby is bound to be beautiful."

Wife. He suddenly stood. "If she comes back, tell her to wait here for me?"

"Sure. I'm on until nine tonight."

He strode through the racks of clothing, heading in the opposite direction of the underwear department. Maggie was going to be his wife. He'd been telling her to get used to the notion.

He rounded the large Christmas tree that a trio of giggling salesgirls were decorating and looked around him. There.

The jewelry department.

Perhaps it was time he took some of his own advice.

Chapter Ten

Trick-or-treating on Halloween was a near impossibility in the rural area of Weaver, Wyoming. Ranch houses were spread too far apart to make the door-to-door variety feasible. So every year the town got together and had a big Halloween party in the gymnasium of the Weaver High School. People who so chose dressed in costume. The few folk around who considered Halloween to be little better than the devil's day went around calling the event the Harvest Festival.

Most folks knew it for what it was. An opportunity for the kids in the area to dress up and be silly and fill their plastic pumpkins with candy and treats, and for the adults to congregate over a keg of beer or a big steaming pot of cider while they nibbled on the potluck dishes everyone brought for supper.

Some would never move away from the long tables of food. Some would dance. Some would sit around and gossip.

Some would take their sweetheart out into the hallway by the rows of lockers or out into the parking lot, and neck.

Over the years Daniel had been known to do his share of all.

This year, however, he found himself being led around by the pinkie by a pint-size bumblebee named J.D. She dragged him from booth to booth as she tried her hand at the games that were set up. When the game was too advanced for her, she seemed to take it for granted that Daniel would win her whatever prize it was she'd set her little heart on.

Though looking down into her bright green eyes made him ache inside, because they reminded him so much of another pair of youthful eyes, he didn't have the heart to deny her.

It was either accompany J.D. around the gym's perimeter or sit at the table the Clay mob had staked out and try not to stare too hard at Maggie. Ever since the day before in the department store, he'd been one unending mass of want. Until he could get that under control and his brain back into control, accompanying J.D. was the less painful choice.

"Dannl." J.D. tugged at his hand as they neared the line of a half dozen school kids waiting for their chance to bob for apples. "I gots to do that." She waved her little starfish hand toward the water barrel where glistening red apples floated.

Daniel shook his head, and went down on his haunches next to the little blond imp. "You think so?"

She nodded fiercely, making the black antennae attached to her head bounce madly. "I gots to."

"Why?"

She looked at him, her delicately arched eyebrows drawing together. "'Cause."

"'Cause why?"

"'Cause I wants to."

"But why do you want to?" He nodded toward the boy who was currently trying his luck. And having little success. "You'll get your hair wet. Probably your costume, too."

Clearly, she hadn't thought of that. She looked down at her bright yellow and black costume. She smoothed her hand down the front of it. Then she looked right into Daniel's eyes and smiled brightly. "You gots to do it for me," she announced, thoroughly satisfied with her brilliance.

Daniel shook his head. "No way, snooks. I don't want to get wet, either."

"But Dannl, I gots to have an apple."

So Daniel Clay found himself on his knees, sticking his fool face into a big barrel of water, trying to snag one of the impossibly slippery, bouncing apples. He heard the catcalls from his brothers, and the peals of laughter from Emily and Jaimie. But damned if he didn't sink his teeth into one of those apples, and when he lifted his head, water dripping from his face and hair, J.D. beamed at him and took the apple from him, sinking her own little teeth into the juicy fruit.

He looked above J.D. to see J.D.'s mother, dressed in a slinky red glittery dress with fringe hanging to her knees and felt the world stop spinning.

With her prized apple in her hands, J.D. and Leandra darted off to the next booth, Sarah struggling to keep up. Daniel sat back on his heels, slicking his hair off his face. Maggie stepped closer, handing him a bunch of paper towels. He dragged them over his face and crumpled them in his fist.

"You're soaked," she said. Even beyond the chatter and the music and the laughter, he could hear her soft voice.

He dashed the soggy towels over his jaw once more and stood. "Hazard of the job." She smiled and he realized her eyes were wet. "What is it?"

She moistened her lips, looking impossibly slender in her flapper outfit. "Would you dance with me, Daniel?" She seemed to be holding her breath.

He tossed the wad of towels into the trash bin beside the apple barrel. He'd do a whole lot more than waltz her around a gymnasium floor, just as soon as the next few weeks had passed. He closed his hand around hers, feeling as much as hearing the soft exhalation she gave. He led her to the middle of the floor. At that moment the teenager who was currently acting as DJ, switched from rousing rock to slow and moody.

Daniel took Maggie in his arms, and they moved slowly

together. Easily together. As perfectly fitted and attuned as the night he'd finally made her his. The night they'd made a child together.

Maggie didn't care if she was being foolish. She only knew that the sight of Daniel, bobbing his head into that cold water again and again in search of the apple that J.D. desired, had moved her deeply.

Had made her believe that things might work out. Might be okay.

Had made her hope.

Hope. Such a fragile thing. Yet so willing to spring back to life, like the crocuses did every spring, sticking their green shoots up toward the sun, even if there still remained a veneer of snow over their heads.

Beneath her cheek she felt his heart beat, steady and sure. His hand, wide palm and long callused fingers, spread over her back, holding her against him. Holding back all the rest of the world, if only for the moments of a beautiful song.

Her fingertips glided through the ends of his hair, thick wavy strands of silk. She felt his warm breath stir the tendrils of hair at her temple and melted against him. One song glided into the next. Still they slowly circled the room, oblivious to the other couples who came and went. Oblivious to the childish shrieks and laughter as games were played and treats collected.

His other hand joined the first on her back, and she linked her hands behind his neck. She sighed deeply when his lips touched her forehead. The corner of her eye.

His low voice rasped along her nerve endings. "I want you."

She pressed her forehead against his chest. He hadn't worn a costume. Just his usual white shirt and jeans. He could have dressed in nothing but his bare skin and she couldn't have been more unbearably aroused by the sight. "Yes," she breathed.

He shook his head, muttering a rueful oath. "Our timing needs some work."

She realized the music had stopped. Couples were leaving the dance area. She drew in a needed breath and felt her mouth run bone dry when he leaned over her, kissing her right there in plain view of God and the entire community of Weaver, Wyoming. "Later," he said against her lips, before striding over to the far side of the gymnasium where Jefferson and Matthew stood near the makeshift bar. He glanced back at her once, and her knees went weak.

Later.

Maggie headed back to the round table where Jaimie and Emily sat, their feet propped on chairs opposite them. She slid off her sequined headband and ran her fingers through her hair. Her eyes strayed toward the far side of the cavernous room.

"I told you."

Maggie glanced at Jaimie who'd spoken and was nodding at Emily. Emily, whose dark, rainwater straight hair was pulled into two high pigtails on either side of her head, à la Raggedy Ann, nodded right back. Her pansy brown eyes were wise and knowing against the smattering of freckles she'd penciled onto her cheeks.

Maggie tried to interpret the look the two women passed between them. And failed. "What?"

Jaimie leaned forward and the top hat she wore on top of her sedately groomed auburn head tipped over her nose. She pushed it back impatiently. "You've been bit."

"By what?"

"By the Clay magnetism," Emily answered. "We recognize a fellow victim when we see one."

"Don't be ridiculous." She snatched up the headband and pretended an interest in the design of sequins. Emily and Jaimie were thoroughly loved by their Clay men. Maggie had no such illusions about her and Daniel.

He'd brought her back here to Wyoming because she carried his child. That was all. If she was foolish enough to dream about more, then that would remain her secret.

What she and Daniel shared was physical. It wouldn't last,

no matter how weak-kneed he made her feel. Or how easily she wove silly dreams about him. He wanted her. For now.

Jaimie leaned forward, rolling her eyes when the top hat slid over her nose again. She took it off and set it on the table. She was dressed as a chorus dancer, complete with top hat and tails. "What ridiculous? Mags, we all saw him kiss you. Half the adults in this place were getting hot under the collar watching the two of you dance together."

Maggie flushed. "It was a slow dance," she defended.

Jaimie and Emily looked at each other again. They just shook their heads and smiled.

"Why didn't Squire come to the party?" Maggie was getting desperate to get Jaimie and Emily onto another topic.

"He claimed he was tired," Jaimie said. "But I think he and Gloria are on the outs again."

"Again?" Emily shook her head. "I really do not understand why he doesn't marry her. She's wonderful."

Jaimie propped her elbow on the table and rested her chin in her palm. She openly watched the men by the beer keg. "Those men of ours come by their stubbornness honestly," she said. "Straight from Squire himself."

Emily shifted in her chair so she could look at the brothers, too. "Jefferson figures that Squire thinks he's had his great love. He can't get past the habit of that."

"You know Squire better than the rest of us," Jaimie said. "He raised you."

"Until he sent me off to boarding school when I was a teenager," Emily said absently. "I wonder if there will ever come a day when they all come home again. Sawyer and Tris, too."

Jaimie snorted softly. "Matthew told me once that Sawyer would rather chew nails than be a rancher. He eats, breathes and sleeps the navy."

"Mmm. I can't really see Tristan giving up the high life of California, either," Emily said. "Still, it's a nice thought having them all here. Isn't it?"

Jaimie nodded. "I just wish Squire and Gloria would get

their act together. She's an attractive woman. If he doesn't watch it, she's liable to tell him to take a hike. There must be other men interested in her. For heaven's sake, you'd think Squire believes that you can't love more than one person in a lifetime.''

"You can," Maggie said thoughtlessly.

Jaimie's eyebrows arched knowingly. "Oh?"

Maggie hopped up, tugging the narrow strap of her dress back up onto her shoulder. "I'd better corral the girls," she said. "They're starting to eye the apple bobbing barrel like its bath time." She hurried off, the sound of Jaimie's and Emily's good-natured laughter ringing in her ears.

She caught up with the trio of little girls and shepherded them back toward booths more appropriate for their ages. But her mind was more on what her wayward tongue had let slip.

You can't be in love with Daniel Clay, Maggie Mae. Not unless you want your heart broken. For good.

She crouched down and absently helped Sarah toss a bean-bag square through the cutouts in a cardboard jack-o'-lantern facade.

Maybe it was the noise and chatter and music that started to get to her. Maybe it was the fact that she'd had to be careful all evening not to breathe too deeply for fear that she'd split a seam in the flapper dress she'd made. Maybe it was the spiraling fear that she was losing control of the situation with Daniel. Or more accurately, the realization that she'd never had control of it.

Whatever it was, the heat in the room suddenly clawed at her. Her stomach lurched warningly. Murmuring to the girls that she'd be right back, she rose shakily, her eyes searching for the rest room. She drew in a long breath, heading instinctively toward the nearest Exit sign.

She slipped through the heavy, metal gymnasium doors and plunged into the night. Sucked in cold, refreshing air. Slowly the nausea abated and she leaned back against the brick wall behind her. The freezing surface raised goose bumps along her arms and legs, but she didn't care. She rubbed her palms over her arms and looked out into the dark night. Realized that the first gentle fat flakes of snow were slowly drifting from the sky.

Matthew's nose for snow hadn't been wrong, after all.

She pushed away from the wall, adjusting the narrow strap of her dress that didn't want to stay up on her shoulder, and turned for the door. The cold night air was good for shocking her nausea away, but a few minutes of it was more than enough. She pulled open the heavy door and went back inside.

The music was slow and romantic again.

She walked around the perimeter of the room, heading toward their table. Smiling faintly when she saw Jaimie had gotten Matthew out on the dance floor. But her smile died when she saw Daniel out on the dance floor, too.

Dancing with Rebecca Morehouse. Weaver's one and only physician. Who also happened to be a stunningly beautiful woman.

Maggie hastily turned away, blindly reaching for a cup of hot cider from the table behind her. She drank it, heedless of its temperature that singed her tongue on its way down.

Well, what did she expect? That he would keep his attention strictly reserved for Maggie? He was Daniel Clay. A man who scribbled the name "Angeline" across half a dozen papers every week. And she was just Maggie. The woman he was marrying because of a baby.

She dropped the empty cup in the trash and strode to their table, where Emily sat with Jefferson and the girls. Maggie joined them and nearly cried with relief when she realized they were preparing to leave. "Mind if I hitch a ride with you?"

Emily's eyes flicked from Maggie to the dance floor, but she didn't say anything. Jefferson picked up Leandra, who snuggled her head against her daddy's shoulder, her little fingers latching on to his thick ponytail like a security blanket. "The girls want to sleep at our place," Emily said. "We need to stop by the big house, though, to get some clothes for Sarah. And J.D., too, if it's all right with you."

Maggie nodded. She just wanted to get out of there. Away from the sight of Daniel holding another woman in his arms.

Apparently while Maggie had been outside, Emily and Jefferson had already made their arrangements with Jaimie and Matthew, because they didn't do anything but lift their arms in a wave as they herded the kids out the door, gathering coats and plastic pumpkins and caramel apples on the way.

Telling herself she wouldn't look back, Maggie did it, anyway. And saw Daniel slowly circling the room, a grin on his face as he escorted the doctor away from the dance floor. Jefferson was waiting at the door, holding it open, and she scooted through, swinging her coat around her shoulders and telling J.D. to pull up her hood.

She sat in the back of their Jeep Cherokee, huddled between safety seats and little girls. When they arrived at the big house, she and Emily climbed out, the girls and Jefferson staying in the warm vehicle as they dashed inside to get Sarah's and J.D.'s clothes for the night and the next day.

Maggie passed J.D.'s backpack to Emily when she paused in the mudroom. Emily added it to what she'd picked out for Sarah. "I don't know why we bother with nighties," she said cheerfully. "They'll probably want to sleep in their costumes."

"Are you sure you want them all? They get so lively—"

Emily waved that off. "Jefferson figures we're gonna have a football team of kids. The more practice we get, the better. Besides, they're getting to be inseparable. Lively or not, they're good. Trust me," she patted her belly, her eyes sparkling. "When this one comes, we'll collect on the favor." She reached for the storm door that had replaced the squeaky wooden screen door. "We're all glad you've come back, you know."

Maggie played with the buttons on her wool coat. She couldn't even summon a faint smile. Though there was no doubting Emily's quiet sincerity. "I know."

Emily sighed faintly. "Daniel is—"

Jefferson tooted the horn, and Maggie could have run out

and kissed his lean cheek. "It's starting to snow harder," she said, and Emily nodded, pushing through the door without finishing whatever it was she'd planned to say.

Maggie stepped out on the porch, watching Emily climb into the vehicle, moving lithely despite her blossoming pregnancy. She lifted her hand, returning J.D.'s wave, blew a kiss and then went back inside, closing the storm door and leaning back against it.

Except for the soft tick of the kitchen clock, the house was silent. Maggie slid off her coat and hung it on one of the pegs beside the assortment of sweaters, jackets, vests, slickers. Coats that had been collecting there for longer than Maggie knew.

She leaned over and removed her high-heeled red pumps and, carrying them with her, she went into the kitchen. The red light from the coffeemaker was on, and she set her shoes on a chair and rinsed the dregs and prepared a new batch ready for the flip of the switch come dawn.

The door to Squire's room beyond the staircase was closed. Rather than going downstairs to her bedroom, she wandered into the little-used living room. Hanging above the fireplace was the portrait of Sarah Clay, the woman who had held the heart of Squire Clay since before her death, and in the thirty-odd years since.

Maggie turned on one of the small side lamps and studied Sarah's portrait. She'd been a petite woman with extraordinarily beautiful blond hair, waving luxuriously down her back, even though it had probably gone against more typical fashion standards of the day. Her eyes, darkly blue, appeared shadowed in the light. As if she discerned Maggie's troubled thoughts.

Lovely. Now she really could add insanity to her list of accomplishments.

She turned away from the portrait, moving across the room to the wide picture windows at the front of the big house. Delicate lace panels hung in the window and Maggie nudged a fold aside to look out into the darkness.

But her attention kept being drawn back to the portrait, and she let the lace fall into place once again. She walked over to the portrait and stared up at it. "What did you have, Sarah Clay," she asked softly, "to hold a man's heart for all these years?"

Those eyes, so blue and gentle, just looked back at her. Maggie swallowed the knot in her throat. She turned off the light and retrieved her pumps. And went downstairs through the rec room and into the guest suite.

Whatever it was that Sarah Clay possessed, that Jaimie and Emily apparently had, as well, was something that simply eluded Maggie.

A sensible person would have accepted that fact long ago. But when it came to one Daniel Jordan Clay, Maggie's sense was nonexistent. It always had been.

She went into the bedroom where the shopping bag from the department store still sat on the dresser. She brushed back her hair and moved the bag to the bed, removing the items she'd selected. Two pairs of leggings. A new bra. A whisper-soft teal nightgown that she'd been unable to resist. Blue jeans for J.D.

She started to fold up the bag, then noticed the slip of paper still in the bottom of the bag. The receipt.

She pulled it out, setting aside the bag. Daniel had paid cash.

She'd selected her items and had dutifully trotted back to the maternity department, only to wait nearly a half hour before Daniel returned. He hadn't even looked at the clothing, for which she'd been grateful at the time. He'd just pulled out his money clip and peeled off several twenties. That had been that.

Her fingers crumpled the receipt and she found her purse, pulling out her checkbook. The one thing she hadn't done yet was to close out her bank accounts in Chicago.

She rooted through her purse for a pen but couldn't find anything but three crayons and a pencil.

Receipt and checkbook in hand, she went into the kitchen,

snatching up the slender gold pen she remembered Daniel leaving on the counter. She wrote fast, then tore out the check and left it, the receipt and his pen sitting smack-dab in the center of the breakfast bar.

Then she went into the bathroom for a shower. She didn't fool herself that Daniel would notice her absence and come racing back to the ranch.

As soon as Matthew's Blazer came to a halt, Daniel hopped out and headed straight for the big house. If he hadn't been talking with the doc, he would have noticed that Maggie wanted to leave.

Probably that morning-evening-sickness thing, he figured. She should've just come and got him on the dance floor. But that wasn't his Maggie. She was so used to doing for herself. Taking care of herself and her blond-headed imp of a daughter.

One of these days, she'd realize she wasn't alone anymore.

He thumped down the outside set of stairs, shrugging out of his down vest and tossing his hat onto the coffee table. Her bedroom door was opened, the room beyond in darkness. But he could hear the shower running.

He thought about going in there and joining her. But he'd probably shock her right out of her proper little mind.

At least one good thing had come from his conversation with the doc. Rebecca had looked probingly at him when he'd asked about sex and pregnancy, but had answered easily enough. Theoretically enough.

He went into his room, then paced back out into the living area. The shower was still running. He yanked the tails of his shirt free and absently unbuttoned it. He needed to get his mind off Maggie standing under the running water with only steam clothing her. Or he really was going to go on in and join her under the water. He'd run his hands over—

Then he saw it. The check.

He reached for the plain blue check blank, filled with Maggie's neat, sloping writing.

The single beer he'd consumed that evening wasn't enough

to make his gut tighten the way it did. He held the check between two fingers, glaring at it. As if by doing so, he could make the writing disappear. That it wouldn't say, down there in the corner of the check, "clothes, etc."

Jaw locked, he crumpled the check in his fist.

"You're here."

For a second, he stopped breathing. Then he slowly turned to see Maggie standing in the doorway to the bathroom. She was bundled from neck to toe in her comfortably worn robe, but strands of hair had escaped the knot she'd caught it up in and clung damply to her neck. His ire multiplied. As much at himself for wanting her so badly that his back teeth ached with it despite the frustration he felt upon seeing the check, as with her for writing the damned thing in the first place.

He closed his fist tighter, feeling the paper crinkle. "You left the party."

The only light on in the place came from the kitchen. But he could still see the way her cheeks colored. Could still see the glisten on her lips when she moistened them. "Yes."

"Why? Were you feeling sick?"

She hesitated, then nodded.

The paper crumpled a little more in his hand. "Are you feeling better now?"

This time there was no hesitation. She nodded and walked into the kitchen, finding a glass and filling it with water.

He followed, and dropped the crumpled check on the counter beside the sink. Her forehead wrinkled, then smoothed as she recognized it. "I'll just write another."

"Waste of paper."

Her lips firmed. Her rounded little chin lifted in a "we'll see" way. If he hadn't been so damned annoyed, so damned hungry for her, he might have appreciated it.

He didn't appreciate it. It only made him more annoyed. And his jeans grew tighter.

She poured the water down the drain after only a few sips. Her robe parted at the neck, revealing a narrow wedge of skin.

His eyes latched on to that sliver of skin that gleamed like an ivory pearl under the kitchen light.

He wondered, not for the first time, what she wore beneath that all-encompassing robe.

He realized that a narrow stream of water was still running into the sink. Maggie was standing there, staring at the glass in her hand as if she wondered how it had gotten there. He reached out and shut off the water and still she didn't move.

"Mag—" His words died when she suddenly looked up at him. No amount of pretending could wipe out the hurt in her eyes. His heart chugged hard in his chest. He had to curl his hands into fists and shove them in the front pockets of his jeans to keep from yanking her to him.

Her lips moved, as if to speak, but no words emerged. She blindly set aside the empty glass.

He couldn't tear his eyes from that wedge of skin her robe revealed at her throat. His hands, no matter what he told them to do, came out of the safety of his pockets and reached for the cloth belt on her robe.

Her lips, soft and tempting, parted a breath. She put her hands on his, and yanked the tie out of them, tightening it as she turned away.

His jaw tightened. He glanced at the paper ball that had once been a check to her stiff shoulders. "So you want to tell me what happened between the party and here?"

"Nothing."

He snorted softly. "Right. While we were dancing we couldn't have stood any closer together without climbing inside each other's skin. Now you're writing damn-fool checks and are about as welcoming as a hard freeze. Why?" Her shoulders, so stiff and proud, trembled. If he hadn't been watching her so bloody close, he'd have missed it.

"Oh, Daniel, stop pretending," she scoffed. "We both know that women are interchangeable for you."

He went stock-still. "Is that so?"

She angled her chin, giving him a view of her tense profile. "I'm going to bed."

"I don't think so," he said softly.

Her eyebrow arched. "I beg your pardon?"

"We're gonna get this ironed out right now. Maybe you don't like confrontations, Maggie, but you better get used to 'em if you continue comparing me to Joe."

Maggie gave the tie on her robe another tug for good measure. She was dismayingly aware of the way the chenille clung to her damp skin. "Just because you don't like the truth doesn't mean I'm comparing you to anyone."

"Truth." His voice lowered silkily. Dangerously. He stepped closer. "There's a concept. Why *don't* we be truthful?"

She took a half step back before she caught herself. His shirt hung loose from his wide shoulders and she forced her eyes away from the way his undershirt—one of those scoop necked, sleeveless kind—clung to his chest. "If you're trying to intimidate me, it won't work."

"No intimidation, Maggie. Just some good, old-fashioned honesty and truth." He lowered his head over hers, his voice flowing over her. "You saw me talking with the doc and you were jealous."

She crossed her arms, needing the few precious inches of space it forced between their bodies. "No."

"Since jealousy is undoubtedly one of those emotions you figure is too *earthy* for your overactive conscience to tolerate, you chalk it all up to me being like Joe."

"Oh, and since when are you an expert in psychoanalysis?"

His jaw hardened and something came and went in his eyes before they very carefully went flat. He straightened and moved away from her, leaving her cold. Bereft. "You'd be surprised," he muttered, raking his fingers through his hair, as if he were suddenly weary. "Rebecca is a friend," he said flatly. "Not much more than an acquaintance. We hardly know each other. Believe me or not."

"Like Angeline is a friend?" Maggie wished the words back when he looked at her as if she'd knifed him in the chest and left him to bleed.

''What do you know about...Angeline?''

Not enough. Not enough to understand why her name makes you wince. ''The papers.'' She swallowed, making herself continue. ''Notes you leave in your room.''

His back was to her, his shoulders tense. But when she would have placed her hand on his back, wondering how she could make amends when she wasn't sure it was even possible, he spoke. ''The only woman I'm involved with is you, Maggie. Accept it or not. And don't mention that name to me ever again.''

He scooped up his vest and his keys and without ever looking back, he left.

Chapter Eleven

When Maggie awoke the next morning, she lay in bed, listening to the hiss of the shower coming from the bathroom. She blinked and peered at her watch. Daniel had gotten off to a late start.

She cautiously climbed from the bed, but her stomach for once stayed steady. She dressed in her new pair of black leggings and a thin, clinging, black turtleneck, over which she pulled a loose-knit red sweater. By the time she finished making her bed, the shower had ceased.

Knowing she was the ultimate coward, she hovered in her room for another solid five minutes before cautiously opening the door. A coffee mug sat on the breakfast counter across the living area. The door to the bathroom was open. She could see the steamy mirror from her vantage point.

She stuck her head out a little farther. Daniel's door was shut.

She scooted into the bathroom and quietly shut the door. Then had to stand there for a long moment while she battered down the ache that rose in her when Daniel's scent—clean soap and the woodsy aftershave he preferred—engulfed her.

When she opened the door again a few minutes later, face and teeth cleaned, and her hair pulled into a neat knot at her nape, she thought perhaps she'd succeeded in missing him.

But Daniel was standing at the counter, sipping his coffee and studying a set of blueprints he'd spread across the wide surface. If he was still angry over last night, he showed no signs of it when he looked back at her.

"Coffee?" he asked, turning again to his drawings.

She cleared her throat. "Ah, no. Thanks. The caffeine."

He didn't comment.

Maggie's teeth chewed the inside of her lip. He wasn't wearing his usual blue jeans this morning, but wore finely tailored black trousers. His shirt, instead of the sturdy cotton he usually wore, was still white, but even from several feet away she recognized it as silk. The clothes only emphasized the impossible breadth of his shoulders and the narrowness of his waist and hips. Even the butterscotch waves of hair had been slicked back from his strong features.

She tugged at the long hem of her sweater and walked past him to get a glass of water. "You're not working on the house today?"

He looked up from the drawings. "Your appointment is today."

She nearly choked on her water. She hadn't even gotten an opportunity to tell Jaimie about her appointment with Dr. Foster. Or the reason behind it. "How did you know that?"

His lips twisted. "Honey, there ain't much about you I *don't* know." He lifted his mug, leisurely sipping. "Jaimie is still sleeping. Matt said she had a rough night. I talked to Emily. She said she'd keep the girls for the day."

Emily was much further along in her pregnancy than either Jaimie or Maggie. Yet she had the girls with her so often, no matter what she'd said last night after the Halloween party. "But—"

Her argument died on her lips when he pinned her with a

cold look. "What goes on between us stays between us," he said flatly. "Don't take it out on the rest of 'em. We watch out for each other. Everybody's glad you and J.D. are back here." He looked back at his drawings. "'Cept you," he added before draining the rest of his coffee.

"And you."

He didn't deny it, and Maggie felt something inside her wither.

"Get some food in you," he said after a moment. "Then we'll leave. I want to stop off to see a guy who does furniture refinishing."

Only a day before she would have argued with him. But that was before she'd seen him bob for apples just to make her daughter happy.

Before she'd seen the torment in his eyes last night and before he'd carefully banked it and walked away without saying goodbye.

Before she'd had to acknowledge, at least to herself, that he'd been right: she'd seen Daniel dancing with the doctor and she'd been jealous. Hideously so. It was a first for her, and not a pleasant one.

She brushed her palms down her sides. "Have you eaten? I could—" she swallowed "—make you some waffles."

He didn't seem to see her figurative olive branch. "Had breakfast with the hands," he said. He rolled up his drawings and slid them into the tube. Then he finally looked at her. "Snowed all night," he said. "Dress warm."

The "guy" who did refinishing must have been nearly a hundred years old, Maggie decided when they stopped off at his hole-in-the-wall shop. She didn't doubt that the man knew his stuff. There were snapshots of beautifully finished furniture tacked up on every inch of available wall space.

But when Maggie heard what the man intended to charge Daniel for the privilege of refinishing the delicate settee, she nearly choked on the exorbitant amount.

She pulled Daniel aside. "That's too much."

He shrugged. "He's upholstering the cushion, too."

"I'm telling you, it's too much. The materials would cost less than a tenth of what he wants to charge you." She tilted her head, lowering her voice even more. "Just because you can afford it, doesn't mean it's right for him to charge you that."

"Maggie, it doesn't matter."

"I'll do it.

His eyebrows peaked. "You?"

"Yes, *me*. For heaven's sake Daniel, I've done a lot of work with wood. I can refinish that settee and anything else you need. I learned how to sew and upholster when I was a teenager."

"I don't want you tiring yourself."

She shook her head impatiently. "I've let you coddle me since I came back to the Double-C. It's driving me up a tree."

"The baby—"

She instinctively pressed her palm flat against her abdomen. "Do you really think I'd do something to endanger this child?"

His jaw cocked. "I'll think about it. I said," he repeated inflexibly when she opened her mouth, "I'll think about it." He ushered her toward the door and told the proprietor they'd be in touch.

She decided it was as much of a concession from him as she'd get.

Dr. Foster was located in the same office as he'd been when Maggie was a patient of his before. The waiting room was the same, with chintz chairs and ladies' magazines littering the glass-and-brass coffee tables.

The only difference was that this time Daniel was with her. The only person to ever accompany her to the obstetrician's office when she'd carried J.D. had been Jaimie.

He sat in the feminine chair, one spit-shined boot propped on the knee of his fine trousers, his hair waving over his forehead, looking wholly appealing.

Maggie wasn't the only one who thought so. She caught

several of the sideways looks he received from the other women also present in the waiting room.

When the nurse finally called Maggie's name, she rose, feeling nervous. What if something was already going wrong? What if—

"Gonna stand out here all day?"

She looked up at Daniel, who'd also risen from his chair. "I—"

He tucked his hand behind her back and nudged her toward the nurse who waited in the doorway leading to the exam rooms. "It'll be fine."

He'd been saying it all along. But honestly, how could *he* possibly know? Then his eyes softened, just a faint warming of that cool silver, and she found herself believing him.

He didn't sit back down, however, when she walked toward the nurse. He followed right along, his warm hand never leaving the small of her back.

With the nurse walking beside them as she escorted them into the doctor's consulting room, Maggie couldn't very well make an issue of Daniel accompanying her. Then they were seated in the twin chairs in front of the doctor's wide desk, and the nurse walked away. But again Maggie didn't have a chance, because the doctor himself entered the room. He gave them a harried smile and sat down, pulling Maggie's chart to the center of his desk.

He flipped it open, studied it, then looked up. He seemed to eye Daniel for a moment, as if he was trying to place him. "Well, Maggie, it's been several years, hasn't it. What brings you here?"

She moistened her lips. "I'm pregnant." And as she said it, she realized it was only the second time she'd admitted it aloud. First to Daniel when she'd told him over the phone. And now.

Dr. Foster nodded, his attention going back to the file. "You're living near Weaver still?" He glanced over the rims of his glasses to see her nod. "Then you must know that Weaver has a fine physician right there. Dr. Rebecca Morehouse. She has hospital privileges here. Surely it would be more conven—"

"Are you saying you don't want me as a patient?" Maggie couldn't bring herself to look at Daniel.

He shook his head. "Not at all. I merely wanted to be sure you were fully aware—"

"I am."

The doctor glanced at Daniel, who remained silent, much to Maggie's relief. Though she figured sooner or later he'd have quite a lot to say about the matter. "Okay," Dr. Foster said. He rose and stuck his head out into the hall. The nurse appeared and he handed over the chart to her. "Phoebe here will take you back to the exam rooms," he told Maggie. "I'll be with you in a few minutes."

Maggie followed the nurse, casting a nervous glance toward Daniel. He'd risen also but, thank heavens, didn't try to follow her and the nurse. He was in the waiting room when she came back out again thirty minutes later with a prescription for pre-natal vitamins and a packet of brochures and information in her hands. "The Preg Pack," the nurse had wryly called it.

Daniel paid the bill while Maggie scheduled her next appointment. She had to nearly bite off her tongue to keep from making an issue over Daniel's assumption that he'd pay the doctor fee. If they were going to have any chance at all, Maggie had to start putting aside her desperate need to control every little thing.

The thought made her stop in her tracks.

He strode on ahead of her across the parking lot toward his truck. It was snowing again. Gentle drifting flakes that clung to the brim of his hat and the shoulders of his black wool coat.

Daniel would change his mind, she fiercely reminded herself. He would.

He reached the truck, then turned to wait, his eyes hidden by the low angle of his cowboy hat.

She clutched the packet of materials to her chest and started walking again. But her heart thundered with the knowledge that Daniel's changing his mind wouldn't be a reprieve for her, after all.

Moistening her lips, she dashed a snowflake off her nose and stopped beside him, hesitating when he opened the truck door and waited for her to climb inside. She fingered the edge of the manila packet. "Dr. Foster says I'm doing fine. That the…baby seems fine, too."

He took the packet from her and tossed it onto the seat. "I know."

"You do?"

"I talked with the doc while you were getting dressed."

Of course. She moistened her lips again and put her foot up on the step. Daniel caught her waist, and she closed her eyes for a moment when he helped her up into the cab.

He started to close the door, then paused, thumbing his hat back a notch. His eyes drifted over her face. "You okay?"

Maggie nodded. "Fine," she whispered. Except she'd done what she'd told herself she wouldn't.

She'd fallen in love with Daniel Jordan Clay.

And he was marrying her for one reason only.

Because of the baby.

If Maggie thought that sleeping in the guest suite with Daniel had been awkward before, it was nothing compared to the way she felt the next morning as she lay in her bed.

What had she become, anyway? She was here, living in the big house with people she cared about, under false pretenses. Living a lie.

She was carrying a baby who would bear the Clay name. If Dr. Foster was to be believed, there was no earthly reason why Maggie wouldn't carry this baby safely to term.

She'd fallen in love with a man who didn't love her.

Sighing impatiently, she tossed back the covers and got out of bed. Lying there moping accomplished nothing. She showered and dressed again in leggings and a sweater. Ivory this time. After tidying her bedroom she went into Daniel's room, stopping short when she found his bed already made. The pile of papers on his dresser was conspicuous by its absence. She nibbled the inside of her lip, glancing over the room. It was as tidy as a freshly cleaned motel room. He hadn't even left one of his leather belts laying about. Not one sock. Not a damp bath towel. Nothing.

The sick feeling swelling in her stomach had nothing to do with morning sickness. She wasn't even sure how long she stood there, looking at the terribly tidy room. But her eyes started burning and she swallowed the knot in her throat before slowly crossing the room to the closet. Her hand trembled as she reached out and nudged the door.

Her knees went weak at the sight of the clothes hanging inside. Daniel's dress boots—the ones he'd worn to her doctor's appointment—were tumbled on the floor. She touched the sleeve of one of his white shirts. If the situation had been different, she'd have slid that shirt off its hanger and buried her face in it. She'd have worn it, feeling closer to him simply by the connection of a shirt.

She hurriedly shut the door and turned away from the closet and went upstairs.

Jaimie was sitting at the kitchen table, making out a shopping list. Maggie could see J.D. and Sarah playing on the floor in the mudroom, pretending they were in a cave, complete with a blanket stretched over their heads from wall to wall.

Getting her vocal cords to work took some concentration, but she finally managed. "Where is Squire?"

Jaimie glanced up at her, and her easy smile faded as she took in Maggie's pale face. "He drove down to see Gloria. He'll be gone several days I imagine. Do you feel all right?"

Maggie swallowed. She wouldn't feel all right until she stopped pretending. "Would you, um, mind watching J.D. for me this morning?"

Jaimie set down her pen. "Of course I don't mind. She and Sarah are inseparable." She reached out and caught Maggie's arms, tugging her down to the chair beside her. "You look like you're ready to pass out. Are you sick?"

"No," she managed.

"Well, you're as white as a sheet. What's upset you?"

Nothing but her own fears. Nothing but the debilitating relief of seeing Daniel's clothing still hanging in his closet. Relief that brought damnably easy tears to her eyes. "Hormones," she said on a choking laugh.

Jaimie's eyes narrowed, and Maggie could practically see the wheels turning in her friend's mind. And it was a relief. To let it all pour out.

Her pregnancy.

Daniel's marriage demand.

By the time she finished, she felt dizzy with the load lifted. Jaimie just sat there, staring at her.

Maggie looked down at her hands. "You're shocked."

"I can't believe I didn't figure it out," her friend said bluntly. "I should have known there was something between you two." Then she smiled brilliantly. "Pregnant. Oh, Maggie." She leaned forward and gave her a tight squeeze. "I'm so happy for you," she said when she sat back. "You're feeling good, though? No problems with the pregnancy?" Her eyes widened. "Good grief, you've spent hours working on your wood orders. Maybe you should be taking it easi—"

"Now you sound like Daniel."

Jaimie still looked dazed. But her smile still flirted with her lips. "How far along are you? You have been to the doctor, haven't you?"

"I saw Dr. Foster yesterday in Gillette. He says everything looks good." So far. She smoothed her palms down her thighs. "I'm sorry."

"What on earth for?"

Maggie frowned, studying her hands. She had a splinter in her palm that she hadn't noticed before. "Coming here under false pretenses. I just…I just wanted to do what was right. Give Daniel some breathing—"

"Whoa. Back up here. What false pretenses? Maggie, how many times have Matthew and I told you that you have a home here? It wouldn't matter what reason you used. You're here. Where you belong."

"But—"

Jaimie wasn't finished, though. "All I want is for you to be happy. My brother gave you a raw deal, and you stuck by him longer than a reasonable person should have been expected to. But this isn't even about him. It's about you being my best friend. You were the one who supported me emotionally. Remember? Who told me to find my place in the world, and damn anybody who didn't like it. When I broke off my engagement to Tony Dayton, everyone thought I was out of my tree, including my own brother, but you understood completely. Tony was all wrong for me; he never would have tried to stop molding me into a suitable wife." She smiled, her eyes glowing. "If it hadn't been for you talking me into visiting and then moving to Wyoming in the first place, I'd have never met Matthew. I think it's wonderful if you find happiness like that with Daniel." She shrugged, laughing softly. "We'll be sisters all over again."

"I didn't say we're—"

"Getting married? Of course you are. I know Daniel. He wouldn't have it any other way."

"Jaimie," Maggie had to stop Jaimie from getting too carried away. "I *have* agreed to marry him, but—" She broke off, closing her eyes and expelling a long breath. "I've been married once to a man who didn't love me." She looked at Jaimie through a sheen of tears. "I don't know if I can do it again," she admitted huskily.

Jaimie sobered. "I know you as well as anyone on this earth. Except maybe my husband. You wouldn't be carrying Daniel's child if you didn't have very deep feelings for him. And Daniel is not Joe. Maybe you think he doesn't love you, but he—well, he's not Joe," Jaimie finished. "Give him a chance. Give *yourself* a chance."

"But people...what will they say?"

"Who cares?" Jaimie caught her hands, shaking them gently. "Mags, how could you be so supportive of me—when I know for a fact that people considered me a flighty nut—I mean, I never stuck with one thing in my life for more than a few months until I came to the Double-C and filled in for you as housekeeper. How on *earth* can you be so hard on yourself?''

''I...slept with him in August,'' Maggie whispered. ''I'd only just told you about your brother. What kind of person does that make me?''

''Human.'' Jaimie glanced toward the mudroom, but the children were oblivious to the discussion going on in the next room between their mothers. ''The first time Matthew and I were together was when you were in the hospital, and we didn't know whether you were going to lose J.D. or not. What kind of person does that make *me?* Mags, you're not your mother. You're not going to walk out on your family ten years down the road. So stop living your life as if you have to make up for her failures. Things work out if you give them a chance. Let yourself love Daniel. There is no shame in that.''

Maggie choked back a watery laugh. ''I should've talked to you a long time ago.''

Jaimie smiled faintly. ''True,'' she agreed. ''But then you always did give the Clay men a run for their money in the stubborn department. And really, Daniel is the one you should be talking this stuff over with.'' She dashed her fingers across her own damp cheeks. ''Now. Tell me. How many weeks along are you? And when is the wedding?''

Feeling lighter after her talk—her confession—with Jaimie, Maggie visited her worktable for a long while, then borrowed one of the trucks and drove out to the building site. The exterior had been painted, and the shingles were in place. No more special work crews were coming in to work. Electrical. Plumbing. It was all in place. What remained of the interior, Daniel planned to finish off himself.

Considering the job he'd done on the guest suite in the big house, she doubted it would take him very long.

She was glad that there weren't a half dozen men working on the house. She wanted to talk to only one man. And she wanted some privacy in which to do it.

She found him upstairs, sweating and stripped down to his sleeveless T-shirt despite the cold air. Working on the window seat he was building in J.D.'s bedroom. She watched for a while, her presence unknown to him, from the doorway. He set one nail after another, and *thwack,* drove it home with one heavy swing of his hammer. Again and again, until she wondered why his muscles didn't rebel against the unrelenting effort.

She drew in a slow breath and smoothed her hair behind her ears. It was freezing in here. ''Daniel.''

He stiffened, cranking his head around. Then blinked as if he were surprised to see her. He probably was. Lord knew she'd given him no reason to expect otherwise. In the days past she'd only come to the house because it would have raised too many questions for her not to.

Daniel focused on Maggie standing in the doorway, looking pretty as an angel in white atop a Christmas tree. Looking at her, he managed to push away the memories he'd been unsuccessfully trying to banish. He wiped his forearm across his sweaty forehead and sat back on his haunches. ''Thought you were gonna work on your Christmas ornament order today,'' he said.

''I was.''

He waited.

''I...wanted to talk to you.''

He glanced around, his jaw tight. ''Nobody keeping you from it, Maggie.''

She needlessly smoothed her hair again, wishing he would put on his shirt. She walked across the room, her footsteps echoing hollowly, and stopped near the sawhorses he'd been using. She balanced the plain-paper-wrapped package she'd brought with her on the sawhorse and tucked her hands up into the sleeves of her sweater, wishing also that she'd not left her coat downstairs in the kitchen. ''I told Jaimie about the baby this morning.''

''I see.''

She couldn't tell whether he was pleased or displeased. His

very lack of reaction unnerved her. She knew he didn't love her. But some type of response would be nice. "She said to tell you she thinks a winter wedding will be perfect."

He hefted his hammer and sent another nail driving into wood. "And what do you think," he asked evenly.

"I think marrying you is probably one of the biggest mistakes I could ever make," she admitted frankly. Her hands twisted together and she swallowed, remembering her bone-deep relief when his clothes had still been in his closet. Then she also admitted the truth. "And I think *not* marrying you is probably an even bigger mistake."

"Well, hallelujah for that," he muttered, driving another nail.

"Look, Daniel. I know I haven't been easy...."

That earned her a quicksilver look.

"But I'm making an effort here."

He nodded and sat back again. "All right." He grabbed a handful of nails from the box on the floor beside him. "Anything else?"

Maggie's words dried up. She wondered at that moment what kind of fool she was, because Daniel seemed about as interested in their marriage plans as he would be over boiling an egg. She shook her head. "No. Not a thing. Except this." She handed him the package.

He took it slowly. "What is it?"

"Open it."

But he already was untying the string and folding back the brown paper. Then he just sat there, looking at the plaque held in his big hands. "You made this."

She swallowed. "Yes. But if you don't like it, just say so. I mean it's really nothing but a..."

"I like it."

"...welcome si—you do?"

"Did you think I wouldn't?"

"Well, I did make it for your home without cons—"

"*Our* home." He stood and set the welcome sign on the window seat. Late-afternoon sunlight glinted through the windows, shining upon the sign. "That's what the plaque says. Or are they just words?" He stepped closer.

She'd spent the better part of that day making a new welcome sign to replace the one she'd originally planned. "They're not just words," she admitted. Not words. A dream.

His fingers touched her jaw. Tilted it toward him. "Everything'll work out, Maggie Mae." His voice was as quiet and soft and gentle as the thumb he smoothed over her lip.

She couldn't have stepped away from him just then to save her soul. And it had nothing to do with the sawhorses behind her. It was him. Drawing her into the misty gray of his eyes.

Hardly breathing, she put her hands on his shoulders. Slid along the hard curve of sinew and muscle to his neck. "Promise?" She stretched up on her toes.

He met her halfway. "I promise," he said in the breath before their lips met.

Then he circled her with his strong arms and held her against him for a long while.

And for the first time in forever, she began to believe.

Chapter Twelve

With word of their engagement out, it seemed as if the big house went into chaos. Daniel supposed that it was no different than a hundred other households when news of a wedding hit, but he wasn't entirely sure. Before a single day passed his whole family had known a wedding was in the works. As well as a baby.

Not that he was entirely averse to the notion of a good old wedding. Even if Maggie did turn three shades of red whenever Jaimie started talking flowers and gowns and such. But that didn't mean that all the twittering and chattering going on wasn't getting sorely on his nerves.

So the next afternoon he found himself accepting the refuge Jefferson offered. Only there was no refuge there. Not when he walked into his brother's kitchen to find Coleman Black sitting, comfortable as you please, at their kitchen table. And Jefferson was nowhere to be found. Damn him, anyway.

''I should've known my brother was up to something when

he called me over here.'' As a greeting, it left a lot to be desired.

Coleman Black's smile was noncommittal. ''He's concerned about you, Dan. So is the agency. Since you haven't bothered to call lately, and I was in the area…'' He leisurely tamped the tobacco in his pipe, then tucked it between his teeth, but made no attempt to light it. ''You're close to being, well, released, shall we say? Why let one incident derail an otherwise promising career?''

''Incident?'' Daniel felt like choking the man, that he could reduce the tragedy in Santo Marguerite to such an insignificant word. If he needed any more proof than he already had that he wasn't cut out for the murky world that Hollins-Winword and Coleman Black operated in, he'd just gotten it. ''I told you I wouldn't be back.''

''But your suspension is nearly over.''

Daniel shook his head. ''You could've suspended me for a week or five years or not at all. I'm out of it,'' he stated flatly.

Coleman shrugged faintly. ''You've certainly told us that often enough. Pardon me if I'd hoped you'd reconsider. Your skills—''

Daniel cut him off with a sharp movement of his hand. ''No.''

The other man studied his pipe for a moment again. ''Jefferson says you're getting married. Is it the same woman you mentioned this summer?''

Seeing nothing but casual interest in Coleman's eyes, Daniel felt some of his impatience drain away and nodded. The quicker he got Coleman out of Wyoming, the better he'd feel. But that didn't mean he planned to bare his soul to his former boss. It was nobody's business what he'd done in the summer. Nobody's except his and Maggie's.

Only he'd excused his actions long enough. He'd left Maggie after the most incredible night he'd ever had, using the excuse of checking in with Coleman to salve his conscience about avoiding morning-afters. When the fact was, he'd been too cowardly to face Maggie the next day. Too cowardly to face himself.

"Have you told her about what happened in Santo Marguerite?"

Daniel didn't fool himself that Cole was asking because of personal reasons. Hollins-Winword operated in the shadows. In the agency's opinion it was fine for the agency to know everything about its operatives, from the number of fillings in their teeth to the occupations and sleep habits of their family members. But turn the tables? Not acceptable.

Nevertheless, if Daniel had thought it would have served one single good purpose, he'd tell Maggie whatever the hell he wanted to and damn the consequences. But he hadn't told Maggie. What would have been the point? It would only turn her away from him. Make her doubt more than ever his ability to provide for them. To protect J.D. and the baby. So he gave Coleman the answer the man wanted, whatever the motives. "No."

Coleman sat forward, cradling his pipe. "What does Jefferson say about all this?"

Daniel snorted. "Like he ever talks about his gig with Hollins-Winword? He was right. I shouldn't have gotten involved with you guys. But I did. It was a mistake."

"I think you're overreacting."

He pushed out of the chair and went to the windows, staring out at the drifting, blowing snow. "Angeline's entire family…hell the entire village…are dead, Cole." He stared out at the drifting white. But in his mind he saw only destruction. Of roughly built homes burned to the ground and once-lush vegetation withered and dead. "And it's my fault. Somehow I tipped my hand, and Arturo took it out on a lot of innocent people. That's hardly overreacting."

Cole finally exhibited some impatience. "If you want to blame someone, blame Arturo and his bloody army. He wanted to control their land. They were expendable."

Daniel shook his head, unsurprised at Cole's answer. Cole's animosity for Arturo Sandoval was practically legendary. It was that very animosity that had no doubt led to the assignment in Santo Marguerite. "I should've known better than to fall for his tricks. You know it. I know it. That's why you suspended me."

"Forget the suspension. I did it because it was the only way we could get you to take a break," Cole corrected bluntly. "Which you did. The agency never said your return to active wasn't desirable."

"It's not desirable to me. So your visit was a wasted trip. We're expanding the Double-C. I'm not going anywhere."

"I expect that willingness to stay here has a lot to do with your young woman."

Daniel snorted. "You going romantic on me, Cole? What'll the guys at the office say?"

Coleman smiled faintly at that. Hollins-Winword possessed nothing so mundane as an office. "I believe it's written somewhere that weddings are supposed to be romantic. Not that I'm speaking from experience. I'll leave love and all that to the rest of you."

Daniel didn't want to think about love.

"How do you feel about the progress in locating Angeline?"

"There is no progress," Daniel stated coldly. Coleman knew that. The man was just trying to get under his skin. Not necessarily because Daniel wasn't going along with the request to stay with the agency, but because it was something Coleman Black enjoyed. Needling people. But Daniel wasn't going along for that ride.

Angeline was gone. End of story. He'd finally accepted the truth.

They heard the slam of a door, then light footsteps. Emily and Maggie appeared in the doorway, Jefferson following them, his arms loaded with shopping bags.

Emily breezed into her kitchen, greeting Coleman as if he was a regular visitor. Jefferson dumped the bags on the table, his eyes meeting Daniel's silently. Without apology. Coleman rose, his attention on Maggie.

Daniel stifled an oath. He didn't need these two meeting. He really didn't. But there wasn't anything he could do about the situation, because Emily did the introducing before the silence had a remote chance of becoming awkward.

Maggie smiled at the man and shook his hand, trying not to let her concern show. She could sense Daniel's tension rolling off him in thick waves.

Then Leandra and J.D. scrambled into the kitchen adding to the confusion as they darted here and there, bouncing a small ball between them.

Maggie smiled and glanced at Daniel. His hands were clenched around a half-empty cigarette pack. Coleman Black was watching the lively little girls thoughtfully, casting a look Daniel's way now and then.

Then the man smiled easily at Maggie. "This is your daughter, then."

Maggie nodded, not sure why she felt wary. She just did. Perhaps it had to do with the way Daniel's knuckles were white around the cigarette pack. Finally she could stand it no more, and she touched his shoulder. He jerked and stepped away from the table as if she'd sprouted fangs and a tail. "I'm expecting a delivery at the house," he announced abruptly. "I'll get you and J.D. later," he told Maggie.

Maggie stared after him. She would have blamed Daniel's sudden departure on the girls bouncing around like jumping beans. But Daniel had been uptight even before they'd entered the kitchen. She looked up at Emily and Jefferson's guest but J.D. and Leandra chose that moment to dash out of the kitchen, talking about needing "makeup like mama."

"I'd better put a lid on that idea," she said, and hurried after the girls. She caught them down the hallway and managed after some concerted effort to redirect their exuberance into the relative safety of Leandra's bedroom. Then Maggie headed back to the kitchen. She stopped before reaching the doorway, though, as she heard Coleman Black speak.

"This J.D. is how old? Three? Four?"

"Nearly four." That was Jefferson.

"Ahh," the other man said softly. "Angeline was four, too."

Angeline. Maggie stepped into the kitchen, drawing three sets of eyes. "Jefferson, could you give me a ride out to the house?"

His dark blue eyes narrowed. Then he nodded. "Let's go."

When Jefferson dropped her off at the house, he offered to come in with her, but she declined. She felt certain Daniel didn't want any company.

Not even hers.

But she'd already lived too much of her life as an ostrich. Letting things happen around her. Daniel had demanded marriage and all that that implied. It was time he learned that communication and sharing and trust was a two-way street.

She found him working in the basement of the house. *Their* house. He was tearing down a perfectly good section of wallboard, as if the devil was prodding him in the backside with a hot poker. "Daniel."

He jerked, but didn't stop.

She shrugged out of her coat and tucked it over the banister, then walked up behind him, touching his tight shoulder. "Daniel, stop. Please."

"Leave me alone, Maggie."

"Who is Angeline?"

"I warned you, Maggie. Don't."

"Who is she?"

He moved out from her touch. "Nobody."

"I don't believe you."

"Add liar to my list of accomplishments." He yanked a section of wallboard down with his bare hand and stared at it.

"Why are you taking down that wall? It was perfectly fine."

"It wasn't painted yet."

"So you tear it down?"

He threw the ruined piece to the side, atop the growing pile. "I decided we could open up this corner of the basement and build you a woodworking shop."

Maybe later she'd feel pleased at his thoughtfulness. That she'd have a place specifically designed for her equipment. That Daniel had done that for her. But she knew that the emotions fueling his bare-handed demolition job were more bound up with the Angeline he wouldn't discuss.

"Is…is she your daughter?"

He jerked and rounded on her, his eyes narrowed. "What?"

"Angeline."

"No," he gritted. "She was just a kid."

"Whose very name sets you off."

"Maggie—"

"Is she the one you see when you look at J.D.?"

His jaw tightened and he turned back to the wall. "I see J.D. when I look at J.D." He wrapped his fingers over the ragged edge of the only remaining piece of wallboard. With one yank, he pulled it right out of the screws.

Maggie jumped back, blinking against the fine powder that puffed out from the wallboard when he threw it at the pile. "You know, Daniel, if we have any chance at all of making this work between us, we have to have some openness between us." Then flushed, all too aware that she was guilty of harboring her own unspoken insecurities. Unspoken feelings. Unspoken love. "Coleman Black," she pressed. "He knew Angeline?"

Daniel shoveled his fingers through his hair, leaving streaks of white powder. His expression was raw, without patience. "I knew Angeline. Nobody else did. And she's dead. So *drop it.*"

Maggie fell back a step. Dead. Dear Lord.

Daniel had turned around again and was staring at the newly bared studs. She lifted her hand to touch his shoulders, but hesitated, curling her fingers against her palm. His entire demeanor shrieked that he didn't want her caring. Her love.

She drew back her hand. Swallowed the questions and the grief she felt for a child she'd never known, but who had obviously touched Daniel. She turned around, spying his big hammer with the claw on one end. She picked it up and held it toward him.

"If this is going to be my workshop, we'll have to take down these studs," she said huskily. "And widen the doorway."

His eyes met hers, and the hammer shook in her hand. Then his eyes slowly lowered to the tool. He closed his hand around the handle, his warm fingers brushing hers. "Right."

They worked side by side for a long while. Until the tension finally drained from Daniel's being and he insisted that Maggie sit down and rest while he finished cleaning up the huge mess they'd made. Then he suggested taking Maggie back to the big house. Or back to Jefferson's. There was no point in her twiddling her thumbs while he started framing in the new room.

But she shook her head. "I'd rather stay with you," she said huskily. "If you don't mind."

He shrugged and turned back to measuring and cutting and hammering. But when he finally called it quits for the day some time later, and they drove back to the big house, she couldn't get over her suspicion that he'd been pleased.

By the next day, though, she decided that she'd probably read something into his expression that hadn't really been there. Because he was gone from the house before she rose for the day. And when she drove over to tell him about Jaimie's plans for that evening, he barely spared her a glance.

"Jaimie wanted to be sure you'd be back for supper," Maggie repeated. "She wants to officially celebrate the engagement." She watched Daniel lift a piece of wallboard into place. "Her words."

"Fine." He fastened the board with smooth ease. Then stepped past her for the next one, hefting it easily despite its size and weight.

She moved out of his way as he fit it into place.

"You need something else?" he finally asked when she once more found herself standing in his way.

Shaking her head, she hurried up the stairs and drove back to the big house. "And men think *women* are hard to figure."

Willie Nelson whined from the jukebox in the corner. Cigarette smoke hung in the air, and three guys were in the corner by the pool table, arguing over an impossible shot. Daniel sat on one of the bar stools at the high bar and stared into the untouched shot of bourbon sitting in front of him, wondering what he was doing at Colbys when he knew that Jaimie was expecting him for her "official celebration" of the engagement.

The engagement.

He reached in the pocket of his vest and pulled out a small velvet box. His thumb popped it open and he set the box on the bar, next to his bourbon. Inside the box nestled two intricately woven platinum bands. One crowned with a glittering diamond with two smaller stones marching out on either side. The rings were deceptively fragile looking.

A lot like Maggie Mae.

His jaw tightened and he snapped shut the box, sliding it back in his pocket. He'd bought the rings that day he'd taken her to the department store for maternity clothes. He'd looked in the jewelry department of that store, but hadn't found what he'd wanted. Two stores later, he had. They'd been burning a hole in his pocket ever since.

It wasn't that Daniel wasn't a believer in marriage. Far from it. If anything, he believed in it too much. His own father, though obviously involved with Gloria Day, had never taken another woman as his wife after Sarah Clay died.

And now Daniel was marrying a woman he'd vowed never to love again because she was carrying his child. He was going to be a father, not only to a baby not yet here, but to J.D. A three-year-old imp who reminded him so fiercely of another little girl. A little girl he'd been unable to protect.

He wondered what Maggie would say, do, if she knew the whole truth about *that*. About Angeline.

He picked up the glass of golden liquor and studied it.

Watched the dim lights over the bar cast a glow over the plain glass. Only he wasn't really seeing it. He was seeing the nervousness in Maggie's eyes when she'd admitted that afternoon that she wasn't sure which was the larger mistake. Marrying or not marrying.

Then the halting, skittish trust that had finally replaced the nerves.

His lips twisted and he set the glass down with a thunk. The bourbon sloshed.

He had never been good at working out his feelings. Expressing himself. He'd never had a need to until Maggie Mae had come to the Double-C. One look at her and Daniel had been a goner. He'd wanted to hold her. Cherish her and laugh with her. But she'd been married. So Daniel had only wished for her to be happy. Only she hadn't been.

He picked up his drink once more, then set it down just as abruptly. Well, no more, he reminded himself harshly. He'd gotten over Maggie Greene a long time ago. They were getting married now because it was the smart thing to do. Because it was the best way for him to provide for her and their child. For J.D. That was all there was to it.

The pool players still hadn't settled their argument, and Daniel strode over to them, sliding a cue out of the rack on the wall. His eyes took in the table at a glance and he leaned over and sank the shot. "It's not impossible," he said at their incredulous looks. He replaced the cue, retrieved his black hat off the bar and drove his truck out of the parking lot, gravel spewing from beneath the tires.

When he pulled his truck up alongside the big house, he was almost surprised that he didn't see Jefferson's truck, or that half the town of Weaver wasn't there. Usually, the Clay clan, when they felt like celebrating, didn't go about it in a small way.

He went in through the back and left his hat on a hook by the kitchen door. The dining room was empty and he went back through the kitchen and headed downstairs.

Sure enough, he heard laughter and music and—

Ah, hell. Two dozen people at least awaited him in the remodeled rec room that had been decorated with white doves and ribbons and about a mountain of foofy wedding stuff.

He managed to tack a smile on his face even before the combined "Surprise" echoed through the room. Jaimie, grinning devilishly, caught his arm and dragged him into the fray. He scanned the crowd, picking out Maggie who was sitting alone on one of the couches that littered the room. She smiled brightly, and he wondered if everyone could see the strain in her eyes as easily as he.

Then he wondered how much that strain owed to the surprise party. And how much it owed to his own deliberate distance that he'd put between them since the day before. Ever since he'd looked into her turquoise eyes and felt his existence spinning out of his control. All because she'd looked at him with some measure of trust. Finally.

"Sit by your intended, sir," Jaimie ordered, pushing a flute of champagne into his hands. Daniel eyed the drink, realizing from one sniff that it was sparkling cider and not champagne, then looked up to see Matthew and Jefferson leaning against the wet bar, beers in hand. Matthew shrugged as if to say, *Go along with her, it's easier that way.*

Feeling a strong urge to grab Maggie and get the hell out of there, he threaded through the people, getting back slaps and hugs. Finally he made it to the short couch.

Maggie looked up at him and a knot tightened in his gut. He grinned, as much for her benefit as for all the rest, and sat down next to her. He lifted his glass and asked, for her ears only, "You okay?"

She lifted her own glass, though she made no attempt to drink. "Just dandy."

"Kiss."

Suddenly the lone call became a chant. Daniel looked around at the collection of friends and neighbors who were hooting and hollering for him to kiss his soon-to-be bride. Then he felt Maggie's narrow fingers searching out his. He glanced at her, hoping he didn't look as surprised as he felt.

She looked back at him, her eyes wide and just this side of panicked. He forgot about the catcalls, the ribald jokes. For a long moment it was just Daniel and Maggie. When he tugged on her hand and she leaned into him and he kissed her cool lips, he did it for them. Not for the people who were watching delightedly.

Her lips softened. Warmed. And then the kiss wasn't quite so gentle. Or so innocent.

"Time enough for that on the honeymoon," Matthew said, tongue-in-cheek when he plunked a bottle of beer loudly and noticeably on the table beside Daniel's elbow.

Maggie colored, yet her eyes didn't falter from his. He ran his finger along her cheek, and he wished they weren't in the middle of thirty-or-so of their nearest and dearest. Because he wanted to do a lot more than touch her face and hold her hand.

Maggie leaned toward him. "It won't last long," she murmured.

"What?"

"The shower." She smiled overbrightly when Jaimie started carrying packages toward them. "I didn't know this was what Jaimie planned when she said *officially celebrate.* And then when I did know, it was too late to stop."

"Where are the kids?"

"Emily got a baby-sitter who is watching them all over at their place."

The stack of gifts grew. Matthew took over, insisting that Jaimie sit still. He practically lifted her off her feet, putting her in a chair next to where Emily sat.

"Normally we'd chow down first," Jaimie said. "But you weren't here when I expected you and we've all been grazing already." She pointed at the spread of food. "Now we want to see some gift wrap flying."

Guests situated themselves around Maggie and Daniel, waiting expectantly.

Why wouldn't they? For all appearances, Maggie and Daniel were marrying for the usual reasons. The only ones who knew about the baby were his immediate family and the staff of Dr. Foster's office.

He glanced at Maggie. "Well, darlin', you'd better show me how this all works. A wedding shower," he added, when she looked at him, confused.

She tucked her hair behind one ear. "*Darlin'*, I've never had a wedding shower before." She took a gift from the top of the heap and handed it to him. "So we'll just have to figure out how it works as we go."

Suddenly Daniel's mood shifted. He fingered the elaborate silver bow on the flat box. She'd never had a wedding shower.

It all sifted into place, and he recognized what he'd known but hadn't thought about. Joe and Maggie had eloped when she was barely out of high school. She'd probably never had the trappings that accompanied most young women's weddings.

He smiled faintly. So here was something new for her, too.

He ripped open the package and stared, dumbfounded, at the contents.

Maggie looked over his arm and gasped. All around them, people laughed and commented and Daniel tilted his head, lifting the extravagantly skimpy black and red teddy out of the tissue paper with one finger looped through an impossibly thin strap.

Just thinking of Maggie wearing such a garment was enough to give him a coronary. He handed it to her. "I think it'll fit you better 'n me."

Maggie eyed the gossamer-thin teddy, feeling as if her cheeks were on fire. But these people who'd surprised them with this shower had done it out of love and respect for Daniel. Not because they wanted to embarrass her. She swallowed and reached out for the teddy, feeling sparks scorch her fingers when they brushed against Daniel's. "I guess we'll see, won't we," she said tartly.

Everybody laughed. The rest of the gifts ranged from the absolute raunchiest—a pair of plastic handcuffs and edible panties—to the most beautiful white peignoir imaginable.

Squire, who was still visiting Gloria, had sent an envelope and card addressed to Maggie. Inside was a deed for a modest chunk of land. Double-C land.

She gasped and looked up, but Matthew and Jefferson and Daniel all watched her as if they already knew what it contained. And approved. Jaimie and Emily smiled as if they understood the stunned surprise sweeping through her. Her hands trembled when she unfolded the card. Squire's writing, slanted and spare. "For my grandchildren, J.D. and ?? And their mother. Welcome to the family, child."

Maggie blinked at the sudden tears blinding her.

Daniel took the note and tucked it back into the envelope, sliding it and the deed into the pile of gifts. "Try backing out now," he murmured for her ears.

She gave a watery smile at his wry words. She knew she wouldn't back out of the wedding plans. And it had nothing whatsoever to do with Squire's generous gift. But that didn't mean she was entirely certain about Daniel sticking to the agreement, no matter what he promised. And she was growing more certain by the minute that if he didn't, she'd be torn to pieces.

Then Jaimie got their attention as she hopped up and snapped off several flash pictures, making everybody complain good-naturedly about seeing spots before their eyes.

They gathered up bows and ribbons and cut the cake. They ate, and some drank. Daniel, she was surprised to notice, stuck with the sparkling cider the rest of the night after his single beer. Though there was plenty of beer and champagne flowing, no one seemed to indulge too heavily. When the party broke up a few hours later, Maggie could honestly say that she'd enjoyed herself.

Mostly because Daniel had sat beside her nearly the entire time, his arm around her shoulder. It felt protective and secure in that spot, and even though they'd hardly said ten words to each other all day, she'd absorbed his close presence like a parched sponge.

Jaimie kicked off her shoes and stretched her feet across Matthew's lap, wriggling her toes. "Ahh. That was fun."

Emily, who had found her spot on Jefferson's lap, yawned and agreed. Her hands slowly moved over her pregnant belly. "So when is the big day, anyway?"

Four sets of eyes turned to them. Maggie looked at Daniel. "Ah...soon."

He nodded. "Soon."

Jaimie threw a wad of ribbons at them. "A *date,*" she chided.

"I guess whenever we can get over to the justice of—" Maggie started.

"What?" Jaimie swung her legs off of her husband's lap. "You're not planning to have some dinky little ceremony in a judge's chambers?"

"Well, I—"

"Friday after Thanksgiving Day," Daniel said. His hand tightened on Maggie's, warningly. "At the Community Church in Weaver."

Satisfied, Jaimie leaned back and stretched her legs once more across Matthew. "Perfect. But it's a holiday so you'll want to talk to the pastor right away. Plus we'll need to get right on the dress."

Maggie blinked, dragging her thoughts from Daniel's statement. "Dress?"

Emily laughed softly. "You know. *The* dress."

"Come on, Mags. You want a real wedding dress this time, don't you?"

Her heart lurched. "But we—" She looked to Daniel for help. He just smiled blandly, confusing her more than ever. He wanted a church wedding. What had happened to standing in front of a judge and saying "I do"?

Chapter Thirteen

"I didn't know that Jaimie had planned the shower," she repeated when Daniel closed the door to the rec room and flipped on one of the small table lamps in the sitting area.

"You said."

She wished she could see his expression. Not that she'd have been able to interpret it. "I'm sorry about the way things got out of hand."

"Like what?"

She spread her hands, her shoulders lifting in a futile shrug. "The church. The dress. You know." She shook her head. "All of it."

"We're getting married, Maggie. We'll do it proper. With the minister and our family and friends there. The white dress, the whole thing."

"I can't wear white," she said inanely. As if the color of her gown mattered; it was the least of her worries.

"Why? 'Cause you wore it with Joe?"

She shrank back at the unexpected comment. "No. Because

I look washed-out in white,'' she said unevenly. ''And for your information, I wore pink jeans and a matching sweater when I married Joe.'' She felt the sharp sting of tears and blinked hurriedly.

He was silent for a long, torturous moment, and she wondered why she just didn't go into her bedroom and shut the door. But she didn't. She stood there, running her fingers along the back of the dark blue sectional couch. Waiting. Waiting.

For what?

''There's a store,'' he finally said in his low, husky voice. ''You can look for your dress there. I saw a wedding dress in the window.''

''Since when do you know so much about wedding gown retailers?''

''Since I bought this at the jeweler right next door to it,'' he said after a moment and pushed something into her hand. Then he stomped up the steps that led directly outside.

Maggie's fingers surrounded the velvety-smooth cube. Biting the inside of her lip, she opened the jeweler's box. The rings were elegant without being elaborate. Delicate without being weak.

She loved them.

She closed her eyes, snapping the box shut. She didn't deserve them. Daniel was marrying her because he was too decent not to. But rings as beautiful as these were meant for someone loved.

Yearning scorched through her, tightening her stomach and making her chest ache. Wedding gowns were meant for brides walking down the aisle toward their true loves. Church weddings were for lovers taking sacred vows with their beloved.

She might be in love, but she was the only one who was. She'd be wise to remember that.

She cleared her throat and slowly followed him up the stairs, grabbing her coat on the way. The sky overhead was black with clouds, and she didn't see him at first. But then she saw the flare of a match and followed it around the side of the house.

And now he was smoking again.

"The rings are beautiful," she said when she finally stopped next to Daniel where he leaned against the house, the tip of his cigarette glowing between his lips. "But I can't accept them." She held out the box, but he didn't take it back and she sighed, finally thrusting it into his hand. He either had to take it, or let the jewelry case fall to the ground.

He made a sound she couldn't interpret, and it was the cigarette that fell to the dirt, where he ground it beneath his boot. He pushed the rings into his pocket. "Why? Because they'll replace *Joe's?*"

She flinched at the way he spat out the name. She automatically ran her finger over the bare spot on her ring finger. She sighed and tucked her hair behind her ear. "Daniel, it's not too late to put a stop to this."

He stiffened beside her. "Is that what you want to do?"

No! The knowledge screamed through her. But she wanted him to be happy. To not rip his bed to shreds in his sleep, then make it in the morning before she had a chance to see it. To not be smoking again, which was something she'd learned long ago that he only did when he was beyond stress. To not grieve for a four-year-old child he refused to discuss. "I...if it's what you want."

He snorted. "Maggie Mae, I could climb to the moon on the back of the things I want."

"You're not making any sense to me."

"Or me." He moved, a large solid shadow. "I want to make love to you until neither one of us has the energy to move much less think. Is that understandable enough?"

She couldn't have said a word if her life depended upon it.

He caught her arms and pulled her up against him. Her coat crinkled softly. "You're gonna be the mother of my child, and all I can think about just now is the way you'd look wearing that sexy little bit of red and black or that virginal white filmy thing from the shower. Or nothing at all. Am I making sense *now?*"

Her fingers curled through the soft fabric of his long-sleeved shirt to the steely muscles beneath. Images from his blunt words whirled. Before she knew what was happening, he lowered his head and closed his lips over hers.

He gave no quarter. Just thoroughly and completely demolished her senses.

When he finally lifted his head, leaving her lips swollen and yearning, the mere act of breathing was nearly impossible for her. His hands molded her hips tightly to him, leaving her in no doubt that he was affected, too. "This is what I want," he gritted.

Lord help her, she wanted it too. But she was so wary of hoping. To believe that this time would be different. That she could love. And not lose. "I'm afraid," she admitted.

He set her on the ground so fast, she swayed. "Because I'm not Joe," he said coldly.

She pressed the heels of her hands to her eyes. *"I'm not talking about Joe!"* Tears burned her eyes. "I'm talking about me. Me. The way you made me feel. That night…with you at the swimming hole—" She bit back a sob and hugged her arms around herself. "I didn't *know* that's what it could be like."

"I should've horsewhipped him when I had the chance."

Maggie trembled at his low words. "It doesn't matter," she said. "He was my husband."

"Yeah, and he gambled and he embezzled. And if that wasn't bad enough, he cheated on you. Was that all okay because he was your husband?"

"No, it wasn't okay!" She stared up into the inky, depthless black sky. "But if I'd been a better wife, he might not have—"

"Bull."

"Oh, Daniel. You just don't understand."

"I understand enough." He closed his hands over her shoulders and turned her to face him.

She stared up at him, trying in vain to see his eyes, but it was just too dark. "Joe—"

"Screw Joe."

She bit her lip, shivering at the disgust in his words. A disgust that was nearly a tangible thing.

"He had your love," he stated grimly. "He threw it away. Even before I—" He broke off, stiffening.

"Joe left me because he didn't want J.D.," she snapped roughly when he stepped away. "And he didn't want me. He wanted his girlfriends. I was never enough for him. Never."

"That's not why."

"Of course that's why." Her voice rose. "You talked about honesty the other day. I was his wife. Do you think I imagined those women? Belinda Gomez? Marlene Switt? Julia Evans? Or Tina? Oh, he did it up right with Tina, though. He actually *married* her. Not that he bothered to divorce me first."

Daniel's restless pacing finally halted. "He married someone else?"

"Yes," she admitted tightly. "Tina Greene. Probably the only woman, other than Jaimie, who really does grieve for Joe." She rolled her shoulders wearily. "She lives in South Carolina. She thinks I was Joe's ex-wife. I couldn't see any point in telling her otherwise. He hurt enough lives as it was."

"Joe and I had a fight the day before he walked out on you." A muscle ticked unevenly in his jaw, the only visible sign of emotion.

She struggled to follow. "About the embezzling?"

"I didn't know about that until later." He gave his head a small shake. "I knew he was cheating on you," he said grimly. "I threatened to tell you if he didn't stop. He laughed. Said you already knew." He lifted his hand, looking for a moment at the wide palm. The long, square fingers. "I saw red."

He lifted his gaze and Maggie pressed her fist against her mouth.

"I would have strangled him with my bare hands if it weren't for the phone ringing in the barn. He was hurting you. Over and over again. And the bastard…didn't…care." He flexed his fingers. "The call was from you," he added grimly.

His hand dropped to his side. "To tell me that the vet had arrived."

"Oh, Daniel." Maggie drew in a shaky breath. "I remember." She'd only had J.D. home from the hospital for a few days.

"He left you the next day. If I'd kept my nose out of it, maybe things would have been different for you. Maybe Joe wouldn't have run. You wouldn't have lost your husband." His voice roughened. "J.D. wouldn't have lost her father."

"My marriage would have ended even if Joe had stayed, Daniel. And it had *nothing* to do with you. It had to do with trust and the complete lack of it." Because she couldn't help herself, she touched his arm. Felt his muscles bunch. "Without Joe, I wouldn't have J.D.," Maggie said huskily. "And I could never regret her. But he never wanted her, Daniel." She drew a shaky breath. "You've given J.D. more attention in just these few weeks than Joe ever did. She's lost nothing. You are the man she's going to think of as her father."

He made a rough sound and moved, dislodging her hand. "Go to bed, Maggie."

She blinked. "I—"

"Just go."

What had she done? Said? They were actually communicating. She'd told him about Joe's bigamy. And now...

Now his fists were clenched as if he wanted to batter the world.

Holding her coat tightly about her, she turned and went inside.

Daniel listened to the door thud behind her and cursed softly. He couldn't go in there after her. Not now. His control was too damned shaky, and if there was one thing he needed to keep, it was his control. His emotions weren't to be trusted. So going after her, telling her he hadn't really meant it, would be sheer stupidity. But there he stood for the longest time, neither going nor staying.

He finally swore low and long and hard. And reached for the door.

He heard the faint hiss of the shower when he reached the bottom step. He went into his room, yanked off his boots and raked his hands through his hair. He lay on the top of his bed, then rose again to pace. Still the shower ran.

Cursing himself and the gut instinct that only led to disaster, he went across to the bathroom and slowly opened the door.

She wasn't in the water, though. She was wrapped in her robe and was watching the plants she'd stuck on the shower floor, giving them a long drink of water. When he opened the door, she turned to him. Her lips, soft and inviting, parted a breath. He waited for a protest that didn't come. And when it didn't come, he told himself that he should be shot for what he wanted to do with this woman.

But he was just a man. What was a man to do when a woman, still bath-damp, looked up at him in that way?

Ignoring the hard knot in his chest, he reached past her and shut off the water. Then slowly tugged on the belt of her robe. And the looping bow she'd tied slid free.

The edge of her teeth sank into her lip and his mouth went dry.

Feeling every ounce of the silent night weighing on them, he tugged once more on her belt and the two ends slipped apart, falling to her sides.

She drew in her breath on a hiss and caught the lapels, holding them together with knuckles gone white. "Don't play games with me, Daniel," she begged, her voice low and uneven. "Not now. I can't take it."

"No games."

Her eyes searched his, and he wondered what she'd see there. If it would scare her into getting as far from him as possible.

Whatever she saw there didn't scare her. Not enough. For her fingers, visibly shaking, released the edge of her robe, and the tiny wedge of skin that had been taunting him turned into a narrow ribbon. From her neck to her navel. And he realized she was wearing that slinky red and black teddy.

In the silence of the bathroom with the shower still drip,

dripping, he could hear her breathing. Even above the monstrous thundering of his pulse in his ears.

Her hand reached up as if in slow motion, and her palm, unsteady and cool, touched his face. Moved tentatively against his whisker-rough jaw.

The need racing through him made him hurt. Her bare toes, peeping out from beneath the loosened edges of the robe, inched closer. He watched her throat work as she swallowed. As she moistened her lips.

He caught her face between his callused hands. Ran his thumb over her soft lips.

She kissed his thumb.

It was a crumb. He took it as a feast. And feast he did. On her lips, that felt like silk beneath his. On the cool, satiny stretch of her lovely neck. On the warm curve of her shoulder when he nuzzled beneath the soft, thick robe.

In the dim reaches of his mind, he became aware of her fingers, threading through his hair. Of her heart, thundering against him.

And finally, finally, he let his hands slide inside the voluminous robe. She mewled and trembled.

His breath hissed as his hands encountered nothing but smooth skin and satin and lace. He didn't dare look at what his hands discovered. If he looked, he'd be gone. He wouldn't be able to stop, no matter what.

After an eternity of waiting, he had her body against his.

"Daniel," she said against him. Taking the opportunity, he thrust his tongue inside. She trembled wildly against him and he held her closer. Tighter. Until she stopped trying to speak. He felt her heart thudding against his. Felt her tongue, shy and tentative, meet his, making him wonder if he'd embarrass himself like a green kid, right then and there.

He turned and she gasped as he lifted her onto the bathroom counter. He didn't give her an opportunity to be flustered. He simply stepped between her legs and scooped her close. The robe fell off her shoulders, hanging on her arms that clung to him.

He tried to be gentle. To be mindful of her tender, soft skin, when he hadn't shaved since that morning, so many hours ago. Her shoulders were perfect. When his lips finally had explored every inch, he told her so.

"It's the teddy," she whispered. "Satin and—"

"You."

Her mouth moved, but no words came out. Not when he ran his finger over her shoulder, tracing one of the narrow straps down to the edge of filmy black stuff that molded and displayed her full breasts without apology or hesitancy. She swallowed back an incoherent sound when he touched the ribbon bow that somehow miraculously held it all together.

Maggie's heart raced as he toyed with the ribbon. Afraid he'd undo it. Afraid that he wouldn't. When his hand moved back up, touching the pulse that raced in her throat, gliding with his smooth-rough touch over her other shoulder, she couldn't help the moan that rose in her throat.

His hooded gaze roved over her. "It's you, Maggie Mae," he murmured. His fingers slid beneath one strap. Toyed with it, making her feel faint with suspense. "Haven't you figured that out by now? Cotton shirts. Woolen coats. Satin and silk. None of it matters." His jaw ticked. "Only what's beneath it." He lifted his hand, and the strap slipped from her shoulder.

She automatically reached to adjust it, but he held her hands. "Are you gonna send me out into the cold night?" He tilted his head over hers and his warm breath stirred the hair at her temples. "Or will you take me into your bed tonight? Into your body?"

She swayed. Daniel didn't mince words. He never had. The image he evoked was more than her weak willpower could withstand.

"We're gonna be married," he said evenly. "J.D. is taken care of for the night, and it's just you and me here. There's nothing wrong with us making love."

She tried to speak. She truly did. To tell him what was in her heart. But so many years of hiding from her heart got in her way.

He made a rough sound and straightened. She wanted to cry out at the painful loss of his warmth. She closed her arms around herself, watching him yank open the bathroom door.

Then he was gone. He hadn't slammed the door. Just quietly closed it behind him. And somehow that was worse than a display of anger. Of temper.

Yanking the robe back over her shoulders, she followed him. Right into his bedroom. He stood by his bed looking at her as if he couldn't believe his eyes. His hair waved darkly gold around his head. With his black shirt and dark jeans he looked like an earthbound angel.

Had any angel, though, ever had molten silver eyes that looked into a person's soul? When angels spoke, they surely didn't do it in husky, gravelly tones that sent a flock of shivers dancing along her spine. "Don't come in here unless you plan to stay until morning," he said, his tone flat.

"My mother had the morals of an alley cat," she announced baldly.

He hadn't so much as moved a muscle. "So?"

"So, I want you to understand."

"Understand what?" He suddenly sounded infinitely weary. He tossed his wallet on the nightstand and sank on the side of the bed.

"Why I—"

"I don't want to hear the reasons you don't want me," he said evenly. "I'm not Joe. I'll never be Joe. And I'm damned sick of being compared to him."

She walked toward him, shivering under her robe. "I don't want you to be," she said surely. "I stopped loving him the day he told me he'd had another affair." She closed her eyes, wishing she could keep her voice even. But the evening had taken its toll. And she felt like a balloon about to burst from all the emotion roiling inside her. "After the first time…I was young. He said he wouldn't do it again, and I believed him. He was my only—the only man I'd ever been with. My father died the year I married Joe, did I ever tell you that? He never got over my mother aban—abandoning us. I couldn't be like her, Daniel. I couldn't. They all looked at me like I was some-one to feel—feel sorry for. They brought me meals when Daddy wouldn't get out of bed for a week. And used clothes when I outgrew my school dresses.'' She hauled in a shud-dering breath, tears burning behind her lids. ''I just wanted my mom to come home. For things to be the way they used to be. But she didn't come home. She never came home and oh, God, I didn't want to be like her!''

''You're not.''

''I am pregnant with your child,'' she said, her throat raw.

''You're not someone else's wife anymore. You're going to be my wife, Maggie. Mine.''

''Because we *have* to! My parents married because they had to.''

He exhaled roughly. ''One of the few things I've ever done in my entire life that I didn't want to do was leave the Double-C three years ago. If I didn't want to marry you, I wouldn't. I could make sure our child was taken care of without that.''

''But you said—''

''I'm marrying you because it's the sensible answer. I want you beside me. And I want it good and legal and honest so you don't have to walk around feeling guilty because you're sleeping with a man without benefit of a wedding ring.''

''You don't love me.''

His low curse rasped over her nerve endings. ''At least we're going into it with honest intentions. Without *love*,'' he spat the word, ''clouding our brains.'' His voice calmed. Evened. ''You're not your mother, Maggie. Maybe you mar-ried a man when you were little more than a child who was cut from the same cloth as her, but you are not like her.''

She didn't have an answer for that. Her toes curled into the thick carpet beneath her feet.

Everything about Daniel tempted her. From the single brush of his callused fingers that made her lose her senses, to his easy acceptance of the garbled story of her childhood.

But it was more.

It was the way he looked at her. With interest in what she

had to say. With humor at the most unexpected times. It was the way he watched over J.D. even though Maggie sensed it caused him some inner pain. It was the way he'd sat J.D. in front of him for her very first real horseback ride and fashioned doll-size reins out of a short length of leather.

It was the way he'd bobbed for apples at a Halloween party.

She touched his hair where it lay tangled and heavy against his brow. She let her fingers trail along his jaw. The rough bristles made her fingertips tingle and she felt such longing to have those whiskered cheeks moving over her once again.

He clamped his hand around hers when she started to slip out of her robe. "What are you doing?"

"Staying until morning."

A muscle ticked unevenly in his jaw. It gave her courage.

She twisted a little and her robe fell to the floor. Nibbling the inside of her cheek, she looked at him. At the bronze cast of his skin. The intriguing web of laugh lines spearing out from the corners of his sooty-lashed eyes. "You make me weak," she murmured.

His gaze captured hers, and she knew in an instant that he understood what she was trying to say and doing such a bad job of. "Say my name."

"Daniel." When had he freed her hand so that it could find a place on his wide chest? "Daniel Clay." Still daring, still scared, she leaned forward to press her lips to the strong, hard, whisker-blurred jaw. "The man I'm going to marry."

She felt a long sigh rumble through him and half expected him to take control. But he didn't. She explored his jaw with her lips, feeling more and more freedom with every centimeter. When she reached his ear, she murmured his name again, and retraced the route.

His hands, she realized, were hard and tight against the mattress. She didn't want him digging his fingers into the bed. She wanted his fingers on her.

Her lips never lost the whispering connection with his jaw. She pressed her hands atop his and found his cool firm lips with her own.

He kissed her back, but again made no moves to take over. The little thrill of control that clenched hard at her center shocked her. She reached for the bottom of his shirt and tugged it from him. It hit the floor with a soft rustle, and Maggie had to take a good long moment to catch her breath at the sight of his broad shoulders, so sharply defined.

Trembling wildly, she touched the pulse throbbing at his neck. Her palms slipped over him, felt the taut muscles in his abdomen jump. His eyes sharpened when she trailed her fingers along the waist of his jeans, dipping into the hollow at his navel when he suddenly sucked in his breath on a long hiss.

He stilled her hands with his own. Stood and pulled the small jeweler's case out of his pocket, pushing it open with his thumb.

Again the beautiful rings beckoned. Then he took out the band with the diamonds and snapped the box shut, tossing it aside. Her hands trembled, but his were steady as he slid the ring into place.

"Now," he murmured, settling her fingertips at the top button of his jeans. "Now."

She moistened her lips. The ring felt natural on her finger. She could have lied to herself and said that it was only because another ring had been there for so many years. But it *would* have been a lie.

His gaze locked with hers, and she was grateful. Because if she looked at what her fingers were revealing with each pop of a button, she'd have lost her nerve. Her chest labored with each breath she drew when her knuckles brushed against him. Bare and undeniably aroused beneath his jeans.

She faltered.

"Don't stop now, Maggie Mae," he rasped.

"I—"

"Kiss me."

She leaned against him with a small cry and pressed her lips to his. His hands closed over hers, lifting them to his chest, sliding his strong arms around her waist.

His head tilted to one side. "Your eyes are as wide as J.D.'s when I took her for her first ride. Are you that nervous?"

"Yes," she admitted on a breathy sigh.

"It's just you and me here, Maggie Mae. Only rule that exists right now is you tell me if you don't like something." His lips curved faintly, though she could see no evidence of humor in his sharp silvery gaze. "Or if you do."

Her heart seemed to stall in her chest. "The, uh, the lamp?"

"Stays on, Maggie Mae. We're not doing anything to be ashamed of." With one smooth tug, he drew the ribbon that held the front of her teddy together. With one sweep of his hand, the lace and satin fell away. "Now we're even." He looked down at his jeans, hanging onto his hard hips with little more than a prayer and two buttons.

Then he shifted her to the bed and shucked his jeans and socks and Maggie couldn't have spoken a coherent word to save her soul. That August night had been dark. But now, the golden pool of light from the bedside lamp danced over his beautiful form. He was…*magnificent,* she thought faintly as he came down beside her.

His hands swept over her, making her cry out incoherently. The soft groan he gave when she touched him in return made her insecurities seem nonexistent. He kissed and touched and tasted until she became mad with need. "Now," she moaned, her mouth open against his chest. "Daniel, *now.*"

He rolled, dragging her atop his chest. "We're not rushing it this time," he muttered. "Slow. That's what I promised myself. I don't want to hurt you."

Her fingers tangled in his hair as he caught one nipple and laved it with his tongue before lavishing the other with the same devastating attention. "Next time," she gasped, closing her hands over him.

His fingers tightened on her hips, lifting her. "Next… time," he agreed hoarsely and thrust into her. Fully. Finally.

Maggie cried out, convulsing. Yet his arms were there.

Holding her close. Holding her safe. After an eternity, she collapsed on his chest, unable for the moment to even move.

His chest heaved beneath her, his breathing harsh and uneven. "Hey. Don't go to sleep on me."

She smiled shakily. She still felt him, strong and deep within her. "Oh, sure."

He suddenly turned, and she found herself staring up at him while he stretched her hands above her head, threading their fingers together. Her neck arched back as he rocked gently, insistently within her.

Had any woman ever been so thoroughly loved?

The wonderment grew, became more distinct within her overwhelmed senses as he drove her relentlessly. Mindlessly arching against him, wrapping her legs around his hard body, she felt every molecule of her body come to life because of him. And again, oh, again, she cried out his name, held spellbound in the grip of exquisite brilliance. Before she could even start to come down off that dizzying precipice, Daniel went rigid, a low, feral sound rising in his throat. His eyes met hers and she saw it all. The unbridled passion. Unashamed. Untamed.

Blessed. Nothing so perfect could be anything less.

Tears streaked from her eyes to her temples. *I love you* hovered on her lips, but she kept the words to herself. Saying them now would solve nothing.

Not when he'd already made it so plain that he didn't want her love. And that he had no intentions of feeling that emotion ever again.

Chapter Fourteen

The next afternoon Maggie stood in the kitchen of the big house and worked her way through the pile of baby clothes she and Jaimie had been sorting through. Daniel was out with Matthew.

And Maggie was no nearer to learning about the little Angeline who haunted Daniel.

She heard Jaimie call her name and set the minute terry cloth infant sleeper on the table.

She went to the stairs and looked up. "What?"

Jaimie appeared at the head of the stairs, laughter on her face. "Come here. You've got to see this."

Maggie went upstairs. The remodeling project was making some progress. But Matthew had been so busy lately with moving the herd to the lower elevations for the winter to get too much done. She knew that Daniel had promised his help, as soon as their house was done. She stopped next to where Jaimie was looking into Sarah's room.

This time Leandra was spending the afternoon and night

with them. And the three little girls were decked out in wedding finery. J.D. had a battered old cowboy hat on her curls and had to keep pushing at it to keep it from slipping over her nose. Her feet were stuck into boots that reached all the way past her knees. She'd stuffed a red bandanna into the elastic waistband of her jeans. Leandra had a pale yellow baby blanket on top of her head, held there by a bright purple headband. Little Sarah was apparently the preacher, with a nursery rhymes book held in her hands as solemnly as if it were the Bible itself.

"I guess the wedding mood has hit them, too," Jaimie giggled softly.

Entranced, Maggie leaned against the doorjamb watching the activity.

"You gots to kiss me now, J.D.," ordered Leandra, scrunching up her lips.

J.D. made a face. "No, I don't." But she leaned forward and hugged her. The hat tumbled over her nose and she pushed it back impatiently.

"My mama and daddy kiss lots," Leandra said firmly. "They gots to love each other lots. It's the *law*."

Jaimie snickered behind the hand she clamped to her mouth.

"Daddy kiss Mama," Sarah chirped. She closed her book with a snap. "Kiss, kiss, kiss."

J.D. finally dropped her hat on the ground. "Dannl is gonna be my daddy."

"Is not," Leandra retorted. "He's a *uncle*. Not a daddy."

"Is too," J.D. said.

"Nuh-huh."

Maggie could see J.D. gearing up. She went into the room, ready to intercede, but J.D. looked up at her, her green eyes glazed with temper and tears. "Dannl is too gonna be my daddy," she yelled, and dashed around Maggie's legs, flying out of the room. They heard her tennis shoes pounding down the stairs.

"Weddings bring out the stress in people. Apparently even little ones," Jaimie said. She gathered Sarah to her and pulled

Leandra over to join her at the child-size table and chairs in the corner. "Ladies, we're gonna talk."

Maggie quickly went after J.D. She skipped down the stairs, nearly reaching the bottom, and cried out when her foot slipped. She instinctively grabbed for the banister, almost touching it with her fingertips, but her balance was gone.

No! Not now!

She fell, tumbling down the last few steps where her head cracked hard against the hardwood floor. And lay.

Still.

There seemed to be a dozen people standing around her when Maggie opened her eyes. Her head throbbed. And her—

She gasped, started to sit, but Jaimie caught her shoulders. "Stay still, Mags. We've called Rebecca Morehouse."

Maggie shifted and felt a sharp pain shoot through her back. She stiffened, seeing stars shoot across her vision. She drew in a slow breath. "I can't lose this baby." If she lost the baby, she'd also lose Daniel. She wasn't sure she could survive either one. She wasn't sure Daniel, who was so certain that nothing would go wrong with this pregnancy, could survive it, either.

"You won't." Jaimie shifted on the floor, drawing her legs to one side. "I just don't believe God will let that happen." She squeezed Maggie's hand. "How is the Christmas ornament order coming?"

Maggie smiled brokenly. But she answered. And Jaimie kept her talking about her wood art, about what kind of stuffing they should have with their Thanksgiving turkey, about a dozen things, all to keep Maggie from sinking into the panic that seeped around the edges of her sanity.

And then J.D. darted back into the room, closely followed by Rebecca Morehouse who took in the situation at a glance. Jaimie managed to convince J.D. that it was okay to leave her mama with the doctor again. And though Maggie desperately wanted the support of her friend with her, she wanted J.D. to be reassured more. "Go with Auntie Jaimie," she whispered.

Rebecca crouched down beside Maggie and opened her bag. She flicked her light in Maggie's eyes, felt along her neck and limbs with her cool, capable hands. "How many stairs did you try to skip, anyway?" She smiled kindly, continuing her exam.

"One too many," Maggie murmured, absorbing the calm, soothing presence of the doctor. "The last two I guess." She grimaced when Rebecca touched her elbow. "I'm about thirteen weeks along," she managed.

"Babies are remarkably resilient," Rebecca soothed. "We'll do an ultrasound for good measure. I don't think you've broken anything. You've got a nice-size lump on your head, though, that I want to get a closer look at." She pulled a cold pack from her bag, squeezing it between her hands before placing it gently against the throbbing ache inside Maggie's head.

"Ohhhh," Maggie winced, closing her eyes.

"You'll probably be stiff and sore for a few days, but I think—"

The front door flew open and Daniel strode in, Matthew hard on his heels. Daniel froze, seeing her lying there. Maggie's hard-earned calm started to waver.

Rebecca pushed to her feet. "Daniel, she—"

He brushed past Rebecca, hunkering down beside Maggie. He caught her hand, brushing her tumbled hair away from her face with a cold hand. His quicksilver gaze searched hers. "You're gonna be fine."

Maggie's teeth chattered and she clenched her jaw. "The baby—"

"Is probably fine," Rebecca inserted mildly. "But I'd like to examine Maggie in my office."

Daniel was already moving, sliding his arms beneath Maggie. She wrapped her arms around his shoulders, taking comfort from his strong, sure arms. Though it ached just to lift her arm, she held the cold pack against the knot on her head, and she buried her nose in the soft collar of his coat, stifling a groan. Jaimie came into the room, carrying a wool blanket which she tucked around Maggie.

"Don't let J.D. be scared," Maggie said.

Jaimie smiled tensely, leaning into Matthew when he slid his arm around her. "We'll take care of her."

Rebecca discreetly touched Daniel's shoulder. "I'll meet you at my office," she said before gathering up her bag and heading toward the door.

"You're gonna be fine." Daniel's low, husky voice rasped against her ear as he carried her out into the cold afternoon. Instead of going to his own truck, however, he strode to Matthew's Blazer, where he carefully settled her in the back seat.

"Déjà vu," Maggie murmured.

He paused, tucking the blanket around her. His eyes were steady. "You and J.D. were okay before. You and our baby will be okay now."

Tears glazed her vision. Discussing the possibility of losing her baby was one thing. Living it, another. A nightmarish other. "Daniel, if I lose—"

His jaw clenched. "You won't," he said. If his conviction alone were enough to ensure it, they would be okay. "Believe it, Maggie Mae."

Maggie Mae. She moistened her lips, wondering if she was insane, because she did believe him. He brushed his thumb across her cheek, then climbed into the front of the truck and tore toward town and Rebecca's offices.

Daniel didn't leave her side, and with each moment that passed as she lay on the table in Rebecca's examining room, she tumbled more into love for him.

Gone was the man with the cold, expressionless looks. The tangible distance. In its place was the Daniel she'd once known, and the Daniel she'd come to know now. The man who gave her strength simply by letting his gaze rest on her face, and by the touch of his hand around hers.

By that evening, Rebecca was finally certain that the only ill effects of Maggie's tumble would be a few days of aching muscles. She cautioned Maggie to laze around for the next few days, just to be extra careful. Then she told Daniel he could take her home.

Home. The Double-C *was* her home now. Whether it was in the big house, or the graceful misty gray lady that Daniel had built. It was all Double-C. And it was her home. Not because of Jaimie or the acres of land that Squire had deeded over. It was because of the man who carried her so surely against his broad chest. Who made her feel beautiful and bright.

And whole.

If only she could do the same for him.

He pushed the front seat forward, ready to set her in the rear of the Blazer, and she stopped him. "I'd like to sit in the front."

"Rebecca wants you to lie down."

"I can lie in the front seat."

From the interior light of the truck she could see a muscle tick in his hard jaw. Then he nudged the seat into place and settled her in the front. He rounded the vehicle and climbed behind the wheel and went still for a long moment when Maggie settled her cheek on his thigh.

He drove back to the ranch, one hand slowly stroking her hair.

Everyone was waiting when Daniel carried her inside the big house. Even Jefferson and Emily were there. Once they were assured that Maggie, bumped and bruised, was fine—as was the baby—they gathered up Leandra and headed to their own place.

J.D. and Sarah both crawled onto Maggie's bed when Daniel finally put her down in the middle of it. It was well after their bedtime, but seeing that Maggie was fine was more important. Though her head ached, she read the storybooks they carried downstairs and listened to their account of supper when Jaimie and Matthew had let them eat in the bunkhouse with Curly and the two ranch hands, Dwight and Monroe.

Finally, however, it was late enough that even their over-excited selves started to droop. Matthew and Jaimie scooted them upstairs to their bedroom.

With all the fussing and commotion suddenly done, Maggie looked across the room at Daniel. He was leaning against the dresser, his arms crossed over his wide chest. His hair was rumpled from his fingers raking through it, and his lean cheeks were gilded with stubble. He looked tired and stressed and so unutterably masculine that she could have cried. If her head hadn't been throbbing so badly, she might have done just that.

As if he read her thoughts, he pushed away from the dresser and shook one of the pills out of the small bottle Rebecca had sent with them. He handed it to her, as well as the glass of water he'd placed on the nightstand earlier. He waited until she'd swallowed, then set the glass aside. "Need anything else?"

Maggie looked up at him, a prayer in her heart that she might have one more blessing in her lifetime. "You." And it was so suddenly so easy. Regardless of what might happen in the future. Saying what was in her heart had never been more right. "I need you, Daniel."

Daniel actually felt his heart jerk. Then she closed her hand around his and brought it to her soft lips, gently kissing his rough knuckles.

"Lie with me." Her voice, low and husky, caressed.

Once, in his life, he'd turned away from her, thinking he was doing the right thing. He'd wanted her to ask him to stay. Had needed it. But she hadn't, and he'd put his heart on ice and gone on.

Now she needed him.

He reached over and snapped off the light and sank down onto the bed beside her.

The quilt his mother had made so long ago was soft and warm against him, and he gathered Maggie close, their bodies fitting perfectly against each other. He could feel her breath, warm and sweet, against his throat.

And peace washed over him like a soft, soothing wave.

Chapter Fifteen

By the end of the next week Maggie was up and around again. Her elbow still ached when she was particularly active. For the most part, however, she was fine and dandy.

A sentiment shared when she drove herself into Weaver to visit Dr. Rebecca Morehouse. She'd already notified Dr. Foster's office in Gillette that she'd decided to seek the medical care of Rebecca after all.

On her way home she stopped at the small post office located in the back of the feed and seed. There was a package there for her that the mail carrier hadn't wanted to leave in the box at the main gate. She wasn't surprised to see the return postmark of the mail-order company she dealt with. It was the latest set of catalogs and copies of new custom orders they'd received. She flipped through the catalog, smiling with pleasure when she saw the color photos of her wood ornaments, then absently riffled through the orders from across the states. There were three from Canada, one from London, even one from Costa Rica. She'd be busy until after Christmas with them.

Waving at Harvey, the attendant who'd handed over the package, she went back out to the truck she'd borrowed from the Double-C.

She drove back home, humming with the music from the radio. It hadn't snowed in several days, and the day was bright and clear. She stopped at the mailbox at the gate and pulled out the bundle of mail from inside, dropped it on the seat beside her and headed up the gravel road toward the house. She parked next to Matthew's new truck and hopped out, carrying the mail with her.

Squire, J.D. and Sarah were heading toward the horse barn and the kittens, no doubt, who were old enough now to be exploring the barn on their stubby little legs. Maggie called and waved to them, then dashed up the back steps, through the mudroom and into the kitchen where she left the mail on the table. Then it was downstairs to the guest suite where she put the last few items they had into the suitcases and boxes sitting on the bed.

They were officially moving to their new home that afternoon.

Tonight J.D. would sleep in her bedroom at the end of the hall with the beautiful window seat and the canopy bed fit for a princess. Maggie would move into the large master bedroom at the top of that grand staircase and sleep in the oceanic-wide bed that Daniel had had delivered. With him.

Thanks to Rebecca's A-okay, Maggie held the secret knowledge close to her heart that when they did climb into that bed, they could do more than just sleep.

Her cheeks heated just thinking about it.

When Jaimie found her staring dreamily into space, she only smiled and shook her head. "You planning to just sit there all afternoon, or let me drive you and J.D. over to the new place?"

Maggie jumped, dragging her thoughts together. Before she could have the night with him, she had to finish the myriad details of the day. Daniel would bring their suitcases and the last few boxes over when he came later that day. He'd had to run into Weaver again for something, and he'd said that he would meet them later at the new place.

Their new home.

"I'm ready."

Jaimie grinned. "I told you everything would work out."

Maggie took one last look at the living area of the guest suite. Then she looked at the diamond ring on her left hand.

So had Daniel. And now she'd even begun to believe in happy endings herself.

Happiness singing through her veins, she corralled J.D., and in minutes they'd set out. Her mood didn't deflate even when Daniel was somewhat later than she'd expected that evening.

She simply left the dinner to warm in the oven in her beautiful new kitchen, fed J.D., then scooted her upstairs to the bath.

It was dark when Daniel finally drove home. It had taken him longer than he'd expected to pick up the scroll saw he'd ordered for Maggie's shop, but when he drove toward the house that Maggie would turn into a home and saw the light shining from the windows, his impatience drained away.

He went in through the back to the scent of roast beef and baked potatoes.

The hardwood floors gleamed with a rich finish. The square mahogany table that Maggie had chosen ought to have seemed out of place among the gleaming, stainless steel appliances, yet it fit.

Carpet, depthless hunter green, cushioned his boots as he passed from the kitchen into the great room. He could hear the murmur of Maggie's low voice and J.D.'s higher pitched chatter drifting down the stairs, and he headed up, then paused, listening to the ordinary discussion coming from the hall bathroom.

Daniel hardly remembered his mother, since she'd died

when he was about J.D.'s age. If he thought about it hard, he figured what he remembered most was the way his mother had smelled of vanilla and flowers.

After that, the only female in the Clay household had been Emily.

His lips curved slightly as the chat between Maggie and J.D. continued. Only now the subject had changed to picking up the toys in the tub and rinsing the bubbles down the drain. He went up the rest of the stairs and propped his shoulder against the jamb, looking through the door she'd left open. J.D., blond hair water-dark and slicked back from her little oval face, was dressed in bright pink pajamas. Duchess—that stuffed horse she dragged everywhere with her—sat like a champion on the top of the counter.

Maggie's hair was pulled back in an untidy knot, and when she leaned over the tub to gather up the rest of the toys, he could see the splashes of water across her loose shirt.

"Having fun?"

J.D. squealed and launched herself at his legs, staring up at him. He swallowed the dull ache inside him and swung her up into his arms.

Maggie pushed to her feet, her cheeks pink as she brushed self-consciously at her damp, rumpled shirt. She looked adorable and he slid his palm around her neck, planting a quick kiss on her lips.

She pulled away, her breathing uneven. "J.D.," she said. "If you want to watch *Lion King,* you need to get to it right now. Otherwise you'll have to go to bed before it's over."

J.D. squirmed and Daniel set her down. She grabbed Duchess and raced down the stairs as fast as her little legs would carry her. Within seconds, he heard the music from the popular video coming from the den where her favorite videos were stored on a shelf low enough for her to use.

He turned and caught Maggie's expression. "Do you know," he murmured, touching her petal-soft cheek, "what it does to a man to see his woman look at him with just that expression you have on your face?''

Her turquoise eyes widened. ''The same thing it does to the woman, I suspect,'' she answered unevenly. Her throat worked as she swallowed. ''I kept supper for you.''

He found himself smiling slowly. Enjoyed watching the hectic color come and go in her cheeks. ''Guess we should get to it, then,'' he murmured.

She tilted her chin, giving him a look so unexpectedly saucy that he nearly groaned. She sashayed past him and he blew out a long breath, watching her hips as she slowly descended the stairs.

He watched her until she was safely down, then went into the bathroom attached to their room. He washed up and put on a clean shirt before going downstairs. He found her in the kitchen, holding a match to one of the two candlesticks she'd set at the end of the table near the two place settings. She'd removed her damp shirt to reveal a clinging blue turtleneck that hugged her figure over the floaty skirt that skimmed her slender ankles.

''I fed J.D. before her bath,'' she said without looking at him. She shook out the match and tossed it in the trash before pulling a platter of sliced roast from the oven. He automatically took it from her, his hands brushing hers, and set it on the table. He caught the sideways looks she gave him as he helped her put the rest of their meal on the table.

''I'm not an invalid,'' she finally said when he nudged her into her chair.

He sat down, too, and looked at her. ''I know you're not.'' Then, drew in a long breath because she'd spent time preparing this meal and he would enjoy it even if his mind was more on the dessert end of things. A place his mind had no business visiting. Not since Maggie's fall.

When they'd finished, however, Maggie placed a crystal dish in front of him and he stared at the dessert she'd planned. Chocolate mousse.

When she sat again and stared at her own serving he knew she was remembering that time, not so many days ago, when he'd wondered aloud which was sweeter. The chocolate or Maggie.

Much as he loved the creamy confection, he couldn't take one more minute of the torture and he pushed his chair back from the table with a soft screech. Maybe they couldn't love each other yet the way he wanted, but he damn sure could sleep with her in his arms. He tucked Maggie's hand in his and led her around to the den. They found J.D. sound asleep, snoring softly on the couch as her movie played.

Maggie shut off the television and the lights as he carried J.D.'s featherweight body up to her room. She didn't stir a whit when they tucked her into her new bed.

Then it was just Maggie and him, standing at the foot of the wide bed in the privacy of their own new bedroom. He'd set a match to the fire in the fireplace, and the flames licked at the kindling, sending golden light dancing across Maggie's hair.

He pulled the clip from her hair, threading his fingers through the moonbeam silk. She tilted her head into his touch, her eyes heavy in the firelight. "I saw Rebecca today," she murmured.

"You doing okay?"

"I'm fine. The baby's fine. Totally fine."

He went still. "What are you saying?"

Her eyes met his. "I'm saying this is our first night in this house and we can, ah—"

"Are you propositioning me, Maggie Mae?"

Her cheeks colored wildly. "Maybe."

He smiled faintly and drew her against him. "It's about time."

Her soft laughter soon turned to soft sighs when he lowered her to their bed and made her his.

He woke well before dawn, not sure what it was that jarred him from his sleep. The fire had burned way down to a faint glow. Maggie was snuggled up against him, her silken legs tangled with his. She was sound asleep.

He gently rearranged her and she sighed deeply, scooting right over onto his side of the bed when he climbed out of it, one creamy arm pulling his pillow next to her cheek.

Moving quietly, he pulled on his jeans and walked along the wide hallway to J.D.'s room. He knew before he reached it that it was her he'd heard. He went into the room and turned on the tiny light sitting on the shelf across from her bed.

She didn't seem the least surprised to see him. Just held up her arms with childlike faith that he'd pick her up.

The hard knot in his gut was sudden and unrelenting. But he sat on the edge of the bed and slid her onto his lap, his jaw clenching when she rested her tousled blond curls so trustingly against his shoulder. "Aren't you sleepy, J.D.?"

She tugged Duchess onto his lap with her. "When you get married wif Mama?"

"Next week. That okay with you?"

She yawned and nodded, sleepily nibbling on Duchess's ear. "'Andra says you're a uncle."

"I'm Leandra and Sarah's uncle," he agreed.

"Yeah, but you gots to be a daddy now."

Daniel nodded, absently rubbing her warm little back.

"Mama gots a baby in her tummy," she piped after a moment.

"Mmm-hmm." Thank God Maggie's fall hadn't ended that fact.

"Dannl?"

"What, snooks?"

"Are you my daddy now?"

He stiffened. But J.D. didn't give him a chance to answer because she squirmed her little body around and threw her arms about his neck, pressing her little girl cheek against his. "I love you, Daddy," she said, her little voice clear and sure.

Daniel heard a soft noise and looked up to see Maggie, wrapped in her robe, standing in the doorway.

The knot in his gut tightened until he couldn't breathe. He nudged J.D. onto her mattress, muttering something. He had to get out of there. Had to—

Maggie fell back in surprise when Daniel thrust past her, striding toward the stairs, thundering down them. She quickly kissed J.D. and tucked her back into bed with Duchess the horse, then followed him.

Only he wasn't inside the house, and she watched in horror as he strode across the cold ground behind the house, seemingly oblivious to the patches of thin snow under his bare feet, or the howlingly cold wind about his bare chest.

She shoved her feet into the pair of lined boots she'd left earlier in the mudroom and yanked her coat on over her robe, snatching up his shearling coat and a pair of rubber overboots, then hurried after him, wincing at the cold air.

She caught up to him when he stopped dead in his tracks and stared into the moonlit night. She walked around in front of him, but he didn't seem to see her. "Daniel." Her breath puffed in the air. "Darling, put on your coat."

"Go away, Maggie," he said hollowly.

Her fingers dug into the coat. "Daniel, it's freezing. Put on your coat."

A shudder ripped across his shoulders. Still he didn't reach for the coat and she swallowed the gnawing anxiety gripping her. She dropped the overboots on the ground and stepped around him, pushing his hands into the sleeves, then yanking the coat up over his shoulders.

She knelt at his feet and pushed and pulled at his jeans until he lifted one foot then the other, which she shoved into the boots. Flipping up the collar of her own coat, she straightened and started fastening the front of his.

"No," he stopped her.

She stared up at him, trying not to cry with panic. Her hair blew around her head and she shoved it out of her eyes. "Daniel Clay, you either fasten your coat or I will."

"Go inside."

"Not without you." She reached again for his coat, managing to get two buttons fastened with her cold fingers before he stopped her again.

"Your fingers are freezing," he said through gritted teeth.

She yanked her hands free and pushed another button through. "I sort of noticed," she retorted, shivering madly. "I'll go in when you come with me."

He stepped back, but she followed. "Dammit, Maggie Mae, get in the bloody house."

"No!" She wrapped her cold hands around his coat and yanked the last two buttons together. "Not without you. Daniel, whatever is wrong, we can solve it *inside.*" She pressed her palms around his hands, rubbing against the cold. "You'll feel better inside where it's warm."

"I don't feel!"

Maggie fell back a step at his hoarse shout. "Wha—"

"I don't feel anything," he rasped. "Not warmth. Not cold. Not love. Not anything. I could hammer a million more nails and I still wouldn't. Now get in the goddamned house."

She raked back her hair, struggling. "Don't swear at me," she said evenly. "Tell me what on earth hammering has to do with standing out here at three in the morning while we freeze off our rear ends!"

His jaw cocked. And his hands closed over her arms. "You'll marry me. I'll provide for you and J.D. and the baby. Because it's the sensible thing to do."

Maggie stared up at him, wishing she could see into his eyes. "I've spent my entire life trying to be sensible, Daniel. But that's not why I'm marrying you. I'm doing that because I love you." She felt him jerk, but her words didn't pause. "And for no other reason. Not because I'm too pitifully loyal to break a promise. Or too afraid to make it on my own as a single parent. *I love you.* Maybe that means my brain is all clouded up, but I don't care.'' The night breeze whipped at her eyes, drying the tears that formed. "Now, please. Come inside. Let me take care of you for once.''

"J.D.—''

"Loves you, too.'' Shivers racked through her body. Cold air easily penetrated the long folds of her robe.

"I can't—''

She threw her arms around him, pressing against him. Needing the touch of him to help her muddle her way through this. "You can do whatever you want, Daniel. From *inside*.''

"I can't feel. I…won't.''

She pressed her forehead against his coat, thinking furiously. "Okay. You don't have to. But, Daniel, I'm really cold.'' She didn't have to fake the shivers in her voice or her arms. "If you…if you want me to warm up, you'll need to take me inside. Okay?''

He swore, low and soft. But he swept her into his arms and strode across the clearing toward the house. Maggie wrapped her arms around his neck and forced herself to think.

The pillaged bedding. The notes that had been there. Then had not.

She pressed her cold cheek into his coat.

His wounded eyes when he'd told Maggie that Angeline was dead. Daniel staring at J.D. as if she'd taken a layer of his soul when she called him Daddy.

When Daniel finally reached the house and set her on her feet inside the mudroom, she was ready. Deliberately she stepped in front of the door when he would have gone right back out into the cold night. "Do you want to freeze to death out there?''

His face was pale, his eyes full of a torment he wouldn't share. "Move out of my way.''

She slowly shook her head. "Why can't you feel, Daniel?''

He shook his head sharply. "Because when I do, bad things happen. Move.''

"Why? So you can go sit on a bar stool in Colbys? I'd

think even that place is closed for the night. What bad things?''

Daniel pressed the heels of his hands over his eyes. ''Forget it.''

She moved and yanked his hands down. Linked her fingers through his with a surprising strength. ''No. What bad things?''

''You like doing this?'' he asked nastily. ''Picking until I'm raw?''

''If you can't feel, you can't be raw,'' she returned swiftly. ''What bad things?''

''I don't want your love,'' he growled.

Later she'd let that hurt. But not now. ''You have it whether you like it or not! *What bad things?*''

''Joe.''

Maggie grimaced. ''We've been through that. Try again.''

His jaw cocked. ''You.''

Her gaze flickered for a moment. ''I'm here. Living in a corner of the world I love. Carrying another child that I'd never dreamed I'd have. Loving you. There's nothing bad there.''

Pushed beyond reason, Daniel turned and slammed his fist against the wall. He heard Maggie gasp behind him. Maybe if she knew the truth, she'd stop picking and picking at him. Exposing every layer of his sins to the singeing light of the sun.

''All right, then,'' he growled. ''Bad. How about twenty-two people dying in a small village because I *felt* that I could protect them against a madman.'' He opened his eyes, staring at the wall. Hoping that his mind wouldn't conjure their faces. Failing. He curled his hand into a fist, concentrating on the sharp ache in his knuckles. ''Angeline's parents. Her cousins and aunts and uncles. All dead, because I didn't follow my *brain* and get them the hell outta there when I should have. They trusted me, and I failed them. In the worst possible way. Angeline, all of 'em.''

Maggie stared at his back, so stiff and unrelenting, even beneath the coat she'd worked so hard to get on him. She didn't believe for one minute that Daniel was as culpable as he believed. And though there were millions of questions and a tidal wave of horror sweeping through her, she focused on the one point she knew would reach Daniel. She unfastened her coat, leaving it on the bench underneath the window. "Tell me about Angeline."

His head tilted and she saw the savage angle of his hard jaw, the hard twist of his lips. "She was four years old," he gritted.

She already knew that. "You cared about her."

"She was a pain in the butt. She followed a person everywhere. Asked a million questions—"

"You cared about her."

He turned his gaze toward her. "I left those people at the mercy of Arturo's men."

"Not intentionally. Not knowingly," she said with bone-deep certainty. Even though she didn't have a clue who Arturo was.

"It doesn't matter!" He raked his hands through his butterscotch hair. "They trusted me. And…they…died."

She yanked several paper towels off the roll and dampened them under the faucet of the utility sink. Then caught his reluctant hand and pressed them to his knuckles, raw from where he'd punched the wall. "You cared about them. Cared about Angeline. And now they're gone. And you're dealing with it by telling yourself it's smarter not to feel anything."

She held on tight to his wrist when he would have pulled away. "I've lost people in my life, too, Daniel. My mother. My father. Babies before they even had a chance at life." She swallowed. "It's not easy to get past the anger and the disbelief and the pain. But it's impossible, if you won't even let yourself feel the grief that you need to feel! Daniel, you have to let yourself *feel* those things to get past them."

"It's not the same."

"Really?" She pressed the towels gently. "Isn't it? You look at J.D. and sometimes see Angeline. It eats away at you inside because there isn't one single thing that you can do to change what happened. You want to beat out at the world around you for going on, for surviving, when a part of you is dying inside."

She blinked at the tears blurring her vision. "I used to think that if I loved someone, I'd drive them away. But I don't believe that anymore. Because I don't believe that you're going away. I believe in you. In your honesty. Your decency. I believe in you because your touch has made *me* feel again. Because I look in your eyes and I see a future. It's not the Double-C. This land that is so much a part of you and your family. It's the way you live your life. It's the man you are. It's you, Daniel. You can say that love clouds your brain, but I think it's really just the opposite. It makes everything so clear. It opens the world for your soul."

She tossed aside the paper towels and looked up into his quicksilver eyes. "And I know that, because of you. Because of what you've made me feel for you."

His jaw clenched. "She was only...four." His arms closed around Maggie, holding her so tightly she wept for the pain she felt in him. "Four. And I couldn't find her. Dammit, we couldn't find her body to even give her a decent burial! And the only way I can get through two days running is to not think about it!"

She pressed her lips to his jaw. Held his head in her palms and brushed her thumb across the hard lines of strain in his lean, hard cheek. "Oh, Daniel," she whispered. "It will get better."

He lifted his head, no sign of agreement or belief in his eyes. "I won't fail you, Maggie. You or J.D."

"I know you won't." She'd expected him to back out of his marriage demand, but she'd known he'd never *fail* her. Or their child. It wasn't Daniel's way. But how could she get him to see that?

"I'll protect you from everything bad in this world."

"We'll protect each other."

He finally drew in a long breath and set her gently from him. His shoulders were rigid. "I want J.D. to have my name," he finally said, and the hard, flat tone of his voice told her more than he'd ever realize.

Maggie's tears overflowed. "Oh, my love. Didn't you know?" He was so impossibly dear to her. He always had been, even when friendship was all that he'd offered. If there was a way for her to help him through his grief, she'd find it. It was the only way he'd open his heart up again to love. "Daniel Jordan Clay," she whispered. "J.D. Jordanne Danielle."

"J.D." He looked stunned. "Why?"

She brushed at her cheeks and told him the truth. "Because I wanted her named for all that was good and kind and decent."

The muscle in his jaw jerked. "You should'a named her after yourself. Or Jaimie, then. Not me."

He sat down on the bench, his hands braced on either side of him, as if he didn't have the energy to stand any longer. Perhaps he didn't. He was carrying such a heavy load on his wide shoulders. Maggie crouched down in front of him, resting her palms on his thighs. "J.D. has the perfect name, Daniel. And not once have I regretted giving it to her. Adding Clay to it will be an honor."

He let out a long, shuddering breath, as if he'd been holding it in for months, and pulled her close to his chest. The words, when they finally came, were low and raw. "It hurts, Maggie Mae."

"I know. It'll get better. I promise." She pressed her lips to the tight cords of his neck. "Come to bed, Daniel. Come to bed and hold me until the sun comes up."

"I forget it all when I'm part of you."

She drew his palm to the faint swell of her abdomen. "We're parts of each other now. We always will be."

He was quiet for a long moment. But his fingers tangled with hers over the child they'd created that warm August night. "J.D.," he murmured, shaking his head slightly. As if he still couldn't believe it.

"Soon we'll have to start thinking about names for this one," Maggie whispered.

He pressed an infinitely tender kiss to her temple and rose, drawing her with him. "Tomorrow is soon enough. For now, I want to go to bed and hold you until the sun comes up."

Chapter Sixteen

Maggie leaned against the wide archway between the kitchen and the formal dining room, waiting for Jaimie, who'd had to make a pit stop at the bathroom, and tried to picture the table Daniel wanted to put in the dining room. They simply couldn't agree on it. He had his eye on one in particular that seated eighteen. She'd told him the table was beautiful, true. But much too large for their needs.

So far neither had relented. The tug-of-war on the issue had turned downright interesting, too. Last night, Daniel had sat her on the floor of the spacious dining room and paced off the dimensions of the table he wanted. She'd pointed out, reasonably enough, the way the oval table *she'd* been eyeing would fit so much better.

Somehow or other, they'd ended up making love on the wide burgundy and navy area rug. Daniel's argument, when she'd given a vaguely scandalized protest, was that they needed to make it really *feel* like their home. Maggie suspected that if the house *felt* any more than it already did, she'd be dead from pleasure.

She smiled faintly, smoothing her hand down her abdomen. Daniel had had only one sleepless night since that first night in their new home. He'd told her, albeit reluctantly, about the agency that had sent him to Santo Marguerite because of his expertise in weaponry and disarming explosives. Hollins-Winword. That he'd gotten involved with the covert agency when Maggie had left the Double-C all those years ago. But he hadn't been willing to discuss Angeline any more than he already had.

So she'd taken matters into her own hands. Though she wasn't sure at all how Daniel would feel if he knew she'd contacted the same investigator who'd been able to track down Joe's whereabouts. The man was even now searching every available source to either confirm Angeline's death or disprove it. One way or another, Daniel needed the answer.

"I should have known you'd be in here admiring your new kitchen. You ready to go to the church?"

Maggie turned to find Jaimie standing near the staircase, watching her with laughter in her eyes and she nodded, gathering up her purse and coat to follow Jaimie out to the truck. Daniel and Matthew were meeting them at the Community Church. It was only Tuesday and the wedding wasn't until Friday, but the pastor wanted them to have a short rehearsal before he went away for Thanksgiving.

Daniel had snorted, saying he didn't need any rehearsal to walk Maggie down an aisle. But Maggie could tell that he really didn't mind.

After the rehearsal, everyone would gather at the big house for supper. Maggie and J.D. would spend the night there until Friday. Until the wedding.

"It being only proper and all," Squire had insisted testily. But Maggie knew that Squire approved of the match. He'd made that abundantly clear with his gift of land.

"Jefferson and Emily and the kids should already be there,"

Jaimie said when they set off. "Matthew talked to Tris this afternoon. He won't make it to the rehearsal, but he'll be here for the wedding. Hopefully Sawyer will be, too. But he couldn't say for sure, because of that court-martial he's testifying in."

"Daniel talked to Tris, too." Maggie said. "He said he'd never heard Tristan sound so overworked, and told him he needed to take off some time."

Jaimie nodded. "He probably won't, though. He's like his brothers. Obsessed with one thing or another. Matthew's obsession is the Double-C."

"Matthew's obsession is *you*," Maggie corrected drily.

Jaimie smiled, sleek with satisfaction. "Daniel is just as bad about you." They rocketed past the big house. "When the Clay men fall in love, they do it in a big way. So he still hasn't told you where you're going to honeymoon?"

"Ah, no. He wouldn't even let me pack." Nor had he said he loved her. Maggie was certain he wouldn't.

"Maybe he figures you won't need any clothes," Jaimie observed slyly, breaking into Maggie's thoughts, and her cheeks heated. She thought Jaimie's statement could very well be true, declarations of love or not.

The Blazer rocked to a sudden halt, and Jaimie started gathering up her purse and assorted other items. Maggie climbed out, too, reaching back for her purse.

A big, warm hand slid up her back, rubbing her neck beneath her hair. Maggie melted and leaned into him. She tilted her chin up to look at Daniel behind her. "Hi."

"Hi." He kissed her forehead and slipped her heavy, oversize purse out of her hands. "Where's your coat?"

"In the back seat. Don't worry. I'm perfectly warm."

His lips skipped along her temple to her jaw and she turned in his arms, tugging his hair until his lips met hers. "Maybe too warm," she added when he finally straightened. "Are you sure you don't mind our sleeping at the big house until the wedding?"

"I'll probably have to spend an hour in a cold shower just to get to sleep without you, but I'll live. Consider it tradition," he added drily. "We've followed nearly every other one for this shindig."

"I'll miss you," Maggie said against his lips.

"Gawdalmighty, Daniel," Squire's voice boomed out from the other end of the small parking lot. "Can't you wait until after the ceremony?"

Daniel shook his head, sliding his arms more fully around her. "Nope." His lips swallowed Maggie's giggle.

But they were interrupted again by J.D., who pelted across the parking lot from the church to wrap her arms around Daniel's and Maggie's legs. "Mama, 'Andra says you gots to stop smooching and come inside to get practiced."

Maggie looked up at Daniel. "Smooching?"

"Think we oughta start limiting the time the girls spend with Squire," he chuckled. "But I'm all for getting more 'practiced.'"

Maggie pushed the truck door closed and pulled the coat around her shoulders, following them when J.D. pulled Daniel's hand toward the church.

Her steps slowed as her eyes drifted from their backs to the cross, rising tall and simply from the snowy ground in front of the small church. Daniel had to have some resolution over Angeline. Until he did, she feared he'd never fully open his heart again. She loved him too much to see him suffering that self-imposed sentence.

"Having second thoughts?"

Maggie blinked, wondering blankly where Jefferson had appeared from. Then noticed the vehicle that was now parked next to Matthew's Blazer. "No second thoughts," she assured.

He nodded, his eyes holding a smile that his stern face didn't. "I'm glad my brother found you, Maggie. You're good for him."

Warmth spread through her. "He's good for me."

He nodded again and started for the church.

"Jefferson—"

He waited.

"Do you think there's a chance Angeline survived?"

He sighed faintly, not seeming surprised at her comment. "It's highly unlikely. Daniel did everything he could to try to find her."

"He told me her only family lived in the village. That all the, uh—"

"Everyone was accounted for except Angeline," Jefferson finished. "But the destruction of the village was absolute. Even Daniel had to acknowledge the unlikelihood of recovering Angeline's body."

Maggie winced. She didn't know the details of what Jefferson had done for Hollins-Winword. But she did know that he'd worked for the private agency for years—far longer than Daniel had. "There's nothing else that can be done?"

"You should be talking to Dan about this," Jefferson said quietly.

"He refuses to talk about her. But I…I wish I could give him something in return for all he's given me. He needs some resolution to this. Closure. Hope. Something."

"You underestimate yourself, Maggie. You've already given my brother everything he wants. You. The baby." He tilted his head toward the church. "That little rug rat who is heading inside right now."

Maggie caught his sleeve. "Please, Jefferson. Won't you help me see if there is any hope?"

He shook his head, a faint smile touching his lips. "You're as bad as Emily," he murmured. "All right. I'll tell you later what I know. If you want to take it further—" He broke off, obviously seeing something in her expression. "Maggie?"

She swallowed and forced a confident smile before heading into the church, leaving Jefferson to follow. If Jefferson was surprised or shocked or dismayed by what he suspected she'd already initiated, that was too bad. He'd agreed to tell her what he knew. The information could only help the investigator she'd hired several days earlier. Speed his task. She'd already sent him every penny she'd managed to put into savings.

The savings that she'd once expected to have to use when Daniel changed his mind about his marriage demand.

Daniel hadn't changed his mind.

She stepped into the small church and felt breathless at the sight of Daniel standing in the chancel with the pastor.

She only hoped he felt the same after he learned what she'd done.

Daniel spotted Maggie hovering near the back pew and lifted his arm, waiting for her to join him. Rather than feeling the claustrophobia any self-respecting bachelor ought to feel at the onset of his wedding rehearsal, all he felt was relief.

Then Maggie joined him, slipping under his arm to stand close to his side.

And he knew a bone-deep satisfaction that in just a few days time she would finally be his. Midway through the rehearsal, however, he realized that Maggie wasn't quite as relaxed as he.

She stumbled over the vows they rehearsed. And her smiles were just a little too quick. Her voice a little too high. And her relief a little too obvious when the pastor deemed them suitably rehearsed for the big event.

During the drive back to the Double-C, however, she seemed to be more herself, and he decided he was reading more into it. Maggie was going to be his wife. She loved him.

He might not be able to feel that particular emotion anymore, but what he felt for Maggie came as close to it as he was capable.

They were the last to arrive back at the Double-C, and they trooped in through the mudroom, adding their coats to the growing pile hanging from the hooks and laying across the washer and dryer. Then into the kitchen where it seemed Clay men and women took up every inch.

Squire sat at his favored chair at the oblong oak table, clearly in his element as he ordered people here and there.

Then it was into the dining room where, miraculously, everyone had a seat around the gargantuan table, even the three little girls.

As Matthew said the blessing, Daniel squeezed her hand beneath the lace tablecloth. "Seats eighteen," he murmured under his breath.

Maggie nearly laughed out loud. Right there in the middle of Matthew's simple blessing. Daniel had a point. There were eleven sitting at the dining room table at that moment. Once Sawyer and Tristan arrived, it would be thirteen. With the arrival of their as-yet-unborn child, fourteen. And Emily's and Jaimie's, sixteen. "Okay," she agreed just as softly.

The next morning Maggie took one of the Double-C trucks and drove over to Jefferson and Emily's home. Daniel had left her bed in the wee hours that morning to return to their own place. She knew that he would use most of the morning putting the finishing touches on her workshop in the basement. So she had several hours to do some of her own investigating.

"You're sure you want to see this?" Jefferson asked. They were seated at the kitchen table.

Maggie nodded, her fingers trembling as she drew a stack of papers toward her.

"Good thing I retired from HW," Jefferson murmured to Emily who sat at his side, their hands folded together atop the table. "If they found out I was showing you this stuff, I'd be out on my can."

Maggie hesitated. "You're not going to get in any trouble are you?" She didn't want that.

Jefferson shrugged. "There's a map of the area where the village was located." He waited while she unfolded it, then pointed. "Hollins canvased the area for information about Angeline. About any other survivors. They got back nothing."

"Did these people know about the danger they were in from this Arturo guy?" She glanced up from the map to see Jefferson nod. "So they knew, but they wouldn't leave, naturally.

They were protecting their homes. Their land. But surely they'd want to protect their families, too?''

Emily shook her head. "It doesn't make sense to me, either, Maggie. If I knew some madman was determined to have his way one way or the other, I'd certainly make sure that Leandra was safe first. Provided for."

"Angeline was the youngest child in the village. The rest of them were sixteen and up," Jefferson put in. "Considered adults, basically."

"But not a four-year-old child. Are you sure there were no relatives her parents might have sent her to?"

"Daniel checked. Hell, a half dozen agents checked. There was no one. I seriously doubt the guy you sent will find out anything new."

She'd thought she would never learn of Joe's whereabouts, either. Yet she had, thanks to the investigator she'd hired then and had hired a few days ago. And look at the miracles in her life that had happened since.

She slowly flipped through the papers, most of which were photocopies of reports. A few fax pages of photos that, despite their grainy quality, made her stomach churn at the desolation that had hit the small village. Jefferson had already explained the chain of events that had occurred before and after Daniel's arrival in Santo Marguerite. About Arturo Sandoval's crazed obsession with taking over Santo Marguerite, and the villagers who were determined to save their homes and farmland no matter what. And Daniel, there to disarm Arturo's army when they finally struck, and there long enough to *catch* the madman. Only somehow, Daniel had been discovered and in a fury, Arturo destroyed anything and everything in his path. Including the land he'd wanted so desperately. "Can I take these?"

Jefferson shrugged. "Don't get your hopes up too high, Maggie."

She slowly folded the map and stood, tucking the papers

into her purse. "Too late, I'm afraid." She left then, heading back to the big house, her thoughts busy.

By the time she pulled up outside the big house, she was thinking again about Emily's comments. As a mother, she'd have done everything in her power to ensure her child's safety. Why wouldn't Angeline's mother have done the same? "The problem with men," she murmured as she hurried down to the guest suite and the telephone there, "is that they think like men."

Two hours and dozens of phone calls later, she wished she'd worked harder at learning Spanish in school. The yellow pad in front of her was covered with phone numbers, reminding her painfully of the slips that had collected over and over again on Daniel's nightstand and dresser.

The phone rang the moment she hung it up after a particularly frustrating call and she snatched it back up. It was Daniel, and her shoulders tightened even more. She knew he wouldn't condone the search she'd begun. But this was too important.

She focused on what he was saying—asking. As in whether she wanted him to take the latest package of catalog orders she'd prepared into Weaver to mail.

She'd forgotten all about the box she'd left in the kitchen at their house. She rubbed her temples. "That would be good. Thanks. Are...you still coming over for dinner?"

"And dessert."

She felt her entire body flush at that.

"I was looking at the mailing label on the box. Do you get a lot of orders from other countries?"

Maggie tucked the phone between her shoulder and ear as she began tidying up her notes. "A few. There's an orphanage in Costa Rica run by American nuns," she said. "They order some of the toys pretty regularly. I send them at cost."

She sat up straight. Orphanages. She fumbled through the notes she'd made, and the obscure reports that Jefferson had given her. "Daniel, did you check the orphanages?"

"What?"

"Orphanages. No, I'm sure I didn't see anything about—"

"Maggie, what the hell are you talking about?"

"Angeline. Daniel, did you check the orphanages in the area?"

"Dammit, Maggie, why are you dragging this out again?" He made a rough noise and in her mind's eye she saw him raking his fingers impatiently through his butterscotch hair. "It's over. Let it lie. Look, I'll drop this stuff off in Weaver, then see you at supper."

"Okay. I love—"

He'd hung up.

"—you," she finished softly.

Was she treading where she had no business? Was she adding to Daniel's pain by pursuing this? What if she found out nothing more than he had? If her actions only caused more pain?

"Oh, Daniel," she murmured. Then she redialed the international operator.

By the time Daniel arrived just before supper, she was a bundle of anxiety awaiting the promised call from her investigator. She considered herself lucky that there were so many Clays in the house talking weddings and Thanksgiving turkeys and football games. If she'd been alone with Daniel for more than two minutes at a time, she knew she'd have been unable to hide her nervousness. As it was, he seemed to be over his earlier irritation as he teased her about wedding jitters, and tucked her into bed with a chaste kiss on the forehead, before joining his brothers upstairs for the poker game that Squire ordered his sons to join him for.

Thanksgiving Day dawned cold and clear.

Maggie spent most of the morning in the kitchen helping Jaimie prepare a traditional feast. Before long, Gloria, who was staying through the weekend before heading back to Casper and her nursing job there, joined them. The men were out taking care of the bare minimum of chores because horses and cattle and cats and dogs didn't care about holidays. Emily and Jefferson and Leandra would be coming over later in the day.

Despite the fact that they were busy preparing a turkey feast, the general topic in the kitchen was weddings. Jaimie's. Emily's. Gloria's to the husband she'd lost about five years earlier. Sitting at the table peeling apples for pie, Maggie let the cheerful chatter swirl around her. She glanced over at the phone hanging on the wall, willing it to ring. Of course, it didn't. Sighing faintly, she reached for the next apple.

A few hours later, the delicious aroma of roasting turkey was filling the house. Jaimie had decided to follow Sarah and J.D.'s example by taking a nap before dinner. Gloria and Squire had gone out visiting for a while. So the big house was quiet when Matthew and Daniel returned. Matthew gave an appreciative sniff of the air and poured himself a mug of coffee before heading upstairs.

Which left Maggie and Daniel alone in the kitchen. She closed the small sketch pad she'd been working in and smiled when he hooked a chair and sank down on it, stretching his long legs across the floor. "I remember a time when we didn't even celebrate Thanksgiving under this roof," he commented.

"After your mother died?"

He nodded, and started to reach for her sketch pad. "Figuring out some new designs?"

She slapped his hand lightly and slipped the pad away from him. "Maybe."

A slashing dimple came and went in his carved face. "I'll show you my...drawings if you'll show me yours."

Maggie sputtered into laughter. He wasn't talking about her scribbles and they both knew it. "Are you inviting me to see your etchings?"

He shrugged innocently.

"I've seen them." Maggie rose and moved past him to check the turkey. "Have you had a lot of success with that line?"

"None this afternoon. So far, anyway. Maybe I'm losing my touch."

She looked over her shoulder at him. "Now you're asking for sympathy?"

"Is it working?"

She tossed the pot holder on the counter. "I do believe you're flirting with me, Daniel Clay. I'm an engaged woman you know."

"So there's still time." He caught her hand and tumbled her onto his lap.

Maggie's pulse quickened. "For what?"

"This." His lips met hers in a tantalizing, tempting kiss that liquefied her bones. "What time is turkey?"

Maggie marshaled her brain cells back to order. "Another hour or so."

"Then we've got time—" He waggled his eyebrows suggestively.

"Oh no you don't," Maggie said, laughing. She scrambled off his lap. "I swear, Daniel Clay, your mind never rises above your—"

"—for a walk." His grin widened when her words died. "I hear walking is good for pregnant ladies. What did you think I was suggesting?" He laughed when she rolled her eyes. But she didn't protest when he hustled her into a coat and they went out into the cold afternoon. They passed the barns and the buildings and still they walked, their linked hands tucked into Daniel's coat pocket.

A lazy snowflake drifted from the gray laden sky, landing on her cheek and she smiled up at him, feeling content. "How many kids do you want?"

He shrugged. The snowy gravel under their boots crunched as they walked. "As many as you want." He cast her a steady look. "I'm at your service."

She laughed breathlessly. "I'm serious."

He stopped walking and stepped around to face her. "Ten. Twelve," he dropped a kiss on her lips and tugged off his gloves, unfastening her coat and pulling her to him before she could stop him. "Doesn't matter, Maggie Mae."

"But you'd like...oh my—"

He grinned and eased his hand over the curves he'd found. "A...large...family?"

"I'll practice making one with you as often as humanly possible," he assured, his warm fingers busy.

"Daniel!"

"If you want to have a dozen kids, that's okay with me. If you want just J.D. and this one," his palm slid down to cover the barely noticeable swell where his child grew. "Then that's okay, too."

She brought his hand to her lips, kissing the callused fingers, the rough knuckles. "If...if you had been able to find Angeline, what would you have done?" He stiffened, but she kept hold. He shifted and Maggie knew he was waiting for her to drop it. But she wasn't going to. Not this time.

"I would have had her buried with her parents," he finally said impatiently.

"If you'd found she was alive."

His jaw tightened into a hard angle. "Dammit, Maggie, how many times do I have to—"

"—but if you had found her safe and well somewhere—"

He swore angrily. "I didn't. Do you honestly think I'd have stopped that fool's chase if I'd believed she was still alive?"

"Of course not. But—"

"She's dead. It's my fault. I've accepted it. Why can't you just leave it be?"

Her heart thudded. "Because I love you."

Something came and went in his gray eyes. "I can't stop you feeling what you do. And you can't make me feel what I don't. So stop trying to fix me, Maggie."

She gasped. "That's not what I'm—"

"I'm not one of your blocks of wood you can cut and chisel into a picture perfect Christmas ornament. If Angeline was alive, I'd have brought her here. She's not. I didn't. And this is the last I want to hear about it,'' he gritted. ''We'd better get back.'' He started walking.

Maggie slowly picked up the gloves he'd left laying on the ground and followed him back to the house. This time they didn't hold hands.

By the time the house was once again alive with people and food and laughter, Maggie wished she'd just left well enough alone. Daniel sat next to her at the big dining room table, loaded down with their Thanksgiving Day feast. But he didn't slide her any quicksilver looks. And he didn't hold her hand beneath the table where no one could see.

And the turkey that everyone else exclaimed over tasted like straw to her.

Chapter Seventeen

"It's a beautiful gown."

Maggie glanced over her shoulder to see Jaimie standing in the doorway to her bedroom. She turned back to the ivory gown and smoothed her fingertip along the heavy satin. "Yes." She dropped her hand and folded her arms around herself, forcing a smile as Jaimie joined her.

"Nervous?"

"About the wedding?"

"Well, it is going to be in," Jaimie glanced at her watch, "four hours. Give or take a few minutes."

Maggie managed a smile. Daniel had barely said ten words to her since she'd broached his off-limit topic of Angeline. She wasn't worried about the wedding. Or nervous about it.

She was worried about Daniel.

"I had the standard wedding-day jitters," Jaimie said easily. She picked up the small spray of roses that Maggie was going to wear in her hair. "As happy as I was to be marrying Matthew, I was still a bundle of nerves."

"I remember."

Jaimie set the roses down on the dresser, her eyes dreamy. "But as soon as I saw Matthew standing there with the minister, waiting for me, I was fine." She blinked and smiled. "Your jitters will disappear, too, I'll bet."

Maggie didn't bother to point out that Matthew had been thoroughly besotted with Jaimie on the day of *their* wedding. Three and a half years later, he still was besotted with his bride.

Daniel wasn't in love with Maggie. He felt responsible for their child. He wanted her. He cared, in his way. But he wasn't in love. And since the day before, Maggie knew he was thoroughly angry.

Could she blame him? He'd made his feelings about discussing Angeline crystal clear. Yet Maggie, thinking she knew better—

"Earth to Maggie."

She realized Jaimie was talking to her. "What?"

Jaimie shook her head, smiling indulgently. "Your daughter and niece are waiting for you to join them for lunch. They think the sooner they shovel their food in their mouths, the sooner the wedding will be. J.D. wants to wear lipstick, you know. And Emily told me when she called a little while ago that Leandra now refuses to wear her dress shoes. Because if her daddy can wear his cowboy boots, then so can she."

At that, Maggie smiled.

"That's better," Jaimie said. She tucked her arm through Maggie's and drew her upstairs and into the kitchen.

Sure enough, two little girls were waiting impatiently. Maggie pulled out a chair and sat next to J.D. But the light lunch, while fixed to perfection by Jaimie, held little appeal to her knot-filled stomach, and she was grateful when everyone else was finished and she could busy herself cleaning up.

Then Squire and Gloria took the children outside to play in the fresh snow that had fallen overnight and Jaimie went to her room to fix her hair, and Maggie found herself at loose ends again.

Staring at the phone.

Wishing for Daniel to call.

But the phone remained stubbornly silent, and she finally went downstairs to her own shower. After, she would give herself a manicure. Then see if she could get her fine hair to hold a curl long enough for the wedding.

But once she settled at the breakfast counter in the guest suite with her emery board and rose-colored polish to replace the pale pink she'd worn for Thanksgiving, she didn't do anything but look at the telephone on the counter.

She had to tell Daniel about the investigator and what he'd found. She couldn't walk down a church aisle with the secret hanging between them. She couldn't.

And if, as a result of her deed, he decided there was to be no wedding, it was better to know before, than after. He had a right to make that choice. He had a right to know.

Her hand trembled as she reached for the phone to dial Daniel's—no, their—phone number. But it rang shrilly as she reached for it and she nearly jumped out of her skin before answering. And ten minutes later when she hung up, tears blurred her vision as she called Daniel.

The phone just rang and rang and rang. And finally, Maggie gave up. She would drive over to the house and see him in person.

Yet when she dressed and hurried upstairs, it was to find Matthew just coming in through the mudroom. And he told her that his brother wasn't at their house, because he'd already gone into Weaver to meet up with Tristan, who had driven straight there from the airport. Then he looked at her, his ice-blue eyes curious. "Shouldn't you be getting ready or something?"

Her opportunity to catch Daniel spun even further away when Squire and Gloria came back in with J.D. and Sarah, who were champing at the bit to take a bath together and have their hair fixed all pretty like big girls and dress in their burgundy velvet dresses. Squelching her frustration with everything she possessed, she joined Gloria in hustling the girls through their baths.

Then Jaimie came along the hallway and ordered Maggie to leave the girls to her so Maggie could finish getting ready. "The wedding is at four," she reminded pointedly. "It's almost two-thirty now."

Daniel was already in town. Maggie went downstairs again and tried phoning the church. But the line was busy. "I don't believe this," she muttered, hanging up after trying two more times.

Obviously, she'd have to catch him before the ceremony. And the quicker she got to town, the quicker she could tell him. She'd just picked up the blow-dryer when Jaimie came gliding into the room, striking in the midnight blue sheath with the tiny tucks along the bodice to accommodate her pregnancy. Muttering about procrastinating brides, Jaimie hustled Maggie into a chair and turned on the dryer. "Matthew's up there looking at his watch every five minutes," she said above the whine of the dryer. "And Daniel called—"

Maggie whirled around. "He called?"

Jaimie pushed her back on the chair with a firm hand, waving the dryer over Maggie's head. "To see when we'd be arriving. Holy kamoly, Mags, would you sit still? You're worse than Sarah."

Maggie sat still. "He didn't…say anything else?"

Jaimie finally turned off the dryer and began winding Maggie's fine blond hair around hot rollers with an experienced hand. "Only that Jefferson and Em were already there. Hurry up and get your dress and we'll go."

"But—"

"We'll finish your hair on the way," Jaimie said, already sweeping a brush and comb and pins into a pink case. "Good thing you're the only one dressing at the church," she muttered.

They heard heavy footsteps thunder down the stairs and
Maggie automatically followed Jaimie's orders as Matthew appeared, closely followed by Squire, wanting to know what on
earth was the holdup.

"You'd think you were havin' second thoughts," Squire
groused as he followed them back up the stairs.

Ahead of her, Jaimie chuckled. Maggie didn't have a laugh
left in her at that moment. She was still having a difficult time
picturing Daniel already at the church. Panic swelled inside
her at the thought. My God, she had to tell him about the call.

By the time they arrived at the church, there were already
cars pulling into the small parking lot. Jaimie pressed Matthew
into service, ordering him to carry the gown, safely zipped
inside a special bag. Before Maggie had an opportunity to slip
away to find Daniel, she found herself closed in the bride's
room with Jaimie and Emily alternately prodding her into
dressing.

Finally she'd had enough. "I need to talk to Daniel."

She saw the look Jaimie and Emily exchanged.

"I mean it." She gathered up the heavy skirt of her gown
and started for the door, but Jaimie barred the way.

"You're not going out there yet," Jaimie said firmly.

"You don't understand. I *have* to talk to Daniel. It's important."

"I'll get him," Emily said after a moment.

They heard organ music when Emily opened the door, and
Maggie felt her knees go watery. Emily was back in minutes,
but Daniel wasn't with her. "He's already in the sanctuary,"
she said. "Waiting for you." She picked up Maggie's bouquet
and stuck it in her hands.

The organist was playing. She'd lost her chance.

She swallowed the knot in her throat, managing to smile at
J.D. and Leandra and Sarah, who were waiting in the narthex
with Gloria. They looked like angels in their ankle-length
dresses of burgundy velvet. Wreathes of baby's breath and tea
roses circled their heads.

Though the inner doors to the sanctuary were closed, she could still hear the whispers of the guests inside the sanctuary. Then the minister's wife opened the narthex doors and the whispers died and music swelled out to meet them.

Her heart in her throat, Maggie hovered anxiously out of sight while the minister's wife fussed with the wide sweeping skirt of her gown.

Emily glided down the aisle, followed by Leandra. Then Jaimie and Sarah.

J.D. marched solemnly into the sanctuary, her hands tight on her small basket of roses. Maggie wasn't worried about J.D. She had complete faith that her daughter would go right to her spot where they'd practiced earlier that week.

"Maggie, dear. It's time."

She focused on the minister's wife, who nodded encouragingly.

Drawing in a shuddering breath, her small bouquet trembling in her hands, Maggie stepped to the center of the wide doorway where the pews seemed to go on forever and ever down an aisle that surely had tripled in length since Tuesday.

Then he was there.

Daniel.

And his quicksilver gaze met hers across the distance. And the aisle returned to normal and her hands stopped shaking. Her fears and her nerves and her anxiety all faded until there was nothing but Daniel. The man she loved.

Maggie appeared between the doors and Daniel felt time crank to a shuddering, jolting halt. Her cream gown was simplicity itself. Not a ruffle or bead in sight. Just her and a sleek sweep of heavy silk that shimmered like an antique pearl when she started down the aisle toward him. Her corn-silk hair brushed away from her lovely face in smooth waves, unhidden by so much as a wisp of veil.

No father escorted her down the aisle. No mother, or even a friend.

Just Maggie. Walking straight and proud and so impossibly beautiful that his throat tightened. Midway down the aisle she passed through a patch of sunlight from the high windows and golden light glinted about her head.

She looked like an angel.

Something hard and tight inside his chest cracked wide, and he thought that he'd been waiting all his life for this moment. For this woman.

Maggie kept gliding toward him, her turquoise eyes shining. He was vaguely aware of the little girls slipping into the front pew with Squire and Gloria.

Then Maggie joined him there in front of their family and friends. In front of a plain wooden cross hanging on the wall behind the minister.

He looked at her as she looked solemnly at the minister. Her hair was pulled into soft waves at the back of her head, fastened with a tiny cluster of roses that matched her gown. "Maggie—"

She looked up at him, her eyes wide. And filled with love. "Are you okay?"

He swallowed, the words jamming in his chest so hard they hurt.

Then she smiled gently. "It's all right, Daniel. Everything is all right now. You see I found—"

"I've waited years for you," he said abruptly, then frowned because the words didn't say everything he felt.

Her lips parted soundlessly.

Uncaring that the minister was clearing his throat nervously or that Matthew was elbowing him in the back, Daniel turned Maggie to face him.

His Maggie Mae. Who filled his heart and his lungs and his soul with her strength. Her love that was wide enough to encompass everything he was. Everything he'd been. Everything he'd cared about.

He brushed his thumb down her silken cheek. "This isn't

about the baby,'' he murmured softly, trying again to express himself. "I want you to know that."

Her eyes filled. "Oh, Daniel. And you need to know—"

"Excuse me—" the minister finally leaned forward, his voice quiet "—could we proceed here?"

Daniel tucked Maggie's arm through his and brushed a kiss over her soft lips. Several chuckles filled the small church, and he looked at the minister suddenly impatient. "Anytime you're ready."

The minister blinked. Matthew hid his chuckle in a soft cough behind him. And Maggie tightened her fingers through his. Her eyes were steady and her hand sure when he repeated his vows and slipped the woven band on her finger. Then she did the same as he, sliding a band that he hadn't even known she'd gotten, on his finger in return.

When the minister pronounced them wed, Daniel turned to her. But he didn't kiss her as the minister had just prompted. He just looked at her, his beautiful Maggie Mae.

Her eyes searched his. "You didn't change your mind," she murmured.

"I wanted to," he admitted in a low voice. "For a while. But I couldn't."

Her eyes glistened. "Because you made a promise?"

He touched her cheek, uncaring that everyone in the church was waiting with undisguised curiosity, and the words he hadn't been able to say were suddenly there. As easy and as natural and as necessary as breathing. "Because I love you, Maggie Mae."

A tear slipped down her cheek and he brushed it away gently. "Oh, Daniel, I love you, too."

"So kiss her already," somebody said from the congregation.

But Daniel already was.

And the guests laughed and clapped.

The music began again, and Daniel turned his bride to walk back down the aisle. He couldn't tear his eyes from her and nearly tripped on her long skirts when she stopped cold, her eyes focused fiercely toward the back of the church.

The laughter and talk and music all dwindled, and he followed her gaze. And froze. "Dear God," he whispered. He looked up to see Jefferson and Maggie exchanging a look. "Maggie?"

She dashed a finger beneath her eyes. "I tried to tell you Daniel, but—"

He barely heard her. He gripped her hand hard, staring at the man and child who'd caused such a stir in the rear of the sanctuary. "How?"

"Orphanages," Maggie whispered. She tugged at her hand and nodded. "Go, Daniel."

He just shook his head. He wasn't going anywhere. The moment Maggie had walked back into his life, he'd known it. He just hadn't admitted it.

He crouched down on one knee, holding on to Maggie's hand like a lifeline.

The dark-eyed little girl studied him for a long minute. He lifted his hand toward her and she took a step forward. Then ran into Daniel's arms.

J.D. slipped under Maggie's free hand, and she smiled reassuringly at her daughter. Despite her gown, she went right onto her knees in front of the child and touched her lustrous brown hair. "Angeline," she whispered, knowing this beautiful child could be none other than the one who'd captured a part of Daniel's heart. All she could do was smile gently, her mother's heart wanting nothing more than to put her arms around the little girl and reassure her. "Welcome."

The girl's eyes flew to Daniel's, and she rattled off a string of unintelligible words. He answered her, his voice husky.

Angeline's eyes were large and wary as she gingerly touched Maggie's hair. The spray of flowers holding back her hair. Maggie welcomed the curiosity as a natural thing.

J.D. slid between Maggie and Daniel, her eyes shy. Then she held out her basket of flowers to the other girl. Daniel murmured to Angeline. And slowly the child smiled and took the basket. The children eyed each other, then smiled. A smile that needed no translations from one language to another.

Daniel rose, his eyes fierce on Maggie's face. "How? When?"

Maggie straightened, her eyes going to the man who still stood in the rear of the sanctuary. "I hired the investigator who found Joe for me," she whispered. "The day after we moved to the new house. I knew you'd be angry if you knew, but, oh Daniel, I *had* to do something." She looked down at the two little girls for a moment. "Jefferson helped by detailing what he knew about Santo Marguerite, but we didn't find anything that you hadn't until we started contacting the churches and orphanages in the area. Then we had a lead. I wanted to tell you, but I was afraid to get your hopes up. And then today," she shrugged helplessly. "Every time I tried to reach you, talk to you and tell you that Angeline was on her way, well, it just didn't work out." She touched his face with trembling fingers. "Coleman Black called me this morning. He pulled all kinds of strings for us. For Angeline. He said to tell you he was sorry he couldn't be here himself."

"There will be reams of red tape," Daniel warned, barely able to conceive of Coleman Black being so...*kind*.

Maggie shook her head, pressing her fingers to his lips. "We've come this far, Daniel. We'll work it out."

Standing there in that church, with miracles all around him, Daniel knew they would. With Maggie by his side, they'd work through the easy times and the tough times. But they'd do it together. Finally.

He suddenly laughed and stood, sweeping Angeline up in one arm and J.D. in the other. He wrapped his arm around all these females who filled his heart. And he looked out at the guests filling the small sanctuary to overflowing, and knew that he was a man blessed. All because of a woman named Maggie. Who had believed in hope and love even when he hadn't.

"My family," he said wonderingly.

Maggie leaned her head against his shoulder, looking up at him with her heart in her beautiful eyes. "No, Daniel," she corrected lovingly. "*Our* family."

*   *   *   *   *

With the help of a certain lovely lady doctor, Sawyer Clay finds his way home to the Double-C. Watch for their story, coming only to Silhouette Special Edition in late 1999.

Coming soon from

Silhouette® SPECIAL EDITION®

A captivating new miniseries duet from bestselling author
Susan Mallery

BRIDES OF BRADLEY HOUSE: If the family legend comes true, two close-knit sisters will dream of the men they are destined to marry when they don an heirloom nightgown on their twenty-fifth birthday. But before those wedding bells chime, Chloe and Cassie must discover the meaning of everlasting love!

DREAM BRIDE (#1231, March 1999)
The sophisticated skeptic: *That Special Woman!*
Chloe didn't believe in fairy tales until a ruggedly handsome stranger swept her off her feet....

DREAM GROOM (#1244, May 1999)
The hopeless romantic: Innocent Cassie yearned to discover true passion in the arms of her reserved, devastatingly gorgeous boss....

You won't want to miss the unforgettable Bradley sisters—and the irresistible men they vow to have and to hold...forever!

Available at your favorite retail outlet.

If you enjoyed what you just read,
then we've got an offer you can't resist!

Take 2 bestselling love stories FREE!

Plus get a FREE surprise gift!

And Baby Makes Three

FIRST TRIMESTER

by

SHERRYL WOODS

Three ornery Adams men are about to be roped into fatherhood...and they don't suspect a thing!

And Baby Makes Three

APRIL 1999
The phenomenal series
from Sherryl Woods has readers
clamoring for more! And in this special collection,
we discover the stories that started it all....

Luke, Jordan and Cody are tough ranchers set in their bachelor ways until three beautiful women beguile them into forsaking their single lives for instant families. Will each be a match made in heaven...or the delivery room?

Available at your favorite retail outlet.

World's Most Eligible Bachelors

**Available April 1999 from
Silhouette Books...**

The Greek Tycoon
by Suzanne Carey

The World's Most Eligible Bachelor: Extremely wealthy Theo Petrakis was built like a Greek god, and his reputation as a ladies' man—and confirmed bachelor—was no mere myth.

Gorgeous tycoon Theo Petrakis lived life to the fullest, so when he came up against the utterly proper Esme Lord, he found adventure in teaching the American beauty his wicked ways. But one tempestuous night had left them with rings on their fingers and a faint recollection of wedding vows. Was their marriage for real...or just their passion?

Each month, Silhouette Books brings you a brand-new story about an absolutely irresistible bachelor. Find out how the sexiest, most sought-after men are finally caught.

Available at your favorite retail outlet.

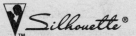

Silhouette ROMANCE™

In March,
award-winning,
bestselling author
Diana Palmer joins
Silhouette Romance in
celebrating the one year
anniversary of its
successful promotion:

VIRGIN BRIDES

*Celebrate the joys of
first love with unforgettable
stories by our most beloved authors....*

March 1999:
CALLAGHAN'S BRIDE
Diana Palmer

Callaghan Hart exasperated temporary ranch cook
Tess Brady by refusing to admit that the attraction they
shared was more than just passion. Could Tess make
Callaghan see she was his truelove bride before her time
on the Hart ranch ran out?

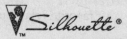

Silhouette®

Available at your favorite retail outlet.

Look us up on-line at: http://www.romance.net

SRVB99

Coming in May 1999

BABY *Fever*

by
New York Times Bestselling Author

KASEY MICHAELS

When three sisters hear their biological
clocks ticking, they know it's
time for action.

But who will they get to father their babies?

**Find out how the road to motherhood
leads to love in this brand-new collection.**

Available at your favorite retail outlet.

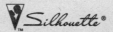